HEARTS PERSUADED

THE QUAKER AND THE CONFEDERATE

HEARTS PERSUADED

JOANNE SUNDELL

FIVE STAR

A part of Gale, Cengage Learning

GALE
CENGAGE Learning·

Detroit • New York • San Francisco • New Haven, Conn • Waterville, Maine • London

GALE
CENGAGE Learning

LIBRARY OF CONGRESS CATALOGING-IN-PUBLICATION DATA

Sundell, Joanne.
　　Hearts persuaded : the Quaker and the Confederate / Joanne Sundell. — 1st ed.
　　　p. cm.
　　ISBN-13: 978-1-59414-883-5 (hardcover)
　　ISBN-10: 1-59414-883-X (hardcover)
　　1. Women soldiers—Fiction. 2. Quakers—Fiction. 3. Virginia—History—Civil War, 1861–1865—Participation, Female—Fiction. 4. Interracial friendship—Fiction. I. Title.
　　PS3619.U557H435 2010
　　813'.6—dc22
　　　　　　　　　　　　　　　　　　　　　　　　　　　2010019610

First Edition. First Printing: September 2010.
Published in 2010 in conjunction with Tekno Books.

Printed in the United States of America
1 2 3 4 5 6 7 14 13 12 11 10

To everything there is a season . . .
and a time for every purpose under heaven;
a time to be born, and a time to die;
a time to plant, and a time to pluck up that which is
planted;
a time to kill, and a time to heal;
a time to break down, and a time to buildup;
a time to weep, and a time to laugh;
a time to mourn, and a time to dance;
a time to cast away stones, and a time to gather stones
together;
a time to embrace, and a time to refrain from embracing;
a time to get, and a time to lose;
a time to keep, and a time to cast away;
a time to rend, and a time to sew;
a time to keep silence, and a time to speak;
a time to love, and a time to hate;
a time of war, and a time of peace.

Ecclesiastes 3:1–8

This is for my sister, Linda Gregg-Biggs, living across the Pond now, in Hereford, England. An avid reader, talented writer, capable artist, and equally apt musician, Linda continues to inspire us with her creative works, wit, and wisdom. One need not purchase a Webster's Dictionary or Roget's Thesaurus with Linda at hand, nor worry over a humorless day. Her gift of laughter and her kind heart have seen me through more than one dark patch. No one has ever suffered from want of Linda's attention. Time is ever the greatest gift we can bestow upon others, is it not?

And so my dear sister, this one's for you.

ACKNOWLEDGMENTS

This historical romance would not have been possible without all of the historians, novelists, Civil War buffs, and Internet academics, who've so ably and meticulously researched, then set pen to paper, chronicling this turbulent time in our nation's history. Beyond these resources, I had the opportunity to visit and subsequently collect invaluable archival data from rich-in-history Virginia and West Virginia bookshops and historical museums. Born and raised in Virginia, I learned early on that the ground I trod was hallowed, the battle cries across fields such as Manassas, the Wilderness, Chancellorsville, and Harper's Ferry . . . still audible, if one stops to listen. My great-great-grandfathers fought in the war. James Gregg was part of the 8th Virginia Infantry, Company C, Confederate States of America. John Shackelford was part of Southall's Battery, Albermarle Light Artillary, Confederate States of America.

Like most, I've accrued a general degree of knowledge about the Civil War, but the writing of this historical romance taught me more; so much more. I hope to share with you, in this two-book Civil War romantic series, what I've learned about women-soldiers masquerading as Confederates and as Yankees, the role of African-Americans fighting for their cause, the treacherous plight of fugitive slaves, and the key role of the Quakers and their rich tradition in Virginia history.

On my very first visit to the town of Waterford in Loudoun County, Virginia, I felt a masterful, historical hand take up mine the moment I began to wander the cobbled streets, and my Quaker hero was at once born in my head and heart. It only took one turn of the research page, reading about women-soldiers in the Civil War, for my heroine to come to life and don her Confederate uniform. My research cried out for a second hero and heroine, both African-Americans, to tell their love story, commanding equal consideration for their rightful place in Virginia history.

Virginia IS for lovers!

CHAPTER ONE

Loudoun County, Virginia—March 1862

Comfort kept hold of Levi's hand, facing all the people gathered at Fairfax Meeting. She spoke her vows clearly, solemnly, with little emotion. "Friends, I take this my friend, Levi, to be my husband, promising, through Divine assistance, to be unto him a loving and faithful wife, so long as we both on earth shall live."

It was Levi's turn now. The lump in his throat, in his chest, refused to clear. He swallowed hard, stood tall, and then grudgingly espoused the same vow. "Friends, I take this my friend, Comfort, to be my wife, promising, through Divine assistance, to be unto her a loving and faithful husband, so long as we both on earth shall live."

Levi's gut wrenched. The only consolation in marrying a woman he didn't love—going against God and his faith and his heart—was that he knew Comfort didn't love him either. He wondered if she felt just as caught, just as dishonest, committing to this pretense of a marriage in front of everyone at meeting merely to fulfill their long-held obligation to each other. Their families and friends had expected them to marry, and now that they'd both reached their majority age of twenty-one, it was time. Levi had wrestled with the idea of talking to Comfort and begging out of their union, but he finally decided he couldn't bring up the subject. To do so would be wrong.

He'd promised to marry her twice now, and saw no possibility of going back on his word.

Levi and Comfort remained standing at the front of meeting but let their hands go. Each wore plain clothes in keeping with Quaker tradition. Comfort was garbed in a gray Linsey-woolsey dress, Quaker cape and white cap, and Levi in black jean-cloth pants and jacket, and a white, heavy cotton shirt. His black broad-brimmed hat rested squarely on his head, taken off only for prayer at meeting.

Levi found his mother's face and swallowed hard. *She knew.* She knew the vows he'd just spoken were untrue. He'd never said a word to his mother about loving another, but looking at his mother's troubled countenance now he could tell she knew. The look of horror on Susan Clement's face penetrated Levi's tough veneer and made him uneasy inside at what he'd just done.

Mind the Light, Levi.

His mother's admonition rang in his head. Countless times growing up she'd cautioned him to Mind the Light and seek the guidance of his Inner Light, which would lead him in all that is right. His action in marrying Comfort was not right. But there could be no going back.

His family had already faced the ordeal of his brother Jonah going off to join the northern ranks. Jonah had been disowned and shunned now by all at meeting. His father hadn't been the same since Jonah's departure. No, Levi could never consider divorce. He'd be disowned and shunned along with Jonah, and such behavior would surely send his father to an early grave. The family worried every day that Thomas Clement's broken heart would never mend. Levi remembered the day Jonah left, and emotions were raw to this day. His father never spoke of Jonah, declaring him dead to the family, but Levi believed his father prayed every night that Jonah was not dead and would return.

Everyone at Fairfax Meeting on this First Day bore witness to Levi's marriage to Comfort Clarke, when it should be Willa standing next to him. *Willa Mae Tyler.* It should be Willa sharing his bed, only Willa. He'd failed her by letting her leave Waterford and he'd failed himself by letting her slip out of his fingers like so much milled dust, one moment sifting through the air, the next gone. He didn't listen when the voice inside him told him Willa was the one for him, and he'd pay for it for the rest of his life.

It wasn't his life that was important now. It was Willa's. She'd marched out of Waterford and Loudoun County with her Confederate infantry unit, determined to be a woman-soldier and fight to avenge the deaths of her brothers at Manassas. The war had caught her up and refused to let her go. It had its ugly hands on her and most probably wouldn't let go until she'd breathed her last breath. Why hadn't he reported her sex to one of the Confederate officers? Maybe they would have let her go rather than punish her. Maybe they would have been easy on her since she was a woman. Levi had threatened to report her, but Willa told him if she were found out and tossed out of her unit, she'd just go and join with another one.

Levi reached up and unbuttoned the top button of his shirt, mindless of any Friends watching. Still standing beside Comfort, he was uncomfortable in his clothes, in his shoes, uncomfortable in the knowledge that he'd failed Willa and Comfort and himself, but most of all, God. Levi had taken a woman that he didn't love and married her at meeting in front of God, with all the Friends witnessing their union where he'd promised to be unto her a loving and faithful husband.

John Clarke, Comfort's father, stood up.

Comfort and Levi took their seats on the front bench.

"I bless this marriage of my daughter to Levi Clement," John declared loudly for everyone present to hear.

Levi listened, or tried to. John continued to speak, mentioning scriptures and talking of their shared Quaker history in settling in Virginia, having emigrated from Pennsylvania seeking good farmland. Levi and Comfort were third generation in Waterford, and John Clarke was proud of their Quaker traditions being carried on in two such fine children. The moment John said *children,* Levi bristled. Levi wanted a family and children, but he wanted them with Willa Mae Tyler, not with Comfort Clarke. Straightening in his seat, the unforgiving bench was a reminder of the hard times ahead for him in his loveless marriage and for the entire Quaker community affected by the war.

After months of Confederate occupation, northern troops had just driven the rebels out. Colonel Geary and his regiment had waited in Harper's Ferry to attack into Loudoun County. They made their assault in time to keep the Confederates from destroying more food stores and burning Waterford and nearby Wheatland and Unison for supporting the North. Levi suspected the Confederates left for reasons other than the northern onslaught. Other battles in other places drew them from Loudoun now.

Levi sat in silence next to his new bride. He felt empty inside. He felt no Inner Light within him on this First Day. No Word came to him, guiding him in all that was right. These were confusing times. So much had changed within him and within the Quaker community since the war began.

War had interrupted their quiet, peaceful way of life on the day the Confederates broke into their meetinghouse the autumn before and took up residence, bringing their weapons inside. It was an awful day in every respect but one: Levi had seen Willa for the first time. He'd known immediately there was a woman hiding in the baggy soldier's uniform. Her sea-green eyes gave her away. They were beautiful despite the anger and hate he read in them—hate for him and for any northern sympathizers. She'd intrigued him from the start. He shouldn't have taken any notice of the woman-soldier but from the moment he'd first spotted her, it was too late to ignore her. He well should have. She represented everything that he did not.

She was an outsider, a non-Quaker. She was a woman masquerading as a man, a soldier willing to take up arms against another. She didn't hold the peace testimony in her heart. Nothing was more dear to Levi's heart than abiding by the peace testimony. Hadn't he been in a struggle the whole of his life to keep his faith and keep his fists at his side? Wasn't his brother Jonah, an outcast now, shunned for running off to join the Yankees and for taking up arms against his fellow man? Breaking with the peace testimony meant breaking with Quaker life and Quaker tradition and breaking faith with God.

The truth of the moment punched Levi in the stomach as if someone had just taken a mean fist to him. He clenched his jaw hard and loosened the second button of his shirt. Despite the cold March day, and despite the fact that no fire burned inside the meetinghouse now, he felt over-warm and sick in his gut. He wanted to charge outside and head down the path along Catoctin Creek to his family's deserted mill. He'd been with Willa there. He wanted to find her there again and wed *her* on this day, and bed *her* on this night. God forgive him. That's what he needed, despite all their differences and all that would always keep them apart. She was his "Willa, love."

Comfort's mother was speaking now. Levi's mother would not be next. He doubted she'd get up and say anything at meeting about a marriage she knew to be a fraud. Susan Clement dared not bless his marriage to Comfort, for to do so would openly defy God and the tenants of their faith. As for his father, Levi doubted he was aware of much these days but his melancholy over Jonah. Levi hoped and prayed that when this war ended, his father's mind would be set right again. By some miracle, maybe his father would know happiness once more. By some miracle, the Quaker community in Waterford could go back to living a peaceful life, rich in the bounty of family and friends, and know some kind of happiness again. Levi's shoulders slumped. He knew it would be a long time before the war that was just getting started would come to any kind of end.

Despite the fact that many in Waterford and the surrounding area held sympathies for the North, and breathed a bit easier with Yankee soldiers now occupying their town, the Confederates would never be far away, and trouble could come without notice.

War had come to stay in Virginia. It crept across their beloved soil from all directions. It crept across the Potomac and the Shenandoah Rivers at places like Harper's Ferry, Snicker's Gap, White's Ferry, and Edward's Ferry, boiling over from border states like Maryland and from nearby Washington; stealing in from across Virginia fields that at one time held the promise of a rich harvest, but now lay flat and dry and fallow. Wasted. All wasted. The community's once-prosperous farms were being whittled away a little more each day, each time a soldier wanted to take food and supplies and kill stock for the army. Only seven miles from Waterford, the townsfolk in Leesburg fought the same daily challenges to keep their families protected and fed, all the while holding sympathies for the South. No matter which town, which side, which war, which victory, which defeat, it was still Virginia neighbor fighting Virginia neighbor. It was still Virginians taking up arms and fighting and dying for their respective causes.

And which cause was Levi's now? He never intended to have any cause in this war, intending rather to help undo the cause for war. Raised as an observant Quaker, he wanted nothing to do with fighting. This war between the North and the South wasn't supposed to be his fight. He wanted no part of fighting, but events had changed that. He'd never take up arms and break with his peace testimony, but he had started on a course, helping runaway slaves and helping secret messages and supplies back and forth from Maryland in support of the northern cause. Although he'd never meant to choose sides in the war, he had chosen and must live with the consequences. By the same token, he must live with the consequences of marrying Comfort, his childhood sweetheart but a woman he no longer loved.

Resigned to his life, Levi would bear the consequences of this loveless marriage. He'd thought he'd kept his feelings hidden, and he hadn't anticipated his mother finding out. He hadn't anticipated her knowing in the very moment he spoke his vows that he didn't mean them. She'd never say anything to him. It was too late now to undo the wrong he'd committed. Guilt-ridden, he'd set yet another burden on his mother's already-worried shoulders. He wished she hadn't found him out, but it was too late now to undo that which he'd done.

He'd do his best to make sure no one else in the family found out. He'd never bring up the subject. As for Comfort, she'd never say anything. She was too proud; one of her failings, he'd always thought. A leader at meeting, she cared about what the Friends assembled thought of her. She wouldn't want anyone to know she wasn't marrying for love and most certainly would never want anyone to know Levi didn't love her. He couldn't remember when they'd begun to fall out of love with each other. Where they had been youths growing up together—attracted to each other from the beginning, having trouble keeping their hands off each other under cover of a haystack or stealing out in back of a barn—somewhere between childhood and adulthood their attraction had started to wear. Comfort was too proud to admit their true feelings, and he was too uneasy with the idea of backing out on his commitment to her.

There was another reason for Levi going through with the wedding. A year before he'd insisted to his family and to Comfort's how important it was to stay in Virginia, in Loudoun County, and protect their property and the land. Many of the Quakers, at news of the coming war, had packed up and moved west to Ohio. Levi believed John Clarke and his family would have moved west if not for Comfort's betrothal to Levi. If they'd gone to Ohio, they'd be safe and settled by now on a new farm. Here in Loudoun nothing was safe. No, he was the reason Comfort stayed. She'd stayed to marry him and start a family with him. There was no going back. He must live with the consequences of his actions on this day, on days before, on days to come.

"Husband." Comfort put her hand to Levi's arm. "Meeting is over. Thee must come with me to sign our wedding certificate. The elders are waiting."

Levi quickly stood. The word "husband" had startled him as much as Comfort's touch. He reset his hat but kept his top shirt buttons undone. "I'll follow thee," he said quietly to Comfort. He knew he should say "wife," but he couldn't, not yet. In time he would. If Comfort took offense by his omission, her serene face gave nothing away. As beautiful as ever, her robin's-egg-blue eyes shone. Her flawless, fair complexion carried the hint of a flush, which became her. She was becoming, all right; that he'd never doubted.

As he followed behind her, watching the natural sway of her curvy hips, ever keeping her perfect posture, he thought back to the days when he'd done this very same thing: following her out behind her father's barn, anxious to run his hands over her curvaceous body and then up to undo her bonnet, freeing her silky blond hair from its captive braid. His whole body had stirred. He remembered it all too well because he didn't feel stirred now.

Another had taken Comfort's place in his heart, mind, body and soul. Another he could never have. Levi's heart wrenched. His loins tightened at the mere thought of the slip of a woman-soldier he'd never see again. He'd held Willa once, but never since then. That one time needed to last a lifetime. Once wasn't enough. It would never be enough. He'd known it then and he knew it now. Never seeing Willa again was his lot in life, a deserved consequence for what he'd done. He'd strayed from his betrothed and bedded a woman who was not his wife.

He couldn't help it.

Willa couldn't help it.

Neither of them had planned for it to happen. Neither of them meant to be intimate with anyone out of wedlock, to break with their own faiths and their commitments to others, ignoring their own moral codes. But they'd done it. Swept up in the moment, Levi had just found out Willa was leaving with her unit, going off to war to fight and probably get killed; while Willa realized for the first time how much danger Levi was in, even though he wasn't fighting as a soldier on either side. There were men who would rather see Levi dead than allow him to live, thinking of him as hiding behind his religion rather than holding fast to it.

Neither meant to love the other . . . but they did.

"Sign here, Levi," one of the elders said, holding a steel-nibbed pen out to him.

Embarrassed by his lack of attention, Levi obediently signed the wedding certificate, just under Comfort's name. His fingers shook, embarrassing him even more. The elders, gathered round to witness the signings, appeared to hold back their smiles. Levi didn't care that they found his wedding nerves humorous; he just wished he could tell them the reason, certain that if he'd married Willa, he'd have a steady hand.

"Levi," his mother called from behind.

Dreading the moment, he slowly pivoted to face Susan Clement. Other Friends stood around and behind her, waiting to offer their congratulations. His mother, he knew, was not about to do any such thing.

"Levi. Comfort." She spoke to the both of them.

Comfort turned around, smiling.

Levi didn't smile, nor did his mother.

"We are all going to thy house now. Do not be late. Thee both need to be on time for the gathering," Susan Clement instructed as if she were teaching schoolchildren.

"Of course, Susan," Comfort replied in the Quaker way. "We will be along in no time."

"Good." Susan nodded, attempting a smile but not quite managing one.

Comfort frowned at her stern look but didn't say anything.

Expressionless, Levi said nothing. His mother glared at him for what seemed an eternity and then at last turned around to take up his father's arm and walk with him out to their buggy. Levi felt every bit of his mother's ire. His father had looked at him and nodded briefly, even smiling for a time at both him and Comfort. His father had no idea Levi had taken yet another turn away from Quaker tradition in marrying for any reason but love. Levi knew he'd never have to caution his mother to keep silent on the subject. She'd never add to his father's already-heavy burden over Jonah.

Jonah had broken faith with the peace testimony and left home, but at least Benjamin and Lucretia and little Grace remained at home, observant Quakers all. Benjamin, Jonah's twin, held little of the rebellious streak that ran through his brother's veins. They were similar in appearance with their brown hair and brown eyes, but not so similar in behavior. As children they'd sparred often, but as adults, only Jonah strayed, going north to fight with the Yankees.

Eighteen now, standing six foot one, Benjamin was a good brother and a good son. If not for the war, Benjamin would be looking for a wife soon himself, even settling down to work his own farm and be a part of the family mill on Catoctin Creek. After the war, Levi meant to restart the mill and have it thriving again. He meant to stay with the land through the war and make sure of it and the mill. For now he needed to look out for his family.

His sisters were growing up and growing prettier by the day, both with dark-blond hair and hazel eyes like their father. At fifteen, Lucretia was almost a woman. Wise beyond her years, Lucretia was blessed with the gift of healing from an early age. She knew more about natural remedies than most and was called upon on occasion by Friends to aid in healing a family member or farm animal. If not for the war, she'd be living a full life in their Quaker community, busy going to school with her friends, learning the scriptures at home and at meeting, and joining in quilting bees where the women socialized. The boys were already looking at her, but there were few social gatherings now, not since last year when the Confederates first occupied their meetinghouse.

As for little Grace, she was thirteen and all goodness. A serious student, she could grow up to be a leader at meeting, Levi believed. Never once had he needed to caution her to Mind the Light. Expert in household duties and ever eager to learn, Grace studied the scriptures with zeal. She set a good example, bearing witness to her heartfelt Quaker beliefs. Grace embraced the tenets of living a quiet, plain, observant, hard-working life, growing up among the Friends. The war troubled her deeply despite her youth, and she prayed extra hard at meeting, waiting upon the Lord for guidance through the difficulties ahead.

Jonah's leaving hit her almost as hard as their father, Levi thought. She struggled to reconcile how Jonah could grow up a Friend, yet turn to participating in war. Like her sister, Grace was wise beyond her years.

"We wish thee well." One Friend after another came up to Levi and Comfort, expressing their good cheer at the vows they just witnessed.

"Thee are both blessed, indeed," the next man said.

"Truly, thee will have many happy years," the next woman followed with her comment.

And so it went until the meetinghouse had emptied, save for the newly married couple.

"Thy mother will be upset if we're late, husband." Comfort took up her Bible from the signing table and started for the door.

Levi wished she'd say his name and not call him husband. He needed more time before he could call her wife. Preoccupied with this thought, it didn't occur to Levi that neither he nor Comfort had shared more than a brief handfasting throughout their wedding and certificate signing. Not even a hug.

Checking the meetinghouse to make sure all was set right again, Levi couldn't help but breathe a sigh of relief that none of the northern soldiers occupying Waterford had charged into Fairfax Meetinghouse and demanded usage for barracks and weapons storage, as the Confederates had. Because their numbers in Waterford were diminished, the Quakers who attended meeting had little need to rebuild new benches. And because they'd been forced last year to combine men and women at meeting, breaking with their long-held tradition to keep genders separate, the members of Fairfax Meeting decided to continue meeting for worship as one body now. The war had already changed many things. This was just one more.

No sooner had Levi stepped outside than a group of Yankee

soldiers approached. Irritated, Levi wished the Friends could have at least this one day without the war hanging over their heads. He wanted his family to have this day for peace and a quiet gathering, unfettered by the sight of guns and men in uniform.

Comfort had been talking with some of the Friends, but walked toward Levi when she saw the soldiers beginning to gather around him.

"It's Sunday and all," one of the soldiers addressed Levi.

"Yes, it's First Day," Levi acknowledged, eyeing the group carefully. He'd no idea what they intended. If it was to take over their meetinghouse, he'd stand in the doorway and do what he could to prevent the soldiers from coming inside.

"First Day?" the soldier repeated, his look puzzled.

Levi wasn't in a mood to teach anyone the Quaker way, mindful of his own turn away from the Word.

The soldier put out his hand for Levi to shake. "I'm Private Ryan and these men, well . . . we're in the same unit and the same mess, eating and sleeping and fighting together."

Levi shook the young soldier's hand, nonplussed by the details he'd shared. The soldier appeared to be younger than he, maybe nineteen, but almost as tall. Levi stood six foot five. The soldier appeared nervous. Levi watched his eyes. He could tell a lot about a person from the look in his eyes. This soldier didn't pose any threat. His eyes were clear and didn't shift. He looked Levi square in the face, despite his obvious anxiety.

"Well, sir, I know you just got done with a wedding, and, well . . . well . . . a lot of us, sir . . . a lot of us miss home real bad." The private looked around at his comrades, twelve in all, and then faced Levi again. "We were hoping that maybe . . . maybe you'd let us tag along for the celebration. We haven't been around families in so long. Would you let . . . would you let us come to the celebration? We'd bring food. We all just got our meat rations and we'd bring 'em. Yes, sir, we would," the private said, shuffling his feet in place, obviously uncomfortable with his question.

Levi's heart gave a little. These were all children, gone off to fight in a war with some never to see home again. These soldiers had mothers and fathers and brothers and sisters and sweethearts, all left behind. Most of their kin would get letters telling them their loved one had fallen in battle. He looked to Comfort. Her heart gave, too; he could tell.

"We're Quakers," Levi informed Private Ryan.

"Yes, Quakers," the private repeated.

"We don't have celebrations with drinking and dancing," Levi explained. "What is thy name?"

"I told you. Private Ryan." The soldier smiled at both Levi and Comfort.

"No, thy God-given name. We Quakers don't go by titles or rank," Levi explained.

"Oh, yeah. My name is Caleb. Caleb Ryan."

"Thee and thy men can come to our house, Caleb Ryan, but understand that we will have a quiet gathering of family and Friends. Thee is welcome, and my wife and I . . . ," he said, swallowing hard, saying it for the first time. "My wife and I would appreciate thee bringing some of thy rations. Thee is welcome to our table and welcome to share our food. Our stores are low, as thee must know," Levi said, making his point clear.

Private Ryan beamed. He turned to his men. "Get your rations and mind your uniforms. We're going to a family celebration."

"Hurrah!"

"Huzzah!"

"We'll wait until thee returns, and then thee can follow us to our house," Levi instructed.

"Yes, sir," the private answered; then he turned on his heels, making a beeline for his camp along with the rest of his men.

"This is a good thing we are doing, husband, inviting the soldiers," Comfort said and put her hand on Levi's arm. She smiled at him, and it was a genuine smile.

"Yes, a good thing," he repeated, mindful of her touch. He'd expected Comfort to rail at him for already being late. She seemed the Comfort of old in this moment, the Comfort whom he'd first fallen in love with, the Comfort who wasn't filled with pride, who wasn't overly critical of others, and who didn't eschew plainness in all things.

Still, he didn't love Comfort.

But maybe over time he'd learn to love her again.

And maybe over time he'd forget that he'd ever loved Willa Mae Tyler.

CHAPTER TWO

Near Manassas Junction, Fairfax County, Virginia—March 1862

The Stone House! Willa had found it. She'd been given an afternoon pass from her sergeant to leave their nearby encampment and now stood at the intersection of Sudley-Manassas Road and the Warrenton Turnpike.

The two-story, red sandstone structure was imposing, despite its obvious damage from rifle fire and artillery shells. The windows appeared intact, probably replaced by the current owners. This was the Stone House—the house where her brother Walter breathed his last breath. This was the house where Walter carried Henry, already dead, in his arms while his own life's blood drained away. Both of her brothers died during the battle at Manassas Junction on Bull Run Creek last year. It was in July, she remembered prayerfully.

Willa had made the decision to disguise herself as a man and muster into Confederate ranks the moment she found out her brothers were dead. She was seventeen then, and now she was all of eighteen. A tomboy her whole life, she didn't think pretending to be a man would prove difficult. So far her disguise had fooled most people; not all, but most. And she hadn't been kicked out of the army, sent home, or captured and sent to any prison . . . yet.

She'd made a promise to herself to fight at Manassas at the Stone House and kill as many Yankees as she could to avenge the death of her brothers. She'd killed Yankees in battle already, just not on this battlefield. Now she approached Manassas and the Stone House with life in her heart, and not death. She had a secret now, a secret to share with her cherished brothers buried on this hallowed ground.

Although she knew she'd never find their exact burial spot, she knew Walter and Henry were buried close. Her friend, Private Shep Carter, had told her as much before he died in the Battle of Ball's Bluff near Edward's Ferry last year—a lifetime ago, it seemed. Shep had been with Walter at Manassas right before Walter died. It broke her heart that Shep had lost his life as so many others did in the battle at Ball's Bluff. She herself had dug his grave and covered him over, assigned to the burial detail at the end of that fateful day. Shep had been kind to her and accepted her, even though he'd guessed she was female. He never reported her to her superiors. Always, she would remember him fondly.

With no battle raging at the moment on the gentle hills of Manassas, Willa was able to approach the Stone House. It sat all by itself in the middle of fields that showed evidence of planted corn, oats and hops. Having grown up on a small Virginia farm in Bedford County, Willa knew all about crops and soil. She could tell that whoever lived at the Stone House now was enduring hard times. The impoverished land told the story.

Willa stopped short, then slowly pivoted in a full circle. A battle played out all around her in her head. She could hear it, feel it, and see the suffering in her mind's eye. Was it a coming battle she envisioned, or a battle that had been fought before? The railroads were close, and they were the reason for many a fight. Each side wanted control of the rails.

Willa clamped her hands over her ears. The cries of wounded and dying soldiers, their gray and blue uniforms bloodied, flanked her on all sides. She knew in that moment that another battle would be fought here at Manassas. More bodies were to join those of Walter and Henry . . . so many more. Willa wanted to run away from the war and the Stone House, but she couldn't.

Dropping her hands from her ears she put a hand to her middle for courage, and then took deliberate steps toward the front door of the Stone House. How queer it felt to be knocking on a door where only last year the house had been barraged with artillery fire and the gunfire of opposing troops. She knew the North had occupied the house before her compatriots did. How queer, too, to know that someone might actually be living here, in the calm before yet another storm. Willa knocked a second time.

The heavy wood door creaked open. A woman stood in the threshold, only opening the door wide enough to see who was outside.

"I'm Private Will Carter." Willa automatically lowered her voice, as she was so used to doing by this time.

The woman opened the door another couple of inches, perhaps not sensing any threat from the young soldier.

Until now, Willa didn't realize that she hadn't planned what to say. Dang it! She should have something prepared. "Uh, ma'am," she said, stalling for time. "My . . . my brothers fought for Virginia and died here in your house last year in July. I was wondering if I could just come inside for a spell. That's all, ma'am. I just want to come inside and spend a few moments where my brothers breathed their last."

The woman cautiously opened the door a little more, looking past Willa as if searching the landscape for more soldiers— soldiers who wanted to take from her and steal what she wouldn't give over. Sometimes soldiers would just want to eat with her and her husband, but more often than not they'd take what they wanted. Satisfied that the soldier at her door was alone, she opened the door wider still. "I'm Jane Matthews, Will. You are welcome to come inside." The middle-aged, kindly woman opened the door fully.

"Thank you, ma'am," Willa said and stepped inside the house. Her body tensed the moment she spied the room and its contents. It looked normal, as if nothing had ever been amiss, as if untouched by the war outside. The place wasn't what she'd expected, but she didn't know what to expect, not really. She stepped farther into the room, walking over to the fireplace, then to the dining area with the table and chairs. Could this have been the table where Walter died? Could this have been where the Yankee army surgeon tried to save him? She ran her fingers reverently over the polished, scratched table surface, mindless of anything but imagining the moment and time when her brother died.

She felt like she was in church now, the little Methodist church she'd attended as a child. She'd sit in the pew alongside Walter and Henry and her parents, fidgeting during the service. Walter would tell her to sit still and shush, then turn around and spark mischief with Henry, causing their mother to tell them all to sit still and shush.

Walter and Henry would always tease her in church, too, because she'd had to wear a dress. Sunday was the only time her mother could force her to wear one. Willa remembered her Christmas ribbon. Her brothers had given the green grosgrain ribbon to her, telling her how pretty she was and that one day she'd give all the boys in Bedford County a fit. She'd left the ribbon home when she'd gone off to war. She'd used it to bind her cutoff hair and then left the tied bundle with her good-bye letter to her parents. Tears stung her eyes and threatened to spill down her cheeks.

"This floor was covered with Yankee wounded," Jane Matthews detailed, breaking into Willa's melancholy reverie. "The basement, too."

Willa quickly wiped her tears, doing her best to hide her emotions. But her tears kept coming. She couldn't stem her feelings, not even in front of this stranger. "Sorry, ma'am," Willa blurted out, trying to hold emotions together.

"You've nothing to apologize for, son," Jane Matthews said gently. If she suspected Willa was a female, she said nothing.

Willa passed for a sixteen- or seventeen-year-old boy to most folks, with her lack of any beard growth and her slight frame and short statue. Her baggy, oversized uniform helped in her disguise, as did her floppy-brimmed hat. She chose to wear it rather than a bummer cap, because it hid more of her than the army cap. Before she left home to muster into the army, she'd cut off all of her waist-length, lustrous, black hair, not trusting that a thick braid could stay hidden for long under any kind of hat. She looked now like the countless young men who'd mustered into army ranks. She was a good shot, too. Few paid much attention to a young man in the army who could shoot, spot-on. Few men in the military would suspect a woman could shoot better than they could.

"Were you here, ma'am?" Willa asked, hopeful that Mrs. Matthews could give her more details of the battle.

She studied the woman closely. Her kind features looked worn, her expression sad. Her blue eyes, at one time likely vibrant, held no sparkle now. Of average height, Mrs. Matthews wasn't much taller than Willa. She wasn't much bigger around the middle either—too thin, Willa thought. Dressed in a cotton blouse buttoned to the neck, wool skirt, and a heavy apron, she looked like a lot of farm wives in Virginia. No silk and satin. No fineries such as Willa imagined women in plantation-owning families might sometimes wear. But with the war going on, she doubted even the rich could afford such luxuries. Of course, Willa didn't know much about how females dressed anyway.

She'd asked Surry these things, if she ever wanted to know.

Choking back new tears at the thought of her best friend Surry, Willa tried to shut out everything but Mrs. Matthews recounting details she could recall about the day Walter and Henry died. Scared to death that Surry might lie dead somewhere, too, Willa did her best to hold her ground and keep herself focused.

"Me and my husband, Henry, we were both here," Jane Matthews spoke up, at first looking at Willa and then on past her, out the window at the fields in the distance. "Henry is out there now, trying to get something done on our land, trying to grow something in all of this wasteland. I swan, it's a fine kettle of fish we're all in, Will. A fine kettle . . . ," her voice trailed.

"Henry? Your husband's name is Henry?" Willa repeated, warming to the same name as her brother's.

"Yes, Henry," Jane Matthews replied, her forlorn countenance on Willa now. "The battle started that day a third of a mile or so north of our house. A brigade of our boys was coming from the Stone Bridge and ran into Yankees advancing on the road out yonder, the Sudley-Manassas Road. Rebels were hiding all around our house, firing on the Yankees until the 27th New York Infantry drove them from here. Drove 'em across the Warrenton Turnpike, and then on up Henry Hill."

Willa listened carefully, intent on the still-shaken woman's every word.

"Wounded Yankees started coming inside here some time after our boys were driven from around the house. They took shelter down in our basement, then anywhere they could," Jane Matthews explained. She started for the basement steps.

Willa followed right on her heels. The basement smelled musty as she made her way down the steps behind Mrs. Mathews. The white stone walls were marked and worn, showing their age. Two small windows allowed in a tiny bit of light.

There was a fireplace along one wall, with posts and beams for support. The area was bare but for a small stack of wood in one corner and several iron candle holders affixed to the walls. It was hard to get a decent breath in the close air.

"Not much left here now. Our stores of food and supplies are near gone. But during the battle, like I said, wounded soldiers came down here looking for shelter. There was blood everywhere, I can tell you that," Jane Matthews declared. "I was trying to help and so was my Henry, even though it was Yankees coming in. They didn't try to hurt us. They were too hurt themselves to care about us, I suppose. The cries from the poor, hurt, young men were the most pitiful thing I'd ever heard in all my born days." She started back up the steps now.

Willa followed.

"The Yankees put a red flag outside of our house, I guess to mark it as a shelter and a place for the suffering. The fighting wasn't over. Henry and me, we just tried to find places for all the wounded coming in. When the basement filled up, we helped lay folks out like spoons lined up on our floor here. Some of 'em were dead already, but Henry and me, we didn't say anything to anybody about it. Rifles were stacked everywhere along our walls. I'd never seen so many guns. Had to be a hundred at least. At first I thought the Yankees were gonna shoot us, with so many guns inside, but they didn't," she said, giving her head a nod as if in affirmation that she and her husband had been spared.

Willa gazed around the large first floor of the Stone House, envisioning all the carnage. Since the Yankees occupied the house, she knew that Walter and Henry were not inside during the time of which Mrs. Matthews spoke.

"The Yankees had a surgeon and two medical officers with 'em, and they tended to all the wounded as best they could," Jane Matthews said, continuing with her account. "We let 'em use our table and anything else they could find to tend to the suffering. Me and Henry, we tried to help with bandages, but we didn't have much to give up. The next thing we knew it was hours later, before candle-lighting is all I remember, and the fighting was over. Then in came our boys. The 28th Virginia Infantry," she proudly announced. "Our boys took charge of things right away. Must have been forty Yankees or so that surrendered. Those Yankees that were wounded and suffering, our boys let 'em stay. And they let one of the Yankee medical officers stay to help. I don't recall any operations being done, but there was so much going on, I just don't know. I do know there was a lot of blood and a lot of trying to stop all the bleeding. Time went on and like I said before, it wasn't candle-lighting time yet, when I saw one of our boys go outside and meet up with a soldier carrying another of our boys in his arms. Must be there were battlefield hospitals set up somewhere, but I don't know about that. I just know our house was still being used as a refuge."

Willa's heart lurched at Mrs. Matthews's words. Willa knew she must be talking about Walter approaching with Henry, already dead, in his arms. She knew the story from here. Shep Carter had told her as much. Dear Shep. Dear Mrs. Matthews.

"That's all I can tell you, Will. It's all I know. I saw the boy, our boy, helped inside and I saw him being put on the table over yonder. He looked real close to death. I knew there wasn't much anybody could do."

Willa went back over to the table, reverently running her hand along its scratched surface. *Walter. Oh, Walter.*

Jane Matthews followed Willa. "He was one of your brothers, wasn't he?" Jane quietly acknowledged.

"Yes, ma'am." Willa fought new tears. "Yes, ma'am, he was my brother Walter. Henry already lay dead outside. Walter had carried him from the battlefield, bringing him to your house.

They were my dear brothers, Mrs. Matthews. They were the reason I mustered in. They are the reason I'm here now," Willa said in a hushed whisper, as if in church. New tears started to fall. This time she let them fall, not caring what Mrs. Matthews might think.

"There, there, dear." Jane Matthews put a hand to Willa's shoulder.

Willa dissolved into tears then, letting Mrs. Matthews hold her close. Long moments passed before Willa pulled out of the maternal embrace. "Thank you," Willa said, a little embarrassed now, uncomfortable at her less-than-soldierly behavior. No matter. What did it matter if Mrs. Matthews guessed her sex—for surely a male wouldn't cry as she just had—and found out she was female?

Jane Matthews smiled knowingly at Willa.

It was all right that she'd guessed. It was all right.

"Dear? I wonder at your staying in this war and this fight? Shouldn't you go home, especially now?"

Willa straightened her spine, immediately alerted to Mrs. Matthews's caution. "What do you mean, especially now?" she queried, bristling a little.

"You're carrying a secret, a secret you came here to tell your brothers," Jane said, her tone sure.

She knows. Willa let out the breath she'd been holding. *She knows.*

Willa was carrying.

She was carrying Levi Clement's child.

"Hold her down, Frank! I'll git the young one. These here two runaways are the ones they're looking for from down Virginia way. I'm sure of it!"

Surry wished she had a gun now so she could shoot both of these vermin who'd just assaulted her and Penny. If they did anything to her little sister, she'd kill them with her bare hands. The white man who had hold of Surry now was bigger and stronger-looking than the one who held Penny. He'd forced Surry to the ground and hovered over her like the angel of death. She was more repelled than afraid, and far more worried for little Penny than herself. These slave catchers were mean and ugly, and Surry had nothing but murder in her heart for them.

Surry had supposed that she and Penny were safe, having made it from across the Potomac in Virginia to the free African-American settlement in Baltimore, Maryland, but she'd supposed wrong.

Maryland was a slave-holding border state, and Maryland had sided with the North. Surry had mistakenly ignored the warnings of those along the Underground Railroad, telling her that she and Penny needed to get all the way north to Canada before they'd be safe and free. Most especially, she'd ignored what Lucas Minor had told her. Lucas had warned her to get all the way to Canada. The war had been going on for a year now. Because Surry wanted to, she believed that folks up north wouldn't still be worried over catching runaways and returning them south. She should have listened to other conductors along the Underground Railroad, to conductors like Lucas. She should have heeded his words and kept hidden, even in the free settlement in Baltimore she should have kept herself and Penny hidden.

Still guilt-ridden over her brother Samuel and her sister Pitty Pat being picked up in Virginia by Confederates soon after they'd started their escape north, Surry blamed herself for their discovery. Even though her little sister had run out from their hiding place to save a hurt puppy on the road, with Samuel chasing to bring her back before the soldiers found her, Surry would always believe it was all her fault. Her family, what was left of it, was her responsibility. She'd failed in keeping Samuel and Pitty Pat safe.

The crushing weight of the oaf atop her just made Surry madder and stronger. In one swift move she kneed him hard in the groin and rolled out from under him.

"You little n—r bitch!" he spat, grabbing his groin in pain.

"Zeke, you idiot," the other man blurt out. "Keep ahold of her. Don't let her git away. There's a good bounty on the both of 'em."

"Surry!" Penny screamed. "Surry! *Surry!*"

Surry got to her feet but didn't run away. How could she, with Penny still held captive? These bastards meant to send them south, back to the Shelby Plantation, and get their money. At least she didn't think they'd kill them.

By now, her captor had gotten to his feet.

Surry faced him, squaring her shoulders and standing tall.

He slapped her hard across the face.

Somehow, she kept her footing. All she saw in front of her now was the bastard rapist Boyd Blankenship from the Shelby Plantation, the ugly white overseer's son who'd hanged her father and raped her, cutting her face in the bargain. This man had the same meanness in him and the same fetid, onion breath as Boyd Blankenship.

"What's the ruckus here?" A Baltimore policeman suddenly came up on them. "Here, now," he said, grabbing the arm of the man who had hold of Penny, shoving him away from her. Another policeman came around the corner, joining them.

Surry breathed a little easier, motioning for Penny to come over to her.

Penny did, running into her sister's arms and holding on for dear life.

"Look here, officer," one of the slave catchers said. "We got a legal right to catch these here two runaways. I got the papers

36

that say so." He took out a wrinkled poster and tried to straighten it out for the police officer. The afternoon sun was fading and the light was poor.

The officer glimpsed the paper, then shoved it back at the slave catcher. "It says there are some runaways from Bedford County, Virginia, from the Shelby Plantation. That's all it says, boys. You can't go picking up Negroes in this free settlement whenever you've a mind to. You two make me sick, trying to get money by hurting these poor people. Now, leave these girls be and get," the officer ordered.

"Hold on, now," one of the culprits said. "You police are supposed to be helping us track down fugitive slaves, not protect 'em. It ain't right, the way you're treating us. We're white like you."

The officer glared at the slave catcher, his expression showing his disdain for the two men and his evident disagreement with their so-called "legal" duty as bounty hunters to catch runaway slaves.

Surry kept her arms around Penny and her eyes on the bastards trying to capture them.

"There's a surefire way to know if these two are runaways or not." The culprit spoke out again. "Just git 'em both to try and write somethin'. Ain't no way slaves know how to read and write. Just git 'em to write somethin', and then me and my partner will leave 'em be. If not, we have every right to turn 'em in and git our money," the bounty hunter insisted.

Surry held her breath, fighting for calm.

The police officer looked both her and Penny over, as if actually considering the bounty hunter's argument. The law said that fugitive slaves had to be returned south, but most of the time the law was ignored in the North. There were still slaveholding states in the North, yes. Maryland was one of them. When pressed, the police had no choice but to enforce the law.

This situation evidently put just such a dilemma before the officer.

"Miss?" the officer said, looking at Surry. "What's your name?"

Squeezing Penny, hoping Penny was listening carefully, Surry carefully repeated, "My name is Susan Smith. This is my little sister, Pattie."

Sighing heavily, resignedly, the officer took out his pad and pencil. "While we've still got the light, I want you to write your name, your address, and what you do for a living."

Surry gently pushed Penny from her and took the pad and pencil.

Both of the bounty-hunting slave catchers smirked, seemingly waiting for the moment they could pounce on both runaways and collect their money.

The other police officer stood next to his partner now, closely scrutinizing Surry and the pad and pencil in her hand.

"I need something for support," Surry told them.

"Use my back," the first officer said, turning around so Surry could do just that.

Surry caught Penny's eye before she started to put anything down. Once she had Penny's attention, she began moving the pencil slowly over the pad:

Susan Smith
Free settlement, Baltimore, Maryland
House domestic worker

She wrote in careful script, rather than printing. When finished, she handed the pad to the officer who'd already turned around and faced her again.

He read what she'd written, smiling broadly once he did. "She's no slave. She can write better than most I've seen. Nope, she's no slave. This girl is educated."

"Goddammit! She's just trying to hornswoggle you," one of the culprits spat. "Make the other one write somethin'! I guarantee you she won't be able to write nuthin'!"

"The little one can't be more than ten or eleven. There's many an urchin around here who can't write yet," the officer intoned.

Surry took control of the situation and took the pad and pencil back from the officer. "Pattie, dear. Please write your name out nice and clear for these officers."

Penny took the outstretched writing materials from her sister.

Surry turned around to let Penny use her back for support.

Her hands trembled slightly, but Penny wrote in near-perfect printing: *Pattie Smith.*

Surry quickly turned around to look at Penny's writing before the officers had a chance to. She'd never been more proud, knowing how scared Penny was, and knowing how smart she was. Penny remembered the name Surry had introduced. She hadn't written Penny Lion but Pattie Smith. Surry handed the pad to the officers and hugged her sister tightly to her.

"Well, I'll be," the officer said, near awestruck that one so young was so educated. Nope, for sure neither of these girls could be runaway slaves from Virginia. They were educated girls. He addressed the two men who'd tried to capture these free Negroes. "You boys best get, now, if you know what's good for you. If you're not out of this settlement in ten minutes' time, my partner and I will come after you and throw you both in jail."

Surry stood tall, with Penny safely beside her.

Both of the brutes skulked away, turning around more than once to utter curses at them.

The officers stayed until the men were well out of sight, then cautioned Surry and Penny to go home and get off the streets. The streets were dangerous. Free Negroes could be kidnapped and sold into slavery in the South, the police cautioned.

Surry didn't need a second warning, quickly ushering Penny off to hide, yet again. Unsure of exactly whom to find to help them continue on the Underground Railroad north, she was sure that they had to go north now, all the way to Canada, to be truly safe and free. She had her best friend since childhood, Willa Mae Tyler, to thank for not being caught this time and sent back south. Since she'd been a slave on a plantation, Surry couldn't go to school and learn to read and write. Almost from the day she and Willa met, both of them no more than seven, Willa had told Surry she'd teach her whatever she learned in school. True to her promise, Willa had done just that. Because Surry was educated, she'd just saved herself and Penny from capture. Willa had saved them.

Home. The sound of the word rang hollow in Surry's difficult thoughts. Home used to be the Shelby Plantation in Bedford County, where she and her family lived together for so many years. Home used to be where she could sneak away and meet up with Willa on the banks of the James, where they'd secretly shared friendship and companionship since they were girls of seven. Home used to be where she had her first crush on Nate Bonner.

But there was no more home for Surry as she once knew it.

Her beloved father had been accused of attempted murder by the monstrous overseer at the plantation and hanged. One of her brothers had run away long ago; then three more ran away after their father had been killed. Surry had no idea if they were dead or alive, if they were caught or had escaped. Nate Bonner was a fugitive slave now, too.

Despite the war, despite the increased danger of traveling, and because Surry believed the dangers at the plantation would be far worse for them now, she had set out along the Underground Railroad with her younger brother Samuel and her little sisters Penny and Pitty Pat. She'd been unable to talk her mother into coming with them. And now Sam and Pitty Pat were likely locked away in some Confederate prison with other runaway slaves. If they were lucky, that is. She prayed they were still alive.

Surry prayed for Willa, too, hoping she didn't lie dead on some battlefield, wishing with all her heart Willa had never joined the army. Surry knew why she'd joined: to avenge the deaths of her brothers, killed by Yankees. The war wasn't about slavery for Willa. Surry understood that and didn't take offense. Surry knew Willa didn't think poorly of colored folks. She knew that.

So many that Surry had loved at home were home no more.

And now there was someone else to worry over. Lucas Minor. Lucas was free. All her life she'd wanted to know about bein' free, thinking there was no such thing, until she met Lucas.

She'd only known him for the short time he helped her along the Underground Railroad, but it was long enough for him to stir her heart and capture her affection. She'd known him long enough to worry that someone so handsome and so wonderful would marry soon. Surry knew that she'd never be the one he'd marry. She wasn't free, and she couldn't stay in Waterford, even if he'd asked her to, which he hadn't. No words had been spoken between them.

Times were dangerous. The safety of her sister was all that was important. The night she saw Lucas for the last time— when he guided her and Penny to Edward's Ferry and helped the ferryman undo the boat ties and let her go—still hurt as much as it did at that moment. The life she wished for with a man like Lucas Minor could never be hers.

Surry forced her worried thoughts to clear. For Penny's sake, she must. The road ahead to Canada would be long and difficult. She must concentrate on their journey and what lay ahead, rather than on who she was leaving behind.

CHAPTER THREE

"Have a swig of John Barleycorn, Taylor," said one of the soldiers sitting around their campfire, pressing the whiskey into Willa's hand.

She'd never tasted hard liquor growing up, never having had the occasion or the desire. Now in the army, she'd tried to fit in as a good old boy and tasted whiskey when offered, but never drank much of it. Usually she'd just take a swig and pass the jug around. This time she passed the jug to the next soldier without a taste. If she drank it, she knew she'd throw up. At night, especially these days, she felt sick to her stomach. Sometimes she'd steal away from the eyes of other soldiers and get sick in the woods. She knew it wasn't because of the runs and didn't worry that she'd come down with dreaded dysentery.

The baby she was carrying had to be the reason.

Levi's baby.

Here she'd thought to forever be a tomboy, never even liking any of the boys she'd grown up with. But she'd given herself to Levi Clement, practically a stranger to her—a stranger who sympathized with the enemy. He was a Quaker and didn't believe in war or slavery.

Well, she didn't support slavery either, but she was born a Virginian and would fight to support Virginia and the South. She would fight to pay her dead brothers the respect they deserved. She'd expected to fight until she couldn't, until she herself was killed. But the unexpected had happened. She'd met

43

someone, someone who had her heart from the moment she first saw him. Somewhere in the midst of war and death and the harsh realities of life, she'd met someone who captured her heart, body, and soul: Levi Clement. She'd gone willingly into Levi's arms, despite all the reasons she should not. She loved him with all her heart and now she was going to have his child. Her life had turned completely upside down in the time it took to first lock gazes with the compelling, tall, dark-haired devastatingly handsome Quaker.

How she wished for Surry's counsel now. How she wished they could sit on the riverbank of the James as they'd done for so many years growing up. She could ask Surry what to do. Surry would know. But she was by herself now, without Surry's counsel, and Willa had to puzzle out this dilemma alone.

If she were back home, married to some young man in Bedford County, and if Surry were back home, married to some young man in Bedford County, couldn't they just go on and continue to share in each other's lives as they'd done before, albeit in secret? Maybe one day they could share their friendship out in the open, colored and white together. Hadn't Willa seen coloreds and whites living together in the town of Waterford? The coloreds in Waterford were free.

Please one day let Surry be free, dear Lord, Willa prayed silently. Then such a fine life it would be, she and Surry visiting each other's homes, exchanging stories of their husbands and their children. Willa's thoughts trailed off.

"I swan, Taylor, you're a puzzle for sure," the beefy private next to her said, forcing her thoughts back to the present. She had the queerest feeling he could read her mind since he'd used the word puzzle. Her heart gave a start. Could he have guessed, sitting so close to her in the firelight, that she was female? On top of everything else, that's all she needed: to be found out and kicked out of the army.

"Whattcha mean?" she asked him, doing her best to sound nonchalant and like every other southern farm boy who mustered into their unit.

"You don't take to drinkin' or swearin' or goin' to town and trippin' the lights fantastic with all the gals just waitin' for us soldiers. You don't get any letters from any sweetheart back home. You stick to yourself like you was some Nancy boy or somethin'."

Willa moved a little bit away from the private. "I'm not a Nancy boy. I'm just here to fight is all," she said in clipped tones, pulling her hat brim down farther, hoping to shut down any more conversation.

"Sure enough," he tossed at her, smiling now. "You sure enough got a right to do anythin' you want, fightin' with us. Sorry to say anythin', Taylor," he apologized. "Don't take no offense, all right? I sure don't want you mad at me on the battlefield. You might be a little guy without much muscle, but you're the best shot in our unit. I know you have all our backs, keeping the Yankees in your sights. You've proven yourself in every skirmish and fight," he said, underscoring his point with a nod.

"No offense taken," she said in her lowest voice, relieved that he hadn't guessed her secret.

Her stomach suddenly seized. She had a far more important secret to keep now: she was pregnant. She'd acted immorally and was going to have a baby without a husband and without the sanction of God's blessing. Her parents would be fit to be tied if they knew.

At once she softened when she thought of her parents. They didn't even know if she was alive. She must write to them, most assuredly *not* telling them about the baby coming, but to let them know she was all right, for now anyway. All those long months ago when she'd left them a letter telling them she'd

45

gone off to fight for Virginia, she'd made a promise. She'd told them she'd come home. Walter and Henry had been killed by the Yankees, and though Willa didn't believe she would be alive to come home, she'd promised her parents she would. Yes, she'd write them a letter this very night and hope to ease their worries. She had a bit of candle left for the task.

As for her worry over the life that grew inside her, the life she and Levi had created, she'd no idea what to do. She'd no idea how she would feel, much less how her body would change. Although she'd been able to bind her bosom to hide her sex, she doubted that after a time she could hide her swelling stomach. Beyond knowing she'd get bigger, she'd never been around babies as a child. Animals, yes. She'd seen animals swell with their babies and even watched horses and cows give birth, but never a person. Afraid of the changes that would overtake her body, Willa was more worried that something might happen to the baby. What if she did something wrong and the baby inside her died?

Willa sucked in a gasp. Scared now, really scared, she suddenly thought of the time years ago when Surry had asked her if she'd ever been scared—really scared. Willa had said no. She'd never had to be afraid like Surry, because Willa was free and didn't have to live under slavery.

Willa would give Surry a different answer now. She was scared, really scared, that she might do wrong by the little one growing inside her. Not worried for her own life in the war—except for trying to fulfill her promise to her parents and come home to them—she worried for her baby's life and what to do for it. Bidding good night to her compatriots, Willa abruptly left their shared campfire and started for her A tent. It was big enough for four, and she knew none of the other soldiers would have gone to sleep just yet. She needed to be alone for a while to think on what to do. After she wrote to her parents, she'd try to figure things out. Maybe a night's sleep would bring her needed answers in the morning.

"Thee must leave. My parents will be home soon. They mustn't see thee! Please, go," Lucretia said.

She'd been frantic with worry the moment Private Caleb Ryan, dressed in his blue uniform, set foot on their porch. She'd been out front sweeping when the tall, good-looking, blond soldier showed up, surprised to see him, yet pleased all the same. The gray day was already cold, with a hint of snow in the air, but the weather would be nothing compared to the storm caused if anyone in her family saw the northerner approach the house. She knew he'd noticed her at her brother's after-wedding gathering—noticed her in the way a boy notices a girl. She'd noticed him, too, even though such a thing was forbidden. He was an outsider. He wasn't a Quaker.

"I won't leave until you promise to give me a chance to get to know you, to at least talk to you," the private insisted, standing in front of Lucretia now, a good head taller than her. He'd removed his hat.

Lucretia was taken aback. Quaker men didn't remove their hats for anything but prayer. All were equal in the sight of God. No one needed to remove his hat. That the soldier had done so stirred her in ways it should not. Despite her panic, looking around Caleb Ryan to see if Levi approached from across the field or if her parents were driving up the lane in their buggy, Lucretia didn't make any promises to him.

"Thee must go and go now!" she repeated, standing firm. Her insides melted, being so close to the attractive, impressive-looking soldier, flattered by his attention. Struggling to rein in her emotions, what did she care that he was of such fine physique and that his presence sent shivers down her spine?

"Lucretia," he said.

"Thee mustn't say my name," she chastised.

"And why is that? You can say mine. It's Caleb."

"I know thy name," she said before she thought better of it.

"Oh," he said, his tone teasing. "And just how is it that you know my name?"

"The same way thee knows mine, I suppose," she threw out without thinking. Flushed with embarrassment, she put her hands to her cheeks to cool them, having set her broom aside the moment she saw the soldier approach.

"You're about the prettiest thing I ever saw," he said, smiling warmly at her gesture. "Even back home I've never seen the like."

Lucretia knew her face had to be pure crimson by now. She took her hands away despite wanting to keep them on her cheeks. Her palms were cold from nervous sweat. "Thee has to leave *now*, Caleb," she insisted a second time.

He didn't miss the fact that she'd said his name. Her rosebud mouth drew his attention, even more than the luster of her blue eyes, the soft strands of dark-blond hair escaping her bonnet, or the comely turn of her chin. "Listen, Lucretia. I don't have much time here. What I mean is that I don't know how long my unit will be stationed here. Coming . . . well, coming to your brother's house the other day and being with your family and all the others . . . well. . . ." He hesitated to finish, looking anywhere now but at her.

"Yes?" she urged, suddenly wanting him to speak his piece.

He looked at her now. "Well, the other boys with me, they all have family and wives and sweethearts to write to them and remind 'em of home. I don't, Lucretia. The simple fact is I don't, but when I saw you . . . when I saw you, the first thought I had was that you might think to write to me. At night when I'm alone before the fighting starts up again, I could take out your letters and know that somewhere there was a pretty girl who thinks of me and cares if I die come morning. I wouldn't feel so alone then," he admitted, now turning almost as red as she.

No matter that she was only a girl of fifteen, Lucretia understood how hard it was for Caleb to admit such things to her. His words touched the woman in her and not the girl. How could she refuse him? *I cannot,* she knew. It wouldn't be breaking with faith and her traditions so very much if she were to just write to him. That should be all right, she resolved to herself.

"Thee must leave now, Caleb Ryan. Thee will be discovered if thee remains at my door. I could go to Waterford tomorrow and perhaps we could meet up there, to the side of the mercantile in the town square. Perhaps, then, if the way is clear, we could exchange our addresses. I will write mine and thee can give me thine. Is that agreeable to thee?" she asked quickly, before she lost her courage.

"Lucretia Clement," he said, his throat thick, "that's about the most agreeable thing I've ever heard."

His husky tone sent new shivers down her spine.

He smiled.

She returned his smile with her own.

"Tomorrow, then?" he repeated.

"Yes, tomorrow," she parroted.

He put his hat back on and turned to leave, soon clearing the steps and heading down the path away from the Clement farmhouse.

"I'm fifteen," she called out to him, shocked at her brazen behavior. "How old are thou?"

The private stopped and looked her way. "Eighteen. I'm eighteen," he called back to her.

He smiled.

She returned his smile again.

Between twilight and candle-lighting, soon it would be time for bed. Levi had chores to finish in the barn. He'd meant to visit his parents and Benjamin and his sisters today, the family farm being very close to the house he'd built for himself and for Comfort. Unfortunately for them all, there wasn't enough work on either of their farms anymore, what with soldiers on both sides of the fight taking from their food stores and crops in the fields. It was bad enough Levi'd had to shut their flour mill down last year, unwilling to keep it running to provide flour for the occupying Confederate army.

Samuel Means, a heretofore prominent lapsed Quaker, had fled to Maryland at the outset of the war. At that time much of his property had been either confiscated or destroyed by the Confederate soldiers. Weeks ago, when the Yankees came into Loudoun County and took control, Means acted as a civilian guide for Colonel Geary and his troops. Levi knew there was no home or business left for Samuel, and wondered what he would do now. He wondered if Samuel Means might know about Jonah. Levi would find Samuel and ask him. It was worth a try. Levi had thought about setting out himself to find Jonah. He still hadn't ruled against taking such action. What stopped him was his family. He had to protect them, and now that included his wife, Comfort. Though he wouldn't and couldn't take up arms to protect them, he must try to keep them safe in ways that were in keeping with their faith.

Right now that meant being alert to troop movements in and out of the county, helping to gather what supplies he could for his family and their Quaker community, using their weekly meetings to share information for the good of everyone, and helping runaway slaves when he could. In Virginia the penalties were severe for aiding and abetting runaway slaves, but Levi held no fear of civilian law. His only interest was God's law, and if he could help slaves trying to flee oppression, he would. He would not commit murder to free slaves, as the abolitionist John Brown had. John Brown had paid for his immoral crimes with his life. As for the war, despite supporting the northern cause, wanting to keep the Union preserved and doing away with slavery, Levi refused to kill his fellow man to do it. If Levi ever committed such a foul deed—breaking trust with God's law and with the peace testimony—then let him pay with his own life.

It was sad to watch their Quaker numbers dwindle. Many had already left for the West, going to Ohio. Some had fled to escape almost certain conscription into Confederate ranks. Levi felt especially low and burdened this evening. After he'd made sure the animals were settled and all was quiet, he stepped outside the barn and took a moment to stare out over the countryside. Never prone to melancholy, still he allowed himself this moment to question the future of their Quaker life and their Quaker community. Some of their numbers had left, but the land, this land that stood before him now, this Virginia soil, was still here. It wasn't going anywhere. Fields might lie fallow, some having been burned and destroyed, but the land was still here.

This was his land, his and his family's and the generation before them. Levi stood his full six foot five and set his jaw. He rubbed his fingers over his day's growth of whiskers. Unlike many Friends, he didn't want a beard, not wanting to look like any of the soldiers in uniform trespassing on his land. Unwittingly, he raised his broad-brimmed hat enough to run his fingers through his dark, cropped-at-the-neck hair; then set his hat to rights again. In silence, as was the Quaker way, he reaffirmed his long-made vow never to leave the land. If he did, it would be in a pine box.

A dog barked in the distance. Levi looked in the probable

direction of the sound. At least it wasn't artillery fire or troops shooting at each other in a skirmish. Few were the days he didn't hear the explosions of war in the distance. Such a gift tonight, hearing only the sound of a neighbor's pet likely giving chase to a rabbit or squirrel. Levi closed his eyes to better appreciate the absence of war from his farm—for the moment, only for the moment.

It grew dark out. He could no longer delay going inside his house. He could no longer delay going in to be with his bride Comfort. He'd yet to say wife with any kind of ease. Worse, he'd yet to bed her. Married on First Day, now it was Fourth Day and they'd yet to consummate their union. It wasn't right and he knew it. He was willing on their wedding night to bed her, but she was not. She'd told him she had a stopping in the mind about joining with him yet. He understood and didn't question her or press her in any way. Hadn't he had a stopping in the mind about marrying her in the first place?

Their marriage already weighed heavily on the both of them. After they'd married and then participated in a festive gathering of family and Friends at their house, he'd thought things might go all right. Now he doubted they would. He doubted she'd ever love him again in the way a woman should love a man. He knew he didn't love her in the way he should. Still, he felt obliged to fulfill his husbandly duties and bed her. They'd never talked about children, but she must want them. Even if she didn't love him completely, she'd love their children. Yes, he felt obliged to give Comfort children. As a Quaker husband, he felt obligated to Comfort.

But as a man he felt obligated to another. Willa Mae Tyler had stolen his heart and he'd love her, and only her unto eternity.

No matter now. Willa could be nothing to him now. He'd married Comfort. He owed his allegiance to her. As it was, he woke up every morning worrying over Willa and not Comfort. He must find a way to shut Willa from his heart and mind, for all of their sakes. Maybe if he could find a way to forget Willa, he could find a way to reach out to Comfort and help make their marriage better and their home a happier place, despite the war. Trudging up the path, stepping onto the porch, he determined to try harder this evening to bring a smile to his bride's face. It was his fault that she wore a frown most days. Tonight he'd change that if he could. It was his husbandly duty.

Night had fallen, and Willa snuffed out her bit of candle, satisfied with the letter she'd just penned to her parents back in Bedford County. She'd put it in the company post in the morning. Her fellow soldiers would be coming in soon. She didn't want them to see her writing a letter. They, none of them, likely thought she could write, since she never did. That she never got any letters already raised questions with them. She didn't want to draw any added attention to herself by writing now, and having them see.

In her letter to her parents she'd asked them not to write her, telling them it was best since she'd be on the move. They'd understand and abide by her wishes, she thought. Inside the letter, too, she'd told them she goes under the name of Will Taylor in the army, and not her God-given name, Willa Mae Taylor. They'd understand that it was part of her masquerade as a man. Her father would smile and her mother would not, ever praying to get Willa to don a dress and be a girl instead of a tomboy.

Fully clothed, Willa drew her oversized gray jacket closer and pulled her wool blanket over her, using her gum blanket for ground cover beneath her. Happy for the cover, she knew that some of the infantry didn't have the luxuries she enjoyed. Some didn't have the cover of a tent and a warm campfire outside.

Some didn't have much food either. Rations were already tight in her unit and the war was young. Willa didn't know much about everything going on, but she'd already determined this war wouldn't be over anytime soon.

To hear officers talk, and picking up on rumors she heard filtering through the ranks, besides knowing they were heading toward Richmond to help defend the Confederate capital city, she had a sense that the conflicts were just getting started. In fact, she knew that conscription in the South was going to be law soon. No more mustering in of your own free will. Nobody had to tell her that the men who joined as volunteers wouldn't think much of men forced into the army by conscription.

Her insides suddenly seized. *My baby? Is my baby all right?* Willa sat up and tried to calm her fears. Lord in heaven, she wished she knew more about what having a baby was like. She surely couldn't ask any of the men around her. If only there was another woman-soldier close. There had to be other women, on both sides, who'd mustered in, pretending to be men. She hadn't spotted another woman yet, but there had to be a few. Some women might have mustered in to follow husbands and sweethearts, too. Some might want to be patriots, like all the men who signed up. No matter their reason, she wished that another woman-soldier was here with her now in her tent, to help her and calm her fears about her baby.

Willa's insides had quieted. She lay back down. A tear escaped her eye, trickling down her face. More tears followed, and soon both temples were wet. She wiped her eyes with shaky fingers and then rolled onto her side. She tried to find a comfortable position but couldn't. Rolling to the opposite side, she choked back her sobs. The other men could come into the tent at any time. She couldn't be crying like a girl. But, she was a girl, a pregnant girl, alone and unmarried, a woman-soldier with a secret to keep.

The reason for her tears had nothing to do with wanting another woman nearby to help and counsel her now. They had nothing to do with missing the companionship of Surry at a time like this, and everything to do with loving Levi Clement and not having him here to counsel her and love her and their expected child. Having been intimate with Levi and now carrying his child couldn't be right in anyone's eyes, not parents' eyes, not the eyes of respectable society and especially not in the eyes of God. But love . . . wasn't it right to love someone? Wasn't it right to love Levi? What choice did she have, once she'd encountered him? None, and she knew it especially when he took her in his arms. They'd seemed safe arms after she'd been in battle and killed men for the first time. All she remembered was Levi taking care of her, washing the blood and fear and pain from her, soothing her, easing her agony over her deeds, and loving her. He'd called her *Willa, love.*

Her tears suddenly dried, and she shut her eyes tight to better remember. In her confusion over everything that had to do with leaving Levi, she'd remembered him calling her *Willa, love,* but only now remembered he'd said so much more. He'd told her he loved her and would unto eternity. She opened her eyes and sat up again. She hadn't wanted him to say the word love, but he had anyway. She hadn't repeated the words back to him, but she'd done so in silence when she'd marched out of Waterford with her company.

Thee I love.

Oh, how she yearned at this moment to have spoken the words aloud to Levi. How she wished she'd told him she loved him, too, and would be his unto eternity. *Thee I love,* Levi Clement.

Without realizing it, she used Quaker plain speech, having picked up some of the Quaker ways while being a party to services at the Fairfax Meetinghouse. Her unit had used half of the meetinghouse for barracks and weapons storage, and on more than one occasion, her sergeant wanted the soldiers to stay for meeting. Against her will, because she found it hard to be in the same room as Levi, she stayed for meeting and had doubtless picked up some of their plain speech. Having grown up in the Methodist Church, Willa didn't think Quakers believed differently than she, but just in a different way. Quakers lived the way of Christ, and so did Methodists. Methodists, though, didn't stick so much to themselves as Quakers did. And Methodists believed in going to war for their country, while Quakers did not. That might be the biggest difference between her and Levi, Willa thought. She knew he'd never allow himself to take the life of another human being. That he loved her, no matter that she'd killed in battle, had to be some kind of miracle.

"You still up, Will?" one of her tent mates said, opening the flaps and coming inside.

"Yep," Willa answered, and then lay back down, rolling onto her side away from him, signaling that she was going to sleep, even though she knew she could not. Every part of her body wanted to be pressed against Levi now. Unashamed of such wanton feelings, every part of her wanted to touch every part of him, just as she'd done on that miraculous afternoon, secreted away in his deserted mill on Catoctin Creek. She could feel Levi's powerful body holding hers, both of them naked, both pressed against the other.

Memory of his masculine essence of clean woods and new tobacco caused her nostrils to flare ever so slightly. Memory of his muscled arms drawing her against his hardness caused her female center to warm. Memory of his deep, pressing, painfully passionate kisses set her body to flame. Suddenly overly warm, she wanted to get up from her gum blanket, strip off her burdensome uniform, and undo the bindings over her breasts, letting the ties burn to cinders. God, how she wanted to let the woman inside her shine for Levi, only Levi.

His dark handsomeness haunted her. She'd never thought to grow up and find the man of her dreams. In fact, she'd never imagined falling in love, the way she knew Surry did. But meeting Levi changed everything in her life, turning it completely around and upside down, all in the span of one magic night. Willa didn't have time to wonder over it anymore, not with their baby coming.

At once, she knew what she had to do.

CHAPTER FOUR

"Penny, keep your coat buttoned and keep right behind me," Surry whispered hard to her little sister, in a rush to make it to the landing along the Choptank River in Delaware, where they had the promise of finding a safe house in New Castle County.

For this part of the journey Surry had no guide, no station-master to lead them. She had to remember the directions. It could rain, maybe sleet, any moment now, making travel worse. Why couldn't there be stars tonight? Especially the North Star. Why couldn't the moon shine brightly to better show them the way? Surely slave catchers laid chase all the way from Maryland.

"Hurry, Penny," Surry urged, knowing her little sister fought exhaustion, afraid she'd become ill again as she had during their run through Virginia. Penny had come down with fever in Virginia, and Surry had worried she might not make it. But Penny had healed, because of Levi Clement's sister Lucretia. The young Quakeress possessed healing powers and used them to help Penny get well. In fact, her little sister hadn't wanted to leave the safe house at the Clement farm, reveling in the company of sisters Lucretia and Grace. Surry still marveled at the fact that some white folks had been so kind to them. Most didn't cotton to slaves, especially runaways. But the Clements had been ever kind, and so had Willa's parents back home.

Scared to death that Willa's parents would turn her and her brother and sisters away that first night they were all on the run from the slave patrol the devil Boyd Blankenship set after them,

Surry still couldn't get over the humanity of the Tylers. She shouldn't have questioned it, not really, not with James Tyler secretly letting her father be buried on his property when Surry's family had no place else to bury him.

Then, the night she and Sam and Penny and Pitty Pat first ran, when they discovered their first safe house deserted with no guide waiting for them, James Tyler hid them all in his barn. Surry could still hear the wild barking of the slave patrol dogs in the distance growing ever louder, coming ever closer. When Willa's mother found out about them hiding in the barn, and about how Surry and Willa had been friends since they were seven, Litha Mae accepted them and even brought them food and supplies for their journey. She wasn't angry at Surry, a slave, for befriending her daughter. Litha Mae had given Surry something else: Willa's precious, green grosgrain ribbon to help Surry feel beautiful again. The ribbon, Surry remembered, had been a Christmas present to Willa from Willa's brothers.

"Willa left this behind," Litha Mae told her, "when she went off to join up with the army and fight Yankees the way Walter and Henry would have continued to do, if they could."

Surry's insides caught at the real reason that Willa's mother had given Surry this special present that belonged to her only daughter. Litha Mae wanted Surry to feel beautiful again, because she'd seen the scar on her face inflicted by her rapist, Boyd Blankenship. Surry had never needed or appreciated anything so much in her life as Willa's green grosgrain ribbon. It wasn't that Surry cared about her looks being marred, even though she'd been called beautiful all her life by the boys at Shelby Plantation. The scar inflicted by Boyd Blankenship wasn't so horrible, running along one curve of her cheek, but it was the fact that every time she looked at the scar, she felt Boyd's murderous, foul body covering hers, abusing her, contaminating her, making her feel ugly inside and out.

That's why her scar was horrible to her. It was a constant reminder of her rape and defilement. When Litha Mae handed her the ribbon, it was as if a part of Willa was with her, telling her to stay strong and be brave, and telling her to put the past in the past and live for today. That's what Surry imagined Willa would tell her. The moment Surry took up her lush, long hair and gathered it at her nape, tying it with Willa's ribbon, she felt beautiful again, no longer the victim of a vicious rape. She could look at herself again and ignore the scar.

When at the Clement safe house, she'd given the ribbon to Lucretia for saving little Penny's life. The young Quakeress didn't want to take the gift, explaining that Quakers were plain people and mustn't wear such adornments. But Surry had insisted. Surry smiled inside, even on the run, when she remembered how Lucretia had tied her thick braid with the ribbon, and then hid it all under her white bonnet.

They were all connected by the ribbon now: Willa, her mother Litha Mae, Surry, Penny, and now Lucretia Clement. They were all kindred spirits, no matter their color, no matter their creed, no matter their differences. They had their gender in common and their goodness of heart. Each of them had compassion for the other, not seeing colored or white, but people, human beings all. It was a tie that bound them: the simple length of green ribbon, now stretching from Bedford County, Virginia, through Loudoun County and on to the shores of the Delaware Bay. Though Surry had given the ribbon over to Lucretia, she felt its binding tie to Willa all the same.

"Surry!" Penny suddenly screamed behind her.

Surry turned around so fast, she almost slipped down the embankment into the dark waters of the bay. Penny had slipped, saved only by the snagging root of a tree along the water's edge.

"Surry! Surry!" Penny yelled at her sister, clinging onto the exposed branch, her feet dangling in the water.

"Stay still, Penny. I'm coming!" Surry made sure of her footing, holding onto a thick-enough outstretched branch of the same tree, and then carefully clamping onto her sister's arm with her other hand. "Let go, Penny. I've got you," she calmly told her sister when she had her hand securely on Penny. In the next moment she'd tugged Penny up the bank to safety.

Penny cried and cried. Surry let her, refusing to shed any tears of her own. This was no way for people to live. This was no way for any human being to have to live, for her little sister Penny to have to live, on the run and hiding in swamps and marshes and forests so thick you couldn't find a clear path, trying to keep from being caught by slave catchers, trying to keep out of the way of the war. They had to fight exhaustion, constant hunger, and insect-spread diseases, knowing that any moment a poisonous snake might find one of them. Any moment one of them might slip into dark waters, on the verge of drowning. They were separated from family and friends, divided from anyone they'd ever known and forced to run for their lives. They'd been forced to leave the borders of their country to be free.

"Bein' free."

Surry's troubled thoughts traveled back in time. She was eight years old, on a riverbank much as this one, telling Willa how scared she was, asking Willa if she could find out what bein' free meant. Willa had found out and told Surry. Surry had cried and cried, as Penny did now, when she found out. Surry wasn't free. She was a slave, a colored girl. She would never know a life of her own, and would always have to do for others.

Surry kept a tight hold around Penny now, fighting for inner strength and peace, for her sake as much as Penny's. No matter how treacherous and impossible their journey north, it had to be worth it, reaching Canada and "bein' free." It wasn't fair

61

that she had to be on the run, but for slaves *it was just the way of it.*

Seth Lion, her beloved father, had always told her slavery was just the way of it. Times were changing and maybe slavery wouldn't always be the way of it in America. Maybe the war would change things. Maybe Mr. Lincoln would change things.

Until then, Surry and Penny had to run for their lives.

"Levi, we must talk," Comfort said, the moment he came inside for the night.

"Yes," he acknowledged, hanging up his hat and coat on pegs by the door. His insides turned a little, enough to alert him to the moment and to what he must do. He must try to be a good husband to Comfort. In every way.

"Supper's ready," she announced and sat down at the set table.

Levi didn't need her to tell him the obvious. She seemed nervous, which was unusual for her. Comfort was a leader at meeting. Comfort was ever cool and in control. She didn't get nervous. His insides folded at the idea that marriage to him was the likely reason she might be now. Guilt set into his bones even harder. He pulled out his straight-back chair and took his seat across from her, not caring what she'd prepared for dinner. No longer hungry, he needed to talk rather than eat.

For her part, Comfort took up a spoonful of beef stew, thanking God in silence for the bounty at their supper table on this chill night. Food stores were low. They'd little left in the way of meat and vegetables and preserved goods. She'd used the last of their smoked beef for this meal. She needed to talk to Levi about securing more supplies. Tomorrow she'd do that. But tonight . . . tonight she needed to talk to him about fulfilling her wifely duties and giving him children. She'd never wanted

62

children, not really. Oh, she loved children: other people's children.

The stew didn't go down easily. She took another bite anyway, hoping to mask her discomfort from Levi. Comfort knew the main reason she didn't like children was because she'd have to lie with her husband to get them. The idea of intimacy with Levi didn't make her insides quake as it once did. She wasn't sure what had happened between her younger days and now, to make such a difference, to cause such a divide in her feelings. How she'd longed for the moments in a time gone by, when each of them was no more than thirteen or fourteen, when he'd pull her behind her father's barn and press his body to hers, running his hands everywhere that he wasn't kissing her. Where had those feelings gone? Where had that excitement at his touch gone?

Scared of her lack of womanly feelings as a grown woman, she went through with her wedding to Levi, knowing she didn't love him the way she should and knowing he might not love her as much as he once did. The war was the reason, she believed, that Levi had turned away from her. She hated the war for that, even more than for the idea of so much fighting and so much death and destruction in the air.

Why, they were Quakers. Quakers didn't believe in fighting. This wasn't a Quaker war. Of course she didn't approve of the North and the South causing harm to one another any more than she approved of slavery, but she didn't feel a part of the war. It wasn't her cause, and it wasn't a Quaker cause. Why, then, did Levi feel it so? Why must he involve himself in such worry over others when, really, he should worry more over her.

There. She'd thought it. Selfish as it was, she'd thought it. Levi should have been more attentive to her before they got married, and he should be more attentive to her now that they were married. Comfort refused to acknowledge that she'd married him because she was too afraid not to. She was afraid she'd be left behind in life if she didn't marry and have children as did all the other Quaker women. Wasn't she a leader? Didn't she have to set a good example for all? *Yes, of course, I do,* she told herself.

Everyone in their community had always expected her and Levi to marry. Levi was the most handsome of all the boys, and now the most handsome of all the men she knew. No one was more tall, dark, and handsome than Levi. And none of the girls were as pretty as she, Comfort admitted to herself, unashamed to do so. Her one fault, she knew, was her inability to think plain in all things as she should. She couldn't help herself. She was beautiful, with her silky blond hair, blue eyes, and perfect curves; and Levi was handsome with his dark, thick hair, lazy slate regard, and muscles that wouldn't stop.

Comfort set down her spoon and took a sip from her water glass. The kerosene lamplight flickered on the table. Everything else in the room was dim around them. Good. She didn't want much light for this conversation, embarrassed by what she needed to say. If she'd married another man—a man she could easily lead around by the nose—she might not be so embarrassed. Levi wasn't so easily manipulated as the boys who'd fought for her attention growing up. It was one of the reasons she'd always liked Levi, because he was the one boy she couldn't sway with the crook of a finger. She had to find the right words for Levi. She couldn't just put up her finger and lead him to the bedroom and get him to bed her. The thought of lying with him, or any man, turned her insides cold. No matter. She must do this. She must fulfill her wifely duties.

"Levi." She looked directly at him now.

He glanced up from his untouched bowl of stew. Food shouldn't be wasted, especially now with their supplies diminishing. Yet he couldn't eat. He'd no appetite for anything but to get this over with. Promising himself to take Comfort to bed when she wanted him to, he'd planned on having forgotten about Willa first. He'd planned on having a little more time to purge Willa from his heart and mind, body and soul. He needed more time to do that. Tonight wasn't time enough. Levi's body tensed, his jaw so tight his teeth felt meshed together.

"Levi," Comfort said pointedly. "We must fulfill our marriage vows and fulfill our duties to one another as husband and wife."

Levi had the sense that she was standing in front of meeting, espousing such a declaration, rather than sitting private with him now. Her words sounded cold and empty.

"After supper we should . . . we should join together in our marriage bed." There. She'd said it. She'd gotten the words out and over with!

"I am finished." Levi scraped out his chair and stood.

"Yes, well . . . ," she said haltingly and stood now. "I am, too."

Levi took up the kerosene lamp mechanically, without feeling, and led the way to their bedroom. They'd slept in the same bed but not touched as yet, each rolling to their side, keeping their distance. Although he'd built a two-story house, with a loft upstairs, they only had the one bedroom and the one bed. In the four days since their wedding vows, they'd yet to roll toward each other and not away. Tonight that would change. Tonight they must lie together as husband and wife. It was just the way of it and what they must do.

Comfort refused to give in to her nerves. She followed Levi into their bedroom, determined to change into her nightdress, unfettered by the fact that he'd be in the room with her when she did. She wouldn't ask him to turn around. She'd face this night and fulfill her wifely duties and get this over with. It was just the way of it. Maybe she'd even like their joining. Maybe her concerns were for naught and she'd warm to his touch and be glad when he entered her. Maybe it wouldn't hurt as she'd always heard that lovemaking would. But, then, she didn't really love him in the way she should, and so it would probably be just as painful as she'd always imagined.

"Willa. Willa, love," Levi whispered at the peak of his passion, unaware he'd said anything. He knew it wasn't Willa he drove into now, but Comfort. Still, he had to imagine Willa's soft, pliant body arching to him, loving him, wanting him, in order to stir his loins enough to make love to his wife. Comfort wasn't anything like Willa, in bed or out. Willa's passion met his, while Comfort lay beneath him as if she were in a coffin—cold, silent, and unmoving but for the slight raise of her hips toward him. He could pretend all he wanted; at least enough to grow adequately hard to plant his seed in his wife, but Comfort would never be his Willa, love.

Levi's stiff shard, driving into her, hurting her, invading her body as if he were a stranger to her rather than her husband, felt like a knife through Comfort's heart. He'd said *Willa, love!* All these months and she'd thought Levi turned away from her because of the war, when it was really because of another woman—a woman named Willa.

Comfort let Levi rut over her now like a frenzied animal, but if it was the last thing she did, she'd find out who Willa was. Instantly possessive of Levi, Comfort forced herself to run her hands over his back, pretending she wanted him closer. She needed him to bed her now, and the next time, and the next. She needed to have Levi's children and be a wife to him. He'd married her and not Willa. He'd father her children and not Willa's. Children would be protection against Levi ever leaving her for another woman. Comfort relaxed a little. Quakers didn't divorce. Tradition spoke against divorce. Still, if she carried her husband's child, she'd feel reassured. It would do her no good to confront Levi over uttering another woman's name during their joining. Obviously, he hadn't realized he'd done so.

No, it would be to her advantage to keep silent on the subject. It would be to her advantage to act the good wife and fulfill her duties and obligations to Levi, feigning interest in lovemaking when she had none. How else could she become pregnant? How else could she ensure that Levi think about her and not another? Jealous of the woman on her husband's lips, she suddenly wondered if she could make him utter "Comfort, love," and not Willa. A challenge now, Comfort pulled Levi closer to her and arched her hips to his, trying to mirror his ardor. *Say my name,* she silently demanded. *Say* my *name!*

"Just a couple of days, sir," Willa repeated, facing Sergeant Massey now, requesting the furlough.

The sergeant frowned down at her, seemingly trying to take his measure about why one of his best privates was asking for a furlough now. Under General Johnston's command, they'd be getting orders any day to be on the march to Richmond. The Yankees were moving in from a couple of places now, by land and water, toward Richmond. This was a bad time for any of his men to be asking for time away.

Sergeant Massey might also receive new orders anytime to join up with Stonewall Jackson's infantry. Jackson's infantry were the best and the fastest in the army, to the sergeant's thinking. Having overheard officers talking at the company post, he knew Jackson wasn't moving toward Richmond now, but northwest, toward Winchester. Must be General Lee had something else in mind for Jackson, instead of heading toward Richmond like the rest of them, the sergeant concluded. Whatever Jackson's movements, Sergeant Massey had put in to join the already-famous officer, thinking his men and his unit would do well to be counted in Stonewall Jackson's ranks. The assignment could prove more dangerous, but then the war was already a dangerous place to be, no matter the battlefield.

Willa tried to wait patiently for her sergeant to decide whether or not he'd give her a couple of days furlough. She had a mission of her own now. It was a mission from which she might not return. Time would tell if she'd rejoin her Confederate soldiers or not. Time and Levi Clement.

"Listen, Private." Sergeant Massey still frowned down at her. "We're moving out soon, south or northwest. I'm not sure. Whichever, I'm depending on your gun. I put stock in you, Private. You're no coffee cooler, waiting till the coffee cools to get to work, hanging at the end of the line and shirking your duties. So just know I'm depending on you. You got that, Private?" he intoned with authority.

"Yes, sir," she answered, standing at attention.

"Put your hand down, son," Sergeant Massey told her. "I don't need a salute from you now, but your word that you'll be back if I give you a furlough."

"Yes, sir," she said again, this time not looking him in the eye. She'd no idea if she'd be back or not. She'd no idea how Levi would take to the idea that she was carrying his child. She'd no idea if he'd want to marry her and make their baby respectable. She'd no idea if it was all right for a Quaker to marry a Methodist. She'd no idea if Levi loved her enough beyond their moments of passion; if he really loved her unto eternity. She'd also no idea how dangerous it would be to travel back into Loudoun County, now that it was occupied by Yankees.

Dressed as a Confederate soldier, she might easily be spotted and found out. Dressed as a woman, she might be spotted and taken for a spy. Her best chance though, she knew, was to disguise herself as a woman and hope to go undetected by the enemy. Funny, she thought, to have to disguise herself as a woman when she already was one underneath her oversized, baggy, soldier's uniform. All her life, she'd only worn dresses to church and never at any other time. Willa's attention from the sergeant strayed further.

Most important of all, she'd no idea if she'd take an enemy bullet, dressed as a man or a woman, traveling into hostile, enemy-occupied territory. She and the baby might not make it to Levi. It was a risk she believed that she must take, for the sake of the baby growing inside her. *My child. Levi's child.* The little one in her womb deserved to be born into this world with two loving parents.

Yes, it was worth the risk to get back to Levi to tell him about their child, for the sake of their child's future. It was also her obligation to tell Levi he was going to be a father. He should be told. It was the right thing to do. Deep down in her heart, she knew it was the right thing to do, despite all that was wrong between them, keeping them apart.

"Private Taylor!" Sergeant Massey raised his voice.

Brought back to the present, Willa stood at attention again.

"I told you, you don't have to salute now," he said, seemingly frustrated with her behavior.

"Yes. Yes, sir," she meekly replied, lowering her hand and her voice, wanting to keep Sergeant Massey fooled about a lot of things.

"I'll give you a pass, but you best get back here soon as you can, all right?"

"Yes, sir," she said again, unable to think of anything else that would suit and that would at least be a half-truth, because he'd said "soon as you can."

"I'm not gonna ask where you're headed, son. You know where the enemy is, and I know you wouldn't be so stupid as to head their way. I hope what you're doing is important. It had better be. Just don't go and get yourself killed, all right?"

She didn't say anything this time, hoping that looking him in the eye was enough to satisfy him.

"Follow me, son, and I'll get your pass. If you tell any of the men I'm doing this," he gritted out, "just don't."

"I won't say anything, Sergeant," she assured him, knowing he was giving her special treatment because he depended on her gun. Likely he thought she might desert, too, if he didn't give her a pass. She knew enough of the sergeant to know that he had a generous heart, besides being a fierce fighter. He didn't want her to get court-martialed or shot for desertion. She'd known from that first time she'd had to kill, following his orders at Ball's Bluff; that he knew what a toll it had taken on her. He knew another thing: she wasn't a coward. He trusted her. Despite her guilt over her sergeant's trust, she had to put the life of her unborn child above all else now.

She had to find Levi.

No matter what, she had to.

CHAPTER FIVE

"I'm thinking on it, Pa. I just wanted you to know." Lucas shuffled his feet, uncomfortable over what he'd just said, at the same time glad his mother was out back hanging the wash and not hearing their conversation.

Nathan Minor made sure the doors to his blacksmith shop, front and the back, were securely closed. Unnerved by what his only son just told him, he couldn't understand the why of it. "Lucas, you're a free Negro here in Waterford. The Yankees are here to help protect us. What are you thinkin', wantin' to go off and fight? White folks ain't goin' to let you, son."

"There are other Negroes, free and slave, who want to join the fight," Lucas said, trying to keep himself in check, not wanting to upset his father any more than he already had. "This is our country, too, Pa," he said, his jaw tight with emotion. "If I can find a fight where they'll let me in their ranks, I'm joining up."

"And like I said, son, white folks ain't goin' to let you in as any soldier. They'll let you join up to cook and carry water and polish their boots, but not carry a gun."

"Maybe so, Pa, but I'm going anyway, to Maryland and up north where I can find a unit that will take me. I have to do this, Pa," Lucas insisted.

"Your mother will have a fit if anythin' happens to you." Nathan didn't add the obvious: that he would too.

Lucas stepped closer to his father. They matched in looks

and in height, both handsome and both standing six foot four. "Pa, it's my duty to fight against slavery. Too many we know have died in slavery, in chains. If any more of our people must die, let them die as free men, not shackled in irons but as soldiers, with our rifles raised high in the cause of freedom. Besides"—Lucas barely spoke above a whisper, his voice hoarse with emotion—"I have to do this as a man. I have to fight for my own people."

Nathan held his tongue. He had no reply to match his son's declaration to join the fight for freedom from slavery. His heart swelled with pride over his beloved son wanting to be a soldier, even as his heart broke over fear that his son might never come home again. Swallowing hard, fighting for composure, Nathan couldn't help but wonder why now? The war had gone on over a year. Why now? Unwittingly, he gave voice to his concerns.

Lucas didn't have an answer for his father. The notion had just come on him, to join the fight and not continue as a guide in the Underground Railroad. Both tasks involved risks. He was used to risks, and wasn't one to frighten easily. There was too much at stake in the cause to help runaways and the cause to free all of the Negroes to waste time being scared. Lucas supposed he'd decided he could do more now as a Yankee soldier fighting than guiding runaways from safe house to safe house. Both endeavors were part of the fight for freedom.

Lucas thought of Surry Lion. Here lately he'd had trouble thinking of anything but the beautiful young runaway he'd helped guide, along with her little sister Penny, out of Loudoun County and across the Potomac so they might continue their escape north. Had it only been a month and a half ago that he'd met Surry Lion? It felt like a lifetime ago when he'd pushed her boat off, putting her safety and that of her sister in the hands of the ferryman. He hadn't wanted to push Surry away, but he had to for her safety.

Just then he thought of his mother. His father had bought his mother out of slavery and married her to set her free. His parents loved each other, despite their uneasy beginning. Lucas had thought of marrying Surry, a slave, and setting her free, too. But Surry was a fugitive and on the run. She wasn't being put up for sale on any auction block.

Lucas was twenty-one and Surry seventeen. He knew another twenty-one years could go by and he'd still carry affection for Surry Lion in his heart. They'd only known each other a week, with her hiding at the Clement safe house most of that week, but it was enough for him to know that Surry Lion made him want to marry and have a family. Until then, he'd never thought much about taking any gal for wife. She'd been a mess when he first saw her, covered in poison ivy, her face swollen and blistered. He'd gone across the fields outside of Waterford to fetch his next passengers, who'd turned out to be Surry and her little sister. His focus had been mainly on Penny. She'd been ill with the fever and his main concern was to get the child inside, out of the elements. Still, something in Surry got to him from the start. Then, when he saw her a few days later, he knew what that something was.

She carried an immediate spark for him. He could see it in her lustrous brown eyes, saw it on her beautiful golden-brown countenance, and in the way she smiled every time he caught her gaze. The gals he knew were after him plenty, and he'd never had trouble catching their eye. But he'd never wanted any of them until Surry. She was the kind of woman he could love for a lifetime. He'd seen her bravery, her loyalty to her family, her intelligence, and her natural, genuine way with folks. Here she was going north, into the unknown, with no one for companion but her little sister. Lucas admired everything about Surry Lion. Her beauty had been hidden when he'd first laid eyes on her, and he didn't think anything of her looks one way or the other. But when her face healed—despite revealing a telltale scar along the curve of one cheek—and when she let down her long, ebony hair, reminding him of crushed velvet, and he could better glimpse her slender, shapely body, she took his breath.

It hit his gut hard that he and Surry could never have a chance to make a life together. He didn't think to set eyes on her ever again, unsure if either of them would make it through such terrible times. Now that he'd decided to join up with a colored unit and fight against the Confederates, he suspected his chances for survival were slim to none. At least he and Surry were not married, with her having to wait at home, worrying over him.

"Son," his father said, breaking into his sober reverie.

Lucas looked at his father, then at his mother. Arletta Minor stood next to her husband. The look on her face near broke Lucas's heart. His father must have told her that he was going off to join the northern army if he could. She said nothing. Her sad expression spoke for her. Tears welled in her ever-kind, aging, brown eyes. Lucas choked back tears of his own and held out his arms to his mother. They hugged for long moments, neither having any words that might soothe their parting.

As she was a recluse much of the time anyway, none of her compatriots noticed when Willa left their provisional camp on furlough. If they had, they would have thought it odd that anyone in their ranks had been given a pass, what with their upcoming push toward Richmond to defend it from the onslaught of northern forces. It was a time to write letters and share a shot or two of John Barleycorn, yes, but not a time to go on furlough, maybe trying to get home for a spell.

The Yankees were pushing into their beloved south now. They had to defend their land, their homes, and their families from the bastard Yankees. This was no time for a furlough. Willa had managed to talk her sergeant into one and still marveled that she had. Of course she would have run off anyway, risking capture and court-martial, because of what she had to do. Finding Levi was all that mattered. Her baby came first. The war came second.

Willa had a plan in terms of the route she'd take, traveling through Centreville and Chantilly out of Fairfax County, into Loudoun County through Aldie, then on up to Waterford. Of course she'd have to avoid any kind of encounter with soldiers, no matter their side. A signed pass or not, Confederates could capture her for desertion, or, if they found out she was female, they could send her to prison somewhere. Yankees would likely just shoot her, dressed as she was in enemy colors. She'd deliberately left her rifle back at camp, but had brought a pistol with her. If she had to, she'd use it.

Willa suddenly realized her Confederate uniform would be a big problem, while she might fare better dressed as a woman. If she were dressed as a woman and not a soldier, she risked the chance of being taken for a spy, traveling alone as she would be. Still, she knew her chances for the journey ahead would be better if she wore women's clothing. Where to find them? What to find? Willa hadn't worn female garb in a long time, and never as a grown-up. She'd figure out what to put on, if only she had access to women's clothing. It wasn't like she could go and borrow from a friend. And she couldn't just walk up to a stranger's door and ask the lady of the house for clothes. Everyone was suspect now. Nobody wanted anyone to come knocking on their door, bringing trouble.

There must be a store or two in Centreville. Willa pilfered through her pockets. She had no money. Even if she did, she'd no way of knowing if any stores would accept Confederate paper. The unforgiving gray morning wasn't helping the situation, and she felt chilled to the bone. Crunching over frozen leaves, Willa made her way in the still-dim light through thick evergreen, toward town.

It was still early, just after dawn. If she hurried, she might get into town before folks had gotten up. More to the point, before shop owners would have gotten up and opened for business. *Hah, business*, Willa scoffed to herself. What with the war, many businesses had shut down. She hoped and prayed she'd find a shop in town, a mercantile at least, that still had a few things for sale.

Lucky, indeed, to neither see nor hear any signs of troop movements, Willa soon reached the outskirts of Centreville. She took her haversack from her back and stashed it in the trees. What little rations she'd brought, she'd stowed in the near-empty canvas bag. Scanning the street, she realized she'd been right. The place was deserted, save for a dog or two roaming freely. When she thought it safe, she quickly darted across the main street and looked into shop windows. Nothing along the first block looked promising. Downhearted and even a little frightened, Willa didn't know if she'd get what she needed before she'd be found out.

Looking up the street and down, she saw no one about; no soldiers in blue or gray. She'd no time to wait and worry over who occupied the town, but hurried on to the next row of buildings, desperate to find a mercantile. A mercantile would surely have what she needed. Forcing herself to slow her step, she peered hard through the intact glass of the first shop she came to, squinting to see anything in the still-poor light.

Then she saw it, there by the counter: an empty dress form! There *had* to be women's clothes inside. Quickly, she tried the door. Of course it would be locked. Maybe the back door would not be. She hurried around back and was right again. By some miracle the proprietor hadn't locked the back door of the mercantile. Just then one of the mongrel dogs, roaming free, ran past her. She held her breath, hoping against hope that the dog wouldn't start barking at her. It didn't, evidently preferring to give chase to some other critter in the alleyway. The moment the dog disappeared from sight, Willa slowly opened the door and went inside, making sure to pull the solid wood door closed behind her. She needed to be deathly quiet. The owner likely lived upstairs.

With enough light coming in through the front window now, Willa scanned the store. Some shelves sat empty while some had rows of preserved and canned goods. Supplies were obviously low. Kegs of liquor and pickles and vinegar lined the floor along the store counter. There were no sacks of flour or sugar or salt in sight. No bins of fruit, dried or fresh. No potatoes. No supply of grain for man or beast. There were brooms and hoes for digging, and shovels and some farming supplies yet to sell. She wondered now if the store had any clothes left.

She walked over to the empty dress form. Her heart sank. No dress, either. When she was about to leave, instinct told her to check under the main counter.

Eureka! There *were* clothes—men's work shirts and pants and women's blouses and skirts—piled in neat stacks beneath the counter. Not a lot, but enough for her to make do. There was a box behind the stacks. Curious, Willa pulled it out. Carefully, quietly, she opened the box. A dress! It must be the dress that belonged on the dress form. Just what she imagined she needed.

Willa took out the long-sleeved, green-and-white-plaid, homespun-cotton dress. Inside the box, too, there were necessaries: undergarments—pantaloons, she suspected. And a thing that looked like it was supposed to tie a woman's body right up, practically the whole top of her.

One of the dogs outside barked. She thought she heard stirrings above her, upstairs. The owners must be waking up. She grabbed up the box, dress and all, and headed for the back door. Hesitating a moment when she heard nothing more upstairs, she went back inside where she'd spotted a wool, hooded cape. She needed a covering. Making sure all was quiet, Willa tiptoed back over to the counter and took up the paper and pencil she'd seen there before. With the light better, she penciled her note for the owners:

I O U for one green plaid dress, the necessaries that came inside the box with the dress, and for one wool, hooded cape.
I will make good on what I've had to borrow, when I can.
Yours very truly,
A Confederate Soldier

She left the note square in the center of the counter, and hoped the owner would understand. This was a matter of life and death. She had to get safely to Levi and tell him about their baby coming into the world. She had to borrow the clothes from the mercantile. Willa believed she'd little choice. Pausing a moment, she stood stock still and shut her eyes. Satisfied all was quiet, she gathered up the box and headed for the back door, this time stopping just by the door to change out of her uniform and into the dress.

In no time she'd removed her heavy jacket, pistol and all, and her pants, shirt and brogans. Still in her long johns and bindings, she was quick to decide she'd leave both on and put the dress over her undergarments for now. There was no time to worry over the funny-looking bindings in the box or the pantalets. Taking up the dress from the box, Willa slipped it over her head, then pulled it carefully over her. It seemed nearly her size, a snug fit over her long johns. She didn't care about what support she did or didn't have, small-breasted as she was. At first the dress felt funny. It didn't feel right, disguising herself as a woman. She never liked dresses and didn't now . . . except she

78

was a woman. And she was carrying Levi's baby. For him, she did want to be a woman. Suddenly the dress felt a perfect fit.

Not that it mattered to her, but she thought the dress pretty, with its white collar and wide sleeves. The folds at the sleeves were sewn low at the shoulder. Gathers over the bodice and the wide skirt drew in at the waist, doubtless to make a body look slender and trim. In her haste to get changed, Willa noticed these feminine fashion details all the same.

She heard something just on the other side of the door. The dogs again, likely ferreting around for food. In a hurry, she stepped back into her work boots and folded her cumbersome uniform and coat as best she could in the dress box. Making sure of her pistol first, she struggled to close the dress box. Twine would have helped, because the box wanted to open because of its full contents. Well, she didn't have twine and didn't see any close by. She found a pocket in the skirt of her dress for her pistol because she needed to keep her gun handy in case of trouble.

As for her hair, she realized she needed to put on the cape and pull the hood up to hide the hair she'd only just remembered was short. She pulled the cape around her shoulders but hesitated to pull her hood up, taking a moment to run fingers through her wavy hair. Startled, she realized her hair wasn't so short anymore, but had grown several inches since she'd first cut it. She'd been so busy hiding it, she'd paid little attention to the fact that it was actually growing. At times she'd missed her thick, waist-long, black locks, but only at times.

Her hair curled now, around her fingers and past her nape. It would be all right to leave her hood off. If only she had her green ribbon to put in her hair to wear as a band. That would match her dress and make her feel like the pretty girl her brothers always said she'd be. Humph, pretty. Ridiculous! She just wanted the ribbon close by, to better remember dear Walter and Henry.

"Mary Louise, I'm going downstairs now."

Willa heard a man's deep voice reverberate through the floorboards overhead. Her heart thudded in her chest. The owners! In the blink of an eye, she was out the back door, overstuffed clothing box caught up in her arms, and hurrying down the alleyway. Thank goodness she'd remembered to put her shoes back on. Still, even in her brogans, she nearly tripped, wearing such a dress for the first time. The skirt was a little longer than she wished, but it did cover her work boots. She hadn't thought about looking for a woman's pair of shoes in her rush to leave. As soon as she rounded the corner to the main street, bright sunlight blinded her. Still, she kept walking when she shouldn't have.

"Ohhhh!" she exclaimed, running into something, someone, causing her to drop the dress box. In a panic, she still couldn't see.

"Here, now, pretty lady, let me help you."

Willa struggled to hold her ground. More than one man stood around her by this time. She blinked hard, trying to see, able to tell at least that she was surrounded. But by which side, Yankee or Rebel, she'd no idea. Her pistol lay hidden in her pocket. Instinctively, she put her hand in her pocket and slowly stood. She left the box on the ground, hoping its contents hadn't spilled out. Standing tall, all five foot two of her, she laced her fingers around the pistol in her pocket and ordered herself to stay calm.

"What's a pretty lady like you doin' out so early?"

Able to focus now, since the sun no longer shone directly in her eyes, she could make out the soldier's colors. *Gray,* thank God the soldier wore gray. She loosened her hold on her pistol, yet didn't take her hand from her pocket. Another soldier bent down and gathered up the box she'd dropped, immediately placing the heavy parcel in her arms, forcing her to let go of her gun. A little anxious that she didn't have her gun handy, she was at least relieved the box hadn't opened to reveal her soldier's uniform. No matter that it was gray like theirs; these soldiers would be forced to take her to their commanding officer.

She needed to think right now—to think like a feminine girl.

"Why, I was out just runnin' an errand for my mama," Willa dripped out, mustering a southern drawl.

"Is that so?" The first soldier who'd spoken kept up his conversation with her.

"It surely is," she answered, forcing herself to continue.

"Well, how about you and me—"

"Aw, c'mon, Eli. We gotta get back. Mornin' patrol's over and we're due back. C'mon, now. Let's don't be botherin' this pretty lady anymore," another soldier broke in.

Grateful for the soldier's intervention, Willa waited, the tension in her body painful. The soldier—the one who was about to make a less-than-gentlemanly suggestion to her—grumbled, tipped his hat her way, and then turned and started down the street. The others followed. She let out the breath she'd been holding.

"Ya'll have a fine day, now," the one remaining soldier who'd come to her defense said, and then tipped his bummer cap to her before turning to join his patrol.

Willa stayed fixed to the spot, watching the Confederate patrol leave. The street had begun to fill up with others starting their day. Riders passed by on horseback. Wagons rolled by. Folks walked past Willa, who stood with her arms full in front of the mercantile.

Lord in heaven! She was standing in front of the very store she'd just "borrowed" from! After a quick glance up and down the street to make sure no more soldiers roamed about, she crossed the main town thoroughfare and made a beeline for the woods and for the spot where'd she'd hidden her pack. Once there, she'd transfer her uniform from the dress box to her haversack. Wise or not, she wanted to keep her discarded uniform with her, in case she would need it again.

If . . . if all went well with Levi, she wouldn't.

"I'm bringing two more slaves here tonight," Levi informed his sisters and his brother Benjamin. All four stood inside the Clement family barn, which was quiet but for the stalled dairy cows lowing at the disturbance. While Levi had wanted to keep to himself his actions to help runaway slaves and not involve his family, he'd been unable to. The first time Lucas Minor guided his passengers on the Underground Railroad to Levi's family farm, his sisters and his brother found out. Not his parents, though.

Still grieving over Jonah's absence, his thoughts not easily distracted, Thomas Clement went through the motions of his day, unmindful of most that went on around him. For his mother's part, Susan Clement might have figured out that he was aiding and abetting runaways in their barn, but she said nothing. A good Quaker, she disapproved of slavery and the ill-treatment of Negroes. Surely his mother knew the danger involved for the family if they were found out by the authorities. The consequences in Virginia would be harsh; still, she said nothing.

Levi bore the burden of involving his family, ever worrying they'd be discovered. Word had quickly spread along the railroad line that there was a healing Quaker at the safe house outside Waterford. From the first time, when Lucretia helped heal little Penny Lion, word spread that the Quakeress knew which herb and which root could heal. Same as Moses, some said. Same as Harriet Tubman—a fugitive slave herself—who risked her life daily, saving and leading many a slave to freedom up north. No Quaker or Methodist who helped in the cause for freedom from slavery came close to the good works of Harriet Tubman, yet it was widely known along the Underground Railroad line that some whites did help Negroes: some like the Clement family in Loudoun County.

Levi had thought about using his own barn as a safe house but he didn't want to chance Comfort finding out, unsure what she'd do or say. He couldn't risk it. Things were tough enough between them without adding this. Her emotions were fragile, especially of late. She'd been acting strange ever since they'd first coupled. Of late she smiled at him more, even fawning over him, when she never had before. He couldn't figure what had changed between them. After that first time together, he'd agreed when she'd asked him to lie with her once a week, every Fourth Day. Some men would think her request odd, but he did not, given their circumstances.

Comfort was used to leading, and he let her lead in this. Comfort was an independent woman, his equal. He'd agreed to the commitment she asked him to make, to bed her once a week. She wanted a family and had said so, often. Theirs wasn't a marriage based on love, though neither gave voice to this fact, but Levi believed they would both love their children. Levi had resigned himself to the fact that he and Comfort were married for life. There was no going back. Children would bring them both the joy they would otherwise miss, living together as man and wife. So yes, he'd agreed to her clinical request that they join together once a week.

"Levi?" Benjamin spoke up, grabbing Levi's attention away from sobering thoughts about his own home life.

"Yes, Levi?" Lucretia parroted her brother. "Will the passengers arrive at candle-lighting?"

Levi pushed back his broad-brimmed Quaker hat and ran his

fingers through his hair, stalling for time to clear his thinking to the task ahead. "No. Later than that. I'm meeting them in a different field. With all the soldiers around, we've had to change their route into the county. Lucretia," he said, first looking at her, and then at Benjamin and Grace, too. "One of the men coming is real sick, I'm told. I don't know what's ailing him, but thee all know the risk. If any of thee doesn't want to be around tonight, I'll understand."

"Brother." Lucretia took his hand in hers. "Thee is right to warn us, but thee knows that I will be here. I can do nothing else than to be here tonight."

"Or me," Benjamin echoed his sister.

"Or me," Grace joined in.

Levi's heart wrenched at the generous nature of them all. They were willing to risk their lives, willing to expose themselves to potential deadly illness. They, all of them, were children of God who believed slaves, too, were children of God in need of their help. Their Inner Light shone. The dim light in the barn suddenly brightened.

"All right, then." Levi broke from their circle and reset his hat. "I'll be back with the men late tonight. Benjamin, have the lantern by the door filled, ready for me to light once inside the barn. Lucretia, come when thee hears the signal, ready with thy medicine bag. Gracie, bring a filled crock of water and biscuits," he instructed.

"God bless thee," he said to them all, his throat tight. In the next moment he was out the barn door, on his way to the appointed meeting place to pick up his latest passengers. If all went well, he'd be back. There was always the chance he might not be.

CHAPTER SIX

"I won't!" Penny protested, closing her tattered pockets as best she could. Backed up flush with the stairwell railing, her thin, worn coat offered her little protection against the question just put to her by the mistress of the safe house.

Surry immediately felt worried. She and Penny had just been taken into a safe house outside of Dover, not far from the waters of the Choptank River, and the owners might toss them out if she and Penny didn't follow all the rules. The rules said go to the loft level and stay hidden and stay quiet. The rules said to hide in the cabinets if necessary. The safe-house owners said they'd give two hard knocks on the wall below, to warn Surry and Penny to take cover.

Right now, Mrs. Cooper, the owner, wanted to know what was spilling out of Penny's pockets before she guided them up the stairs to the loft. It was unusual to know the names of the folks taking them in, not to mention dangerous for all parties.

"Penny, show her what's in your pockets. Show *me*," Surry begged.

"Children, we don't have time to lollygag. More slave patrollers come every day to our Delaware Bay shores searching for slaves. They even come to our doors now, without notice, and sometimes with a federal marshal. Thee *must* hide."

Surry realized Mrs. Cooper must be a Quaker, saying "thee." The Clements had used the same plain speech.

Mrs. Cooper stood next to Surry, trying to coax Penny out of her corner. "I just want to know what thee has hidden in thy pockets, child. Come on and tell us. We've little time. The patrollers will be on their rounds soon and I must get thee hidden in the cupboards. As soon as it's clear, I will bring thee and thy sister a bit of food."

Penny opened her pockets at the word food. Their contents spilled out all over the wood landing.

"Penny, what on earth . . . ?" Surry knelt down immediately to collect the leaves and clumps of grass and dirt littering the floor. Mrs. Cooper might get mad. Surry couldn't afford for Mrs. Cooper to get mad. It didn't occur to Surry why her sister might be stuffing her pockets with leaves and grass.

"Don't get mad at me, Surry. Please don't get mad. I was hungry, that's all," Penny blurted out, starting to cry.

Surry froze in her crouched position, her hands at a standstill over the dirt and leaves and grasses, over what her sister had been secretly eating because she'd been so hungry. Surry's insides seized at what their lives had come to; at the fact that her dear little sister was eating dirt because she didn't have anything else to put in her stomach. In that moment Surry felt like the worst of sisters for not taking good care of Penny. She thought of Pitty Pat and Sam, too. She hadn't taken good care of them, but let them be captured by Confederate soldiers. God only knew where they could be now. *It's all my fault,* Surry cried inwardly. Hot tears fell. She couldn't stop them any more than she could stop the hurt in her heart over what had become of their family. All because their skin was the wrong color.

Her father had always told her, "It was the way of it."

But Papa, it's no way for us to live.

"Never mind that, child." Mrs. Cooper put a hand to Surry's arm and guided her to a stand. "I'll take care of the floor. Thee must take care of thy sister now and get upstairs. Come along, now," she encouraged, and guided both runaway girls up the remainder of the steps. "Children, as soon as it's safe, I will bring thee food and water. I promise thee both," Mrs. Cooper said, her throat tight with her own tears.

Willa hung back in the woods outside of Waterford, at the edge of the thick pine along the Old Waterford Road. Hidden by the trees and thick underbrush, she wanted to stay out of sight of any possible passersby—any Yankee soldiers on patrol. Loudoun County was Yankee country now and every move, every sound, every change of mind was important. She backed farther into the woods, finding a sturdy tree to lean against to help her find the courage she needed for the day ahead.

This was the most important day of her life—hers and her baby's.

No matter that she had to break from social convention; no matter that her parents wouldn't approve; no matter that the war had her surrounded; no matter that she was a soldier who'd committed to the fight; no matter that she was a Methodist; no matter that the blond she remembered from Fairfax Meeting-house had obvious affection for Levi; no matter that Levi had said, "Willa, love" after their night of lovemaking but might not feel the same now. No matter to any of that on this, the most important day of her life and her baby's.

Willa must find Levi. When she did, she'd tell him the truth, all of it. She'd ask him to take her for wife, despite the war, despite all of their differences, and despite the expected disfavor of his family and hers, at their unexpected union. She'd tell him how much she loved him and always would, especially with their child on the way. *Until death I am thine, Levi,* Willa vowed silently, unaware she was thinking in the Quaker way, repeating the vows a bride might make.

Heavy gunfire in the distance vibrated through the trunk of the tree she leaned against. As if shot, she pulled away and began checking her clothing out of habit to see if she'd taken any fire. Instead of running her hands over her bulky uniform, she ran her fingers over the folds of the green-and-white-plaid dress she'd borrowed from the mercantile back in Centreville. Yes, she'd best check her dress and make herself presentable as an ordinary young woman, walking along the Old Waterford Road, out on errands like anyone might be on this bitter cold morning.

Pulling her wool cape closely around her shoulders, its hood up over her head, she checked the ties of her overstuffed haversack, not wanting it to come open along the way. She'd thought about hiding it in order to hide her Confederate uniform in case she were found out, but a voice inside told her to keep it with her. Willa didn't want to listen to the voice telling her she might need her uniform again. She shrugged her shoulders, refusing to get downhearted.

She'd no time for worry. She'd no time for anything but finding Levi. Her baby depended on her to find his father. Willa froze, not because of the piercing wind kicking up around her now, but because she'd thought *his*. In that moment she knew she carried a son. The same voice she didn't want to listen to a moment ago, she listened to now. Adam. She'd name her son Adam. Adam Clement. Adam was the first man. Methodist or Quaker, it was fitting to call her first son Adam.

Willa heard a wagon approach. She crouched down low to hide. The roads and woods had to be full of Yankees. She wouldn't allow herself to be caught on such a day. Rising enough to see who approached in the wagon, she breathed a little easier to see that it was a man and a woman in civilian dress, a Quaker couple it appeared. It gave her an idea. Making sure of her pistol, she straightened her cape and hood, picked up her heavy haversack, then marched out into the road.

The driver pulled up short when he spotted Willa.

She waved her arm, hoping her friendly gesture wouldn't cause alarm.

"What is thee doing jumping out in the road like a wild rabbit? Does thee not know it's dangerous?" the man in a dark frock coat and black hat shot down at Willa. The unsmiling woman in plain Quaker dress sitting next to him said nothing.

"Thank you for stopping," Willa quickly offered. "I struck out on foot early this morning from nearby. . . ." She struggled to think of where.

"Goose Creek?" the woman spoke now.

"Why, yes, from Goose Creek," Willa echoed.

The woman at last smiled, evidently more comfortable now with their encounter.

Willa understood her concerns. "Thank you, ma'am, for stopping. I'm that tired, I am. And the morning is ever so cold. I'm on an errand from Goose Creek and I need to find Friend Levi Clement?"

"Is thee a Friend?" the woman asked.

"No, I am not. I am a Methodist from the meetinghouse in Goose Creek. It is urgent that I find Levi Clement. It truly is, ma'am."

"We are acquainted with the Clements, of course," the woman offered. "I am Letty Janney and this is my husband, Isaac. We are going in the direction of the Clement farm. Might we give thee a ride?"

"Oh, yes. Pl-please," Willa answered right away, so cold her teeth chattered. Grateful for the ride and her good luck, she hurried to the back of their wagon and climbed in.

Turning around to make sure his passenger was safely inside, Isaac Janney quickly giddyupped his team. Likely he didn't want to stay stopped in the road any longer than was necessary during these uncertain times.

The weather worsened by the minute.

Willa hunkered down in the open wagon, trying to stay out of the biting wind, knowing she'd be better to stay out of sight of any passing Yankee soldiers. It was safer to travel with the Quakers than alone, but it offered no guarantee against discovery and capture. She felt almost happy traveling with the Janneys. They hadn't asked her too many questions. And they were acquainted with Levi. Yes, it felt good to be among Friends.

Willa's heart quickened, thinking of seeing Levi soon. Anxious to see Levi again, to have him hold her and kiss her and tell her he loved her, she pictured his handsome face with just a shadow of whiskers, his penetrating slate regard, his slow grin, his tall, muscled frame, his masterful arms around her, pressing her to him. Her whole body ached for want of his touch. It was hard to sit still in the bed of the wagon, and Willa imagined being in Levi's bed. Instead of keeping her eyes open and alert to the danger around her, she shut them tight, imagining Levi's powerful body over hers, imagining his touch, his masculine essence, his manhood taking her womanhood over and over and over. . . .

"Miss!" Letty Janney called out to Willa from her front wagon seat.

Startled, lost in thought over Levi, Willa had trouble returning to the present. When she did, she had no idea how long the trip had been or if there had been any passersby. She was that angry with herself for her inattention.

"Miss," Letty Janney repeated. "The Clement farm is yonder."

Willa looked in the direction Mrs. Janney pointed, at the farmhouse in the distance, down a long lane. Surrounded by open fields and rolling, treed hills, the Clement farm made her think of home. Her family farm wasn't as big and certainly this wasn't her home, yet strangely, she felt like she'd come home. Hopping out of the wagon, pulling her haversack behind her,

Willa couldn't wait to clear the lane and reach the farmhouse.

"Thank you for your help," she said, beaming at the Janneys. She knew she must look silly to them, smiling brightly on such a cold, bitter day—another day of war and destruction and hunger and fear and death—but she was too happy at the thought of seeing Levi again.

"God go with thee, child," Letty Janney bade, the hint of a smile on her lips.

"And you, Friends. And you," Willa said, then turned on her heels and set out down the lane. She glanced behind her once, long enough to notice the Janney wagon pulling away. The wind blew hard now, making her way more difficult. Her cape flapped and her hood fell away. Dark clouds threatened overhead. Glad for the weight of her cumbersome haversack, Willa had the feeling that but for it, she'd blow away on the next gale. Drops of rain sliced across her face. Too late to worry over getting wet. Willa hurried as best she could the rest of the way.

Finally she reached the house, climbing up the steps in her sodden dress, glad for shelter from the storm. The wind blew across the wide porch, howling past like banshees after a battle. Unnerved by the eerie sounds, Willa hesitated before knocking on the large wooden door. She hated for Levi to see her looking so poorly, but there was nothing to be done for it.

"Hullo!" Someone called from behind her. Willa turned around to see who it was.

"Hullo!" Lucretia yelled across the wind and sleet, soon clearing the steps, coming to stand in front of Willa.

Willa recognized the young woman. She was one of Levi's sisters. Willa remembered her from all the times she'd seen the Clement family come and go from meeting.

"Thee must come inside." Lucretia stepped right past Willa and opened the door.

Willa hesitated, suddenly scared to see Levi, suddenly scared

to tell him what was in her heart. All her bravado of only moments before drained away.

"I don't want to mess up your floor." Willa said the first thing
that came to mind to stall for time.

At this, Lucretia took hold of Willa's arm and practically
dragged her inside the house, then quickly shut the door. "Here,
let me help thee with thy wet things," Lucretia offered, at the
same time taking Willa's heavy pack from her, then undoing her
cape and taking if from her, as well.

Willa stood motionless, numb, her senses shutting down to
the task ahead. Any second Levi could walk into the front room!

"I'm Lucretia Clement. What is thy name?"

"Wha—?"

"What is thy name?" Lucretia repeated, dabbing Willa's face,
then her own, with an antimacassar doily from the headrest of a
nearby chair.

"Willa Mae Tyler," Willa answered before thinking whether it
was wise.

"Willa Mae Tyler?" Lucretia parroted. She remembered that
name. She stopped dabbing her face and studied Willa carefully.

No one else had come into the front room; not Levi, or
anyone else in the family. Willa eased a little, only then realizing
that Lucretia Clement gave her a queer look. "What's wrong
with my name?" Willa questioned, on her guard now.

"Why, nothing," Lucretia assured her, slowing undoing her
bonnet. "Nothing is wrong except that this belongs to thee."
Untying her wet bonnet, letting it slip to her back, she pulled
her heavy braid around, then began untying the green grosgrain
ribbon holding it together.

It didn't register at first, what Lucretia was doing or why it
mattered. Why would she be removing a ribbon from her hair
and telling Willa it belonged to her? Willa never had any such
finery except the beautiful green ribbon her brothers had given

her for Christmas, the same green ribbon she'd left on her pillow at home before she'd run off to muster into the army. That was the only—

"Here," Lucretia pulled up Willa's hand and placed the ribbon in it.

"Is this mine? I mean how . . . how did . . . ?" Willa sputtered, suddenly clutching the ribbon to her, reveling in its familiar touch, at once feeling a tie to her brothers and home.

"When I heard thy name, Willa, that's when I knew," Lucretia explained. "A friend gave it to me for helping her sister. It was thy friend Surry Lion."

Willa's heart stopped. "*Surry!* Surry gave it to you! Surry was here? Surry is all right?"

"Yes, she and her sister used our barn for a time, escaping north. I helped her sister get well, and that's when Surry gave me the ribbon. She told me the story of how she'd gotten it from thy mother, when she and her brother and sisters hid in thy family's barn when they'd first started their escape north," Lucretia said, wanting to explain things fully.

"Thank you," Willa whispered, hugging Lucretia to her. "Thank you for telling me Surry is all right. Thank you," she repeated, hot tears raining down her cheeks. She pulled away from Lucretia, ever grateful for their tie, the ribbon in Willa's hand proof of it. Willa put the ribbon to her cheek, thinking of her parents and Surry. Her parents had helped hide Surry and her brother and sisters. That meant her mother knew about Surry now, about their long-standing, secret friendship, a white girl friends with a colored girl.

Thank you, Mama, Willa silently professed, relieved that her mother knew, hoping she understood. Surry's mother had, after a time. Esther Lion had accepted Willa as her daughter's friend, despite all the reasons Esther Lion should not. Willa wondered how Esther Lion fared now, and the rest of Surry's family. What was it Lucretia had said?

"You said Surry's one sister was with her?"

"Yes. Penny."

"What happened to her other sister and her brother?" Willa asked, anxious to hear. Afraid for Surry and her family, Willa didn't think there had ever been a time when Surry and her family were not afraid, bein' scared having been the fabric of their lives. Looking at Lucretia now, she waited to hear the fate of two more in the Lion family.

"Her brother Sam and her sister Pitty Pat were captured by Confederate soldiers in Virginia. Surry and Penny had stayed hidden and couldn't help them. As for anyone else, I'm sorry, Willa, but I don't know," Lucretia apologized.

"Oh, please, Lucretia." Willa took up the girl's cold hands. "Do not distress yourself. You've brought me so much joy in telling me that dear Surry is all right. You must warm yourself and not worry over me. I know that Surry is escaping north. I know that for sure now. She made it this far, dear Lucretia. Thank you," Willa said again, vowing to include Lucretia in her prayers every night from now on.

Voices trailed into the front room from the kitchen at the back of the house. Willa heard a man's voice. Was it Levi's? Her heart pounded. She couldn't find a good breath. Quickly, she shoved her ribbon in the pocket with her pistol, when she'd rather wrap the ribbon in her hair to look pretty for Levi.

"Why art thou here, Willa, if not in search of thy friend, Surry Lion?"

"To find your brother Levi," Willa answered absentmindedly, thinking to see him enter the room at any moment.

"Levi? Thee came to see my brother?" Lucretia repeated, incredulous.

More voices could be heard reverberating from the kitchen, female voices included. Every muscle in Willa's body tensed.

94

"Shall I wait here for Levi?" she asked of Lucretia, not looking at the young Quakeress, but at the hallway to the kitchen.

"Levi lives in his own house, just across the field a piece."

"Where?" Willa shot at Lucretia. "Which field? I must find him!"

"But the storm. Thee must not—" Lucretia didn't have a chance to finish.

Willa had snatched up her heavy haversack and cape and was already out the door and down the steps, out of range of any warning, when she'd have done well to have stayed and listened.

Glad to have seen the last two fugitive slaves safely off in the early morning hours, Levi trekked into Waterford, despite the storm brewing. He didn't go on horseback, regretting it now, what with the weather. However, he had been concerned that the occupying troops might confiscate his mount. No matter on which side or the fight, the cavalry, blue or gray, was ever in need of horses. Others in Loudoun had had their property confiscated, including many animals.

No, Levi didn't want to take a chance on his horse being taken. Now with the Confederacy calling for conscription, "for every able-bodied man between eighteen and thirty-five to volunteer," and even though northern troops occupied Waterford at present, there would be more pressure on him to muster into the army. It didn't matter that Levi was Quaker; some folks didn't care. All they saw when they looked at him and his brother Benjamin were two southern men who refused to fight, who were cowards. The insults never came from other Quakers, but from outsiders, even some he'd called friends before the war. The war had changed some of his neighbors from well-meaning folks into just plain mean folks. It was out of fear and desperation that they said such things. Levi understood.

Maybe that was the same reason, out of fear and desperation

over his struggle to keep his peace testimony and over his struggle to do away with the causes for war in their lives, that Levi had taken to carrying his Bible of late, the scriptures often bringing ease to his agitated thoughts. He checked his deep coat pocket, making sure it stayed shut, protecting his Bible. Facing into the wind and weather, Levi looked ahead. He'd reached the outskirts of Waterford.

Instead of going to the meetinghouse, as he'd told Comfort he'd do, he needed to see Gideon at the mercantile. Gideon would know about the Loudoun Rangers forming up under Samuel Means, of all people. Samuel was a Quaker, even though a lapsed Quaker. Levi needed to talk to Gideon and find out the facts.

Levi had already lost one brother to the fight. He didn't want Benjamin to be lured into one, too. If a northern fighting unit was forming right under Benjamin's nose, the lure might be too great for him to hold to his peace testimony. Unsure of the future, Levi picked up his step into town.

Exhausted from her trek to Levi's house, Willa had been too busy dealing with the elements to think about why Levi might live in a house separate from his family. The rain had lessened, but still came down. She stepped onto the front porch, noticing how well-built the white clapboard house appeared. There were outbuildings, too. Levi had done a fine job on his house, Willa thought. The porch was wide, fronting the entire house and even wrapping around one side. She set down her burdensome haversack by the door and didn't hesitate to knock this time.

A woman opened the door and not Levi.

The blond!

The beautiful blond from Fairfax Meetinghouse!

Comfort said nothing, not opening the door wider and not inviting the drenched woman inside her house. She didn't recognize the stranger, but knew from her dress she obviously wasn't a Friend. "Yes?" Comfort greeted, none too friendly.

Too in shock to speak, Willa said nothing.

"What does thee want?" Comfort grew suspicious. This woman could be a Confederate spy coming to her door, cooking up trouble.

"I-I'm looking for Levi Clement. Is-is this the right house?" Willa managed to get out, her spirits sinking lower and lower.

"Who art thou to be looking for Levi Clement?" Comfort asked warily.

"Nobody, really," Willa muttered in her own defense.

"Thee must have a name," Comfort pressed, thinking she needed to know a name in order to report this spy if need be.

"Willa Mae Tyler is my name," Willa responded, before she thought better of it.

Willa! Comfort had heard that name before, on Levi's lips when they'd first coupled. He'd said "Willa, love" at the peak of their joining.

So, this is his Willa, love, Comfort spat to herself. Filled with sudden jealousy over the slight woman on their doorstep, Comfort hated her. She shouldn't. Hating was wrong. But she did. Striking out the only way she knew how, she made sure of *Willa's* attention before she spoke. "Well, I am Comfort Clement, Levi's *wife*," she said evenly, then slammed the door in Willa's face.

Willa stood face-to-face with the slammed door for long moments trying to comprehend what had just happened. *Levi is married! He's married to the beautiful blond . . . to Comfort!*

Willa's insides folded and her knees went out from under her. She collapsed in a heap next to her haversack, not knowing if Levi was inside or if he'd overheard them. What did it matter? What did anything matter now? Levi hadn't meant it when he'd told her he'd love her unto eternity, calling her his Willa, love.

He'd never meant it.

Beyond cold now, Willa went dead inside, but for the life she had growing in her. No bullet on any battlefield could hurt worse than this moment, now that she knew Levi had never meant it when he'd said he loved her.

CHAPTER SEVEN

Mindless of the rain, that it had stopped, and mindless of the hour, Levi had a lot on his mind, walking home on the Old Waterford Road. He'd had his talk with Gideon and he didn't like what he'd found out about the Loudoun Rangers. More trouble was coming to Waterford, more trouble for his family.

He needed to keep his family protected, and short of killing, he would. Something up ahead caught his attention. Soldiers, a group of Yankee soldiers were gathered in a circle, blocking the road. A caravan of wagons, too, probably full of arms and supplies. Supplies were scarce in the county now. Some of the wagons probably had foodstuffs confiscated from his neighbors' farms. Begrudging this sort of theft, Levi picked up his step. He'd pass this surly lot and get to his own place before the soldiers tried to confiscate anything there.

"Captain, she's a spy for sure!" Levi heard one of the soldiers shout.

She? Angry the soldiers might be bothering a helpless woman, Levi stopped outside the circle of blue uniforms.

"Go on, now, Quaker." One of the soldiers waved him on.

Levi tried to see over the soldiers and get a look at the woman they surrounded.

"I said keep moving," the soldier snarled, stepping away from the group and turning on Levi.

Unable to get a clear glimpse of the woman, Levi could tell she wasn't very big. Shame on these men. Shame on them.

"Quaker, don't you know you're interfering with United States business here? Now, get going," the same soldier demanded, his rifle in hand.

"What? Is thee going to shoot me?" Levi spat out. "Is thee going to shoot me for trying to help keep an innocent woman from falling victim to thy war?" Taller than the soldier, and many others in the circle for that matter, Levi still couldn't get a clear glimpse of the woman they surrounded.

The soldier raised his rifle, pointing it at Levi.

Angry at the soldier and pretty much at the world, Levi pushed down the rifle barrel and pushed past the line of soldiers, to the middle of their circle.

Willa!

His heart slammed against his chest.

He'd dreamed about seeing her again, wishing it, wanting it. But not like this!

Relieved to see her alive, he was frightened for her now, really frightened. He hardly recognized the slip of a woman in front of him in a dress, drenched and exhausted, her vacant eyes dull and with no life in them, looking like a little girl lost. What was she doing here, in enemy territory? Was she here to find him? The notion that she might have come back to find him, risking her life for him, caught at his chest and made him fall in love with her all over again, even in this impossible moment.

"Quaker, you want to go to prison with this Confederate spy?" a big man threatened, taking hold of Levi's arms. Another soldier grabbed his other arm.

Levi shook both men off. "Confederate spy? What makes thee think this innocent woman is a spy?" he demanded.

Willa looked at Levi now.

Levi took heart. She was coming back to him.

"She's got a Rebel uniform in this here pack of hers," the captain said. "I don't think there's anything more you need to know. Now, get going, Quaker." The captain motioned for his men to part so Levi could leave.

Levi held his ground, looking at Willa. "That's not proof of anything. Lots of mothers and wives and sisters in these parts have lost loved ones. It's not a crime to carry their belongings," Levi shot out pointedly at the captain.

"I said get!" the captain snapped out.

Willa blinked when the captain yelled. She looked hard at Levi, as if seeing him for the first time. Her words were for the captain, but she kept her eyes on Levi. "Yes. I was carrying my brother's uniform. That's all. I'm from over in Goose Creek. Yes, I'm going back to Goose Creek now, is all," she said, her voice barely above a whisper.

The captain turned on Willa. "You're going to prison for spying. I'll get the truth out of you one way or the other," he threatened.

Willa switched her gaze from Levi to the captain.

"You're a pretty little thing; I'll give you that. Lots of pretty little things carry enemy intelligence. Lots of pretty little things leave my soldiers wounded and dying on the battlefield. I'll get the truth out of you," the captain vowed, clamping his hand around Willa's arm. "Men, get rid of the Quaker. Send him on his way now!"

"But I know her!" Levi shouted, shaking off the soldiers trying to push him away. "She's a Quakeress from Goose Creek Meeting!" he said, struggling to come up with a plausible story the soldiers might believe. "She's a leader at meeting and just came to spend time with us at Fairfax Meetinghouse." Frightened for Willa and upset that he couldn't think of more to say, his hand went to his pocket, the pocket holding his Bible. At once, he pulled out the frayed leather volume and held it before Willa. "Here, Friend Willa. Thee left this at meeting."

Willa looked at Levi, then at the Bible.

101

"Take thy Bible, Willa Mae Tyler," Levi encouraged. *Come back to me, Willa, love. Come back.*

The captain appeared to be considering Levi's words, perhaps not wanting to arrest a Quaker woman as a spy. Most of the Quakers in the county supported the North. Evidently this woman didn't, and had lost a brother. It wouldn't go well at headquarters if he arrested a Quaker, much less a female Quaker. The pathetic creature, pretty as she was, really didn't look like any kind of spy to him. He and his men had already wasted too much time on this Quakeress. He was already way behind schedule, getting the arms and supplies delivered.

"Take your Bible, miss," the captain said, letting go of her arm.

Willa reached out and did just that, her fingers brushing Levi's for the briefest of moments. She looked up at Levi, her eyes filled with sadness. "Thank thee, Friend Levi," she whispered.

Levi nodded to her when he ached to take her in his arms and take her home to his bed. But then he couldn't. He already had a wife at home—and in his bed. He looked at Willa, wondering how she'd react if she knew. It would break her. He might as well take one of the rifles aimed at him now and shoot her dead, telling her such a thing that he'd gone and married someone else unto eternity. He studied every detail of Willa's expressionless face. Her eyes held no sparkle, no welcome for him. He could feel her pulling away, when moments before he thought she was coming back to him. Sick with dread, he wondered if she *did* know what he'd gone and done.

"We're going in your direction, miss," the captain said, taking hold of her arm again. "Let's get you in one of the wagons and give you a ride home. The day's too miserable for you to be walking."

The wind picked up. Snowflakes danced in the air. Levi

watched the soldiers help Willa into one of the covered wagons. She started to pull her hood over her head, but hesitated and turned to look back at him once, only once. He thought she smiled. That smile, imagined or not, was all he had left to hold onto of Willa Mae Tyler. God only knew how long he stood there, watching the Yankee caravan disappear from sight, taking Willa away from him. His chest hurt, his heart ripping in half yet again. He'd let her go before, just as he had now. He felt helpless to help her. Should he go after her? No, he shouldn't. It was too dangerous for her. Torn between following his heart and doing what was right, Levi stared after her. She'd already gone. It was best he leave her be, and he knew it.

"God go with thee, Willa, love," he whispered over the wind.

Levi started down the road toward home. At least Willa hadn't gotten herself killed. But why had she come back? The pain in his chest hadn't eased. Somehow he didn't think it ever would.

A soldier helped Willa from the wagon, and then handed her pack down to her. The other wagons lumbered on, soldiers on horseback guarding both sides of the supply caravan. Three soldiers had ridden inside the wagon with Willa, their rifles ready. They gave her a quick nod, then trained their eyes back onto the woods surrounding them. Snow spat through the late afternoon air. Willa shivered. Her damp clothes weighed her down, keeping her cold. So did her melancholy thoughts. She couldn't shake them off, either.

Gunfire suddenly cracked through the air.

Willa dropped to the ground beside the wagon, instinctively taking what cover she could. A soldier dropped next to her, stretched out, writhing at first, then going still—dead still. His surprised eyes stayed open. Blood trickled out one corner of his mouth. He was the driver. Willa went for her pistol, peering through the wagon wheels, trying to see who'd attacked. Rifles fired from the wagon. Their fire was returned from the woods. Willa could tell there were more guns in the woods than the three shooting from the wagon bed. They had to be Confederates attacking them. The fact that she was about to be killed by friendly fire didn't register with her, she was still so upset over Levi's rejection of her. That bullet had already killed her. She felt dead inside, but for her baby.

The soldiers above her, shooting from the wagon, weren't returning fire anymore. Willa knew the reason. She'd be next. With as little movement as possible, she heaped herself over the dead soldier's body. The only thing she could do was play dead herself. In war, soldiers often shoot first and ask questions later. It would be easy for the Confederate soldiers to mistake her for the enemy. Mistakes happened in war. She didn't want to be a mistake, not with the life growing inside her.

Somehow in that moment, Willa knew something else. If she lived through this day, she'd go back to her unit and fight the enemy until she couldn't anymore, fight the reality that Levi hadn't meant it when he'd said "Willa, love," and that he didn't love her unto eternity. She'd fight the Yankee cause Levi supported, fight the Yankees who killed her dear brothers, fight the enemy who wanted to take their Virginia soil from them and killed their families. God forgive her, but she would fight.

Motionless over the dead soldier, her eyes shut, Willa could do little else but lie there and await her fate. A bullet might come, any second now, killing her and her baby. Her lids fluttered. Dang it! She wished she could keep them still. She tried not to breathe so anyone would see.

Hoofbeats! Willa felt them vibrating along the ground, even through the dead soldier's body. Gunfire cracked, repeating in the air. More horses now; she could hear them coming from another direction. Cavalry from the woods, charging into the road, shooting, but not at her. Daring, she opened her eyes only a slit, only enough to make out the danger around her.

Dead men littered the road, dead men in blue. The guards from the supply caravan up ahead must have come back to engage the enemy. They must be the ones lying dead in the road, their horses wandering around, skittish, having lost their riders.

Willa saw men in gray, blurred somewhat, but she could make out their uniform color. She dared not open her eyes, for fear she'd be shot. Luck was with her so far, but in war a soldier's luck could run out at any time, without notice, spilling out and disappearing into the earth beneath.

"You can get up now, miss."

Willa's eyes flew open. She stared at two brown leather boots positioned in front of her. Slowly, cautiously, she tilted her head up to see the rest of the man standing in the boots. On her stomach, over the dead soldier, she lifted herself up and off of him, never taking her eyes from the man who had her cornered.

"Pretty smart, what you did," the imposing soldier said the moment she stood in front of him.

"What do you mean?" she asked, doing her best to appear composed.

The tall, well-uniformed soldier smiled. "Playing dead so we wouldn't shoot you is pretty smart in my book, miss," he said.

"Oh . . . yes," she answered haltingly.

"Are you all right?" he asked.

"Me?"

He laughed.

Willa chuckled herself, nervously reacting to the soldier's laugh rather than from anything lighthearted. This was all too bizarre, this game of life and death.

"Miss," he said, his face serious. "You best take up your things and get on home. It will be dark soon, so go on, now," he told her, his tone fatherly.

Willa thought he must be an officer, the way he wore his uniform so well. He had an unusual hat on, unlike any others she'd seen. It had a plumed feather tucked into its brim, and one side of his hat was pinned up. That hat had to go against regulations, even for an officer. She wondered why he didn't question her about what she was doing traveling with the Yankees. If she'd been in uniform he certainly would have. But she wasn't. She was in a dress. This officer didn't take her for a spy or soldier or the enemy. If he did he wouldn't be letting her go now. He seemed every bit the Virginia gentleman, wanting to help a Virginia gentlewoman and show her respect.

"I can't spare my men to escort you," he said. "Time's wasting. You get along, now," he repeated, and then put a hand to his hat, giving her a slight nod before turning and walking to the middle of the road.

Willa listened as he barked out orders for his men to take up the wagon reins and get the caravan moving again. In Rebel hands now, the arms and supplies would go for the Confederate cause and not the Yankees'. Willa had the feeling these soldiers operated on their own, separate from the main army. It was just a feeling and no more. She admired them nonetheless, for their bravery and expert fighting skills. The carnage in the road, the lives lost on this day, meant there were women and children at home who would get letters soon, letters to cause them a lifetime of tears. Willa cried inside for them all. But it wasn't her job to stay and bury the enemy dead. It was her job to get back to her unit and rejoin her comrades. Still, as she took up her heavy haversack and began walking away from the bodies littering the road, she hoped the Confederates would see to them.

Levi needed to make sure all was well at his family's place

before heading to his own. The Yankees who'd stopped Willa might have come here first, and taken things: food, animals, whatever they wanted for their troops. This pilferage was only going to get worse. Levi knew it. No matter the color of the uniforms coming to take what they wanted. Finished checking the outbuildings, especially the barn, Levi started for the house. Lucretia suddenly popped out the front door and hurried down the pathway toward him.

Something was wrong.

Levi tensed, waiting to hear.

"Levi! Levi!" Lucretia reached him on the path, out of breath.

He waited, hoping this was only about food being taken.

"Levi? Does thee know a Willa Mae Tyler?" Lucretia blurted her question.

His insides turned sick with worry now that Willa had been here and that she knew, she must know, what he'd gone and done. He looked at his little sister, her face so innocent in the dimming light.

"She was here, Levi. Willa Mae Tyler was here looking for thee," Lucretia said excitedly. "She said thee is a friend. And, Levi, thee won't believe this. She's a friend to Surry Lion! Remember the sisters we helped escape north?" Lucretia kept on, not waiting for her brother to answer. "Isn't it just the most amazing coincidence? Levi, Willa was so nice and so pretty. Is she a friend to thee, Levi, as she said?"

There was only one thing on Levi's mind now.

"What did thee tell Willa when she came looking for me?" he asked more harshly than he intended.

Lucretia shot her brother a puzzled look. "Why nothing, except thee doesn't live here but across the fields. She didn't stay to talk, but practically flew out the door, in the direction of thy house," Lucretia finished, her look still dubious.

"Little sister, this is important." Levi forced his tone to soften.

"Did thee say anything about me? About Comfort and me?"

"No, brother. There wasn't time," Lucretia said. "Wh—"

Lucretia had no time to finish her question.

Levi was already down the path and charging across the field toward his own house.

"No, husband. Not a soul. No one came to our door today," Comfort lied, still consumed with jealousy over the woman who had most definitely come to their door today: *Willa Mae Tyler.*

"Thee is sure?" Levi asked a second time.

Comfort knew what this was about, and she was having no part of it. She refused to tell him word one about the intruder. Watching Levi, knowing his heart as she did, it was all she could do to hide her fury. She was mad at him, yes, but far angrier with Willa Mae Tyler.

Levi took little notice of Comfort, relieved that Willa didn't know he was married. She hadn't found out. Thank God. He lit a second lamp. Why had she come back to find him? Thank God she wasn't captured as a spy.

Mindlessly, Levi sat down at the supper table, turning his empty plate in slow circles, first one way, and then the other. Willa had taken his breath today, drenched, exhausted, worn-out look and all. He thought of that first time, long ago yet not long at all, when he'd cared for her after she'd first fought in battle. In shock from the fight, she'd let him clean the blood and dirt from her and then remove her uniform with its telltale traces of war, only then to let him hold her close the night through. He longed to find her, to run out in the dark and find her and take her to his deserted mill, laying her down on their bed of flour sacks, and hold her the night through, just as he'd done that first time.

But he couldn't. It wasn't his right. She wasn't his. He couldn't be hers, not now that he'd married someone else. He shot an accusing look at Comfort. She stood at the cast-iron stove, her back to him. This wasn't her fault. He shouldn't blame Comfort. This was all his fault. He suddenly scraped back his chair and got up. He needed air. The air inside felt too close, too warm, too oppressive. "I've got to check the barn," he called over his shoulder to Comfort, and then shut the front door behind him.

"Be back soon, husband. Supper is almost ready," Comfort called out, her words falling on deaf ears. She turned back to her stove, stirring the soup so hard now, she nearly splintered her wooden spoon. This had been a terrible, terrible day. Its awfulness had nothing to do with the war and everything to do with another woman. Willa Mae Tyler. Levi loved Willa. Comfort knew it. The knowledge made her sick to her stomach. Where had he met this Willa? Comfort had never set eyes on her before. She knew most folks in Waterford and many in the surrounding towns, but she'd never set eyes on Willa Mae Tyler before.

Levi evidently had.

"Ouch!" Comfort burned her finger on the side of her pot. Forcing herself to calm down, she needed to think on a plan to keep her husband home, to keep him from running off to find *his Willa, love.* Comfort was a good Quaker. Levi was a good Quaker. Comfort found solace in this. Quakers don't divorce. Levi had married her before God, in the eyes of all bearing witness at meeting. They both signed their wedding certificate, and the papers were all in order. There would be no divorce.

Comfort turned around quickly, staring holes through the shut front door. Uneasy, she wondered if Levi had just run off to find Willa. Maybe he hadn't gone to the barn but had left her and run off, despite their marriage vows.

Comfort forced herself to calm down yet again. Levi would never leave his family. He would never leave, what with Jonah still off and the Yankees covering the countryside. Levi meant to protect his family and the Friends as best he could. More to the point, Comfort knew Levi would never leave the family mill and his farm and his land.

There. Comfort felt much better at having remembered Levi's steadfast connection to the land. He'd told her as much. When her family, her father John Clarke especially, spoke of leaving Virginia for Ohio, for better farmland and to avoid the war, Levi had registered his vehement protest at ever leaving himself. Levi said he'd never leave the land.

Humph! Comfort scoffed to herself. Even to find *his Willa, love,* Levi wouldn't run off.

Feeling reassured, Comfort stirred the soup pot carefully, letting the bits of chicken and vegetables simmer and cook. That's precisely what she needed to do with her troubled thoughts. She needed to let them simmer until she had a good plan to keep Levi happy at home. If she didn't keep him happy, he wouldn't bed her once a week and she'd never have his child. Comfort desperately wanted to give Levi children. He'd love her again if she did. She knew he would. She prayed he would.

Slowly stirring her soup, Comfort determined to come up with a new recipe, a new plan to recapture Levi's affection. She'd had him all to herself since they were children. There had never been anyone in town or the entire countryside that had ever stolen Levi's attentions from her, until now, until his *Willa, love.*

Comfort kept stirring. She wouldn't quit until she'd thought of something to drive a wedge between Levi and his feelings for the interfering, unwelcome Willa Mae Tyler.

CHAPTER EIGHT

"What's it mean, being a free man, Surry?"

Surry's insides folded at her little sister's innocent question. It took her back years, to the moment when Surry had put the same question to Willa. She'd asked Willa to find out what bein' free meant. Surry knew the answer now. It meant everything.

"When will we be there?" Penny asked. "When will we get to freedom?" Penny followed with another question, not waiting for Surry to answer her first one, too busy leaning over the side of the boat now, her gazed fixed on the icy, choppy waters of Lake Ontario below.

"Penny, get back up here!" Surry pulled her sister away from the edge of the boat and onto the safety of the deck.

The fishing-boat captain looked down from his wheelhouse, peering hard through the window, seeming to make sure of his passengers. Accustomed to secretly picking up runaway slaves in Rochester, New York, he most likely didn't want to lose anyone over the side who'd escaped this far, especially a child.

"Come, sit here." Surry took Penny's hand and guided her to a nearby row of crates. Surry sat down. "Come, Penny," she encouraged, keeping a tight hold on her sister.

Penny tried again to head for the boat's edge.

"If you want me to tell you what being free means, you'd best sit," Surry admonished.

Grudgingly, Penny obeyed this time.

Surry kept her hold on Penny, just in case she'd make a dash for the edge. She held onto Penny for another reason. What she was about to say was important. It was the most important thing to hear in all of her sister's eleven years.

"Being a free man means you don't have to run, doesn't it, Surry?" Penny suddenly blurted. "It means you don't have to eat grass or fall down or hide or be scared anymore, doesn't it?"

Surry swiveled slightly and took both of Penny's cold hands in hers. "Yes, that's exactly what it means," she managed to answer, her throat tight with emotion. For the first time in their difficult, two-month-long journey, Penny smiled, really smiled, her face aglow with happiness, beaming despite her suffering, despite having to leave her childhood behind in Bedford County. Surry hugged Penny close. "You're a brave girl, a very brave girl," she whispered over the top of Penny's head, cradling her, gently rocking her, their easy sway keeping time with the steady waves carrying them to Canada and to freedom.

New tears threatened. Surry held them back. She didn't want to cry on such an important day. Fighting the instinct to look behind her, she kept her eyes on the waters ahead. So many were left behind, never to know freedom: her mother, her two youngest sisters, Sam and Pitty Pat, and her brothers who had run from the plantation. If only they were all with her. Her melancholy thoughts trailed along. Instinctively, Surry glanced at the heavens, knowing that at least her father already knew freedom from his shackles.

Papa, she prayed silently. *I know you keep watch over us all. I miss you so, Papa.* Stricken with new emotions, wishing with all her heart for her father's comfort in these unknown waters, she at once felt his presence washing through her. She felt his arms enfold her and Penny, holding them, loving them and guiding them. Giving in to her tears, her tears of joy from knowing that she and Penny were not alone on their journey to freedom, she let them fall.

"Toronto's up ahead!" the captain shouted from the deck above.

Penny jumped up and ran over to the edge of the boat.

"Be careful!" Surry yelled, jumping up herself and running to join Penny, to share in their first look at Canada, their first look at freedom. The wondrous city stood in the far-off distance as a beacon of light, marking the end of their long, dark journey. Suddenly mindful of their shabby attire, Surry started smoothing out the wrinkles of Penny's tattered, wool coat.

"Surry, don't," Penny said in sisterly annoyance and shrugged her off, finding a spot at the railing just out of Surry's reach.

Surry understood and let her be, taking time to straighten her own clothing and check her hair. Untied now, it fell over her shoulders and down her back in a mass of soft curls and waves. Reaching into her pockets, she wished she had a tie. She wished she still had Willa's beautiful green grosgrain ribbon. That would make her feel presentable on this important day. Willa. More than the ribbon, she wished Willa stood next to her, gazing out from the boat railing toward Canada, together as best friends on this secret adventure.

"Oh, Willa," Surry whispered over the waters. "I'm going to be free now. I'm going to find out what bein' free truly means. I wish . . . I wish you were here with me," she said, choking back sobs. "I wish you and Lucas were here with me," she said, struggling with new emotions at the thought of Lucas Minor.

She didn't think her heart could sink lower, not having the rest of her family or Willa with her on such a day, but it did. It did at the thought that she was leaving Lucas Minor behind, too. She'd no right to grieve over him. Why, she'd hardly known him for more than a week. Her spirits plummeted even further. That week was all she'd had and all she'd likely ever have with the most irresistibly wonderful man she'd met in the whole of her eighteen years. Drawn to him from the first, without meaning to be, she'd begun to dream of life with him. He wasn't in her reach. He was free. She was not. But in Canada she'd be free, just like him. In Canada she'd be worthy of him. In Canada he'd look at her differently and maybe, just maybe, he'd fall in love with her as she had with him.

Surry straightened her spine and tried to shake off such foolish thoughts. The very idea that she was in love with a man she'd only known a week was ridiculous. But she was. The truth of it hit her straight through her heart. And now that she was going to be free, maybe Lucas would love her, too. Unwittingly, she put her fingers to her lips, feeling his warmth, even on this chill day. She'd never felt his kiss, yet she imagined his mouth covering hers now. Her mouth ached for his. She ached to know his touch, on her lips and everywhere else. So what, that she had such wanton thoughts? What did it matter anyway? There was no chance for a life with Lucas Minor. There was no chance she'd ever know his touch. She ripped her hand from her mouth, angry she'd put them there as she'd thought of Lucas.

Looking in Penny's direction, making sure her sister stayed safe, Surry stared out over the uneven waters to the shores of Canada West. Forcing her thoughts on what lay ahead, she tried to imagine what life would be like for her and for Penny. She must think about the two of them and not of the many left behind. In Canada no one would treat them badly for being runaway slaves. In Canada no one would be prejudiced against them, thinking themselves superior. In Canada they'd find work and shelter, with everyone friendly. Lonely at first, soon she and Penny would build a new home together and not have to look behind them, afraid that bounty hunters or mean overseers laid chase.

In Canada they'd be free at last. Thank God, free at last.

The end of May, the twenty-third to be exact, Willa touched her chest for luck, touching the spot over her heart where her green ribbon lay tucked inside her breast bindings, ready to help take the Union garrison in Front Royal, Virginia. A part of Stonewall Jackson's foot cavalry, she was proud that her unit had been ordered to join Jackson's army and not continue under General Johnston, to march toward Richmond to defend the Confederate capital. When she'd made her way back to her unit near Centreville, returning from her so-called furlough, she'd found out. No matter that Jackson's infantrymen were known for the speed of their forced marching, no matter that her baby had to be three months along, she determined to keep up, glad to have any distraction from bitter memories of Levi Clement!

Still devastated that he'd gone off and married someone else, she rued the day she'd ever met him. Yes, he was her baby's father, but she'd never tell him about baby Adam. Never. Adam was hers alone to protect and keep safe, hidden away from the cruel outside world, for a time. But only for a time. She didn't think this awful war would be over in six months. That's how long she figured she had to go before she'd give birth. Her part in the fighting, though, would have to be.

Willa didn't know anything at all about motherhood, but she couldn't imagine bringing her child into this world and continuing with her masquerade as a woman-soldier. Although she was able to protect baby Adam now, once he was out of the protection of her womb, she could not. She'd return home, to Bedford County, to her parents, and hope they'd accept her back, her and their grandchild.

As ridiculous as it sounded, given the war and the fighting and the poverty and loss that made up everyone's lives now, civilian or military, Willa thought of social conventions. She knew her parents wouldn't approve of this unplanned pregnancy, and she hoped they'd understand. She'd have to find some way to tell them so they wouldn't reject her. Not for a moment did she think they'd turn her and her baby out, but they might turn their affections from her and her baby, even though she knew they loved her.

Willa had a more pressing worry now, wondering how long she could keep up appearances as a male soldier. She'd no idea how much her belly would swell or when it would. For now, her uniform trousers and jacket hung on her body. She'd deliberately worn oversized clothes since she'd mustered in. She thought there was plenty of room for her belly to swell with no one the wiser. Here lately, she'd felt better, too, and didn't get so sick come evening. If luck stayed with her, she'd continue to feel all right. Counted among Jackson's infantry, she'd been able to keep pace, and keep her identity secret, but she didn't know how long her energy would hold. At night, at first camp, she'd hit her blanket and fall asleep immediately, often not staying up long enough for her evening's ration. That couldn't be good for baby Adam. No, from now on she'd have to make sure she ate enough to keep up her strength for his well-being.

If she revealed her gender to her superiors now, she could get out of the military. She didn't think they'd punish her, except to send her home. Of course, she would go home when Adam was born, but not yet. She'd signed on as a soldier, and as long as she could load and point a rifle, she wanted to do her part for Virginia, for the South, and for Walter and Henry. She owed it to her dead brothers and to the future of her unborn child. If fighting was the only way to bring peace and make a better world for Adam, then fight she would, for as long as she could. Besides, heading toward the fight in Front Royal, she didn't have to think about Levi. Bent on keeping her weapon loaded, able to fire off two shots a minute, she didn't have time to think about the man she'd once loved, and now hated with every breath in her.

She hadn't meant to hate Levi.

It was just the way of it.

Levi stood near the Waterford town triangle, unhappy to hear the recruitment cry from Samuel Means for any Union sympathizers to join the Independent Loudoun Guards. Means had been given the authority to raise a company of cavalry and also given the commission of captain. Levi didn't approve. Quakers didn't abide by titles, all men being equal. Levi would never call Samuel Means captain. Pro-Union feelings ran high in Waterford and in Lovettsville. Means counted on this. Just at that moment, Samuel looked right at Levi. Levi turned away, scanning the crowd, looking for his brother Benjamin. He worried that Benjamin might have already signed up to muster into the guard.

Time was, a year ago, a month, even a day past, Levi might have heartily disapproved of Benjamin joining the fight, but now Levi felt caught up in his own inner struggle not to join up himself. How many more times could he break with his Quaker faith and still keep it? Levi swallowed hard, knowing he wasn't the same man he'd been before the war started. He'd vowed to never act in support of any side in the war, but he'd already broken with that vow by helping courier messages back and forth across the Potomac and by helping runaway slaves along the Underground Railroad, all in sympathy with the northern cause. Like it or not, he'd chosen a side.

And, like it or not, he'd married a woman he didn't love, breaking with his faith, with God, and with all bearing witness at meeting. He lived a lie with a woman, bedding her on a schedule that had nothing to do with affection, going to sleep on those nights knowing he'd dream of Willa and imagine her body next to his and not Comfort's. Before the war, before he'd met Willa, he would have married Comfort, thought he was in love, kept with tradition and been none the wiser. But that was before, when he'd never thought to question anything outside of Quaker restriction. Now . . . now he loved Willa Mae Tyler, an outsider, not a Friend, a woman-soldier, and not his wife.

And, God forgive him, now he wanted to answer Samuel Means's call to arms. His gut wrenched from wanting it. The changing times had changed him, when he thought he'd never consider such a move away from his faith and his commitment to peace. Levi didn't even know when it had happened; all he knew was that it had. He stopped just short of raising his hand to Samuel Means and volunteering for his guard. So much was at stake if he did. His enlistment would crush his father, in the wake of Jonah being gone. It would crush Levi, too, as a Quaker, a man of devout faith. With no moral or spiritual compass left inside him, his Inner Light stamped out, there would be little left of the man he once was. No, as hard as it was now to keep his fist relaxed at his side and not raise it to join the Independent Loudoun Guards, for now he must Mind the Light.

"Brother," Benjamin said, putting his hand on Levi's shoulder from behind.

Levi wheeled around, knowing full well what was coming.

"I . . . I'm going to join up," Benjamin declared, standing tall, facing his big brother. "Thee can't stop me."

Levi studied Benjamin. Three years younger than him, Benjamin had grown to be almost as tall and almost as muscled as Levi. Brown haired and brown eyed, good-looking like Jonah, Benjamin had worked hard all his life, in the fields and at the mill. He didn't have any experience with weapons, and other than getting into scraps with Jonah, Benjamin didn't know much about fighting. Yet Benjamin wanted to join the fight. It wasn't a surprise. He was Jonah's twin. He'd been holding himself in check every since Jonah left, Levi suspected.

Benjamin stared Levi down, his jaw tensed. "I said thee—"

118

"I'm not going to stop thee, Benjamin," Levi interrupted. "I'm not."

Puzzled, Benjamin kept his brow furrowed. "I don't understand. Thee has to be mad at me. Thee *has* to be."

"No, thee is wrong, Benjamin." Levi put his hand on his brother's shoulder. "I'm not mad. I understand. I will tell our parents that thee has gone off to help our neighbors in Goose Creek for a time. Thee has Friends at meeting there. There will be no questions."

"Thee . . . thee would lie for me?" Benjamin said in disbelief.

"Yes, but not for thee. For Father. I will lie for his sake."

Benjamin breathed a heavy sigh. "Thank thee, Levi. Thee is a good brother. I promise I will come home when I can and visit, and that way maybe Mother and Father won't think anything's wrong. But our sisters—"

"I will explain to Lucretia and Grace. I'm sure they will say nothing. They will worry about thee and so will I, but they will keep silent," Levi reassured him.

Benjamin nodded at Levi. "So, it's all right with thee, what I'm doing?"

"It's all right," Levi reassured him a second time. "But it won't be all right if thee gets thyself killed," he tried to joke.

Neither brother smiled.

Both knew the risks involved.

"Go along," Levi told him, his throat dry and raw with feeling.

"Yes, well . . . I'll be seeing thee," Benjamin said, starting to turn, but then hesitating. He gave his brother a hug then, in front of all the would-be soldiers forming up.

Levi hugged Benjamin back. It might be the last time the brothers would see each other in this life.

Benjamin broke away first. "Fare thee well, brother."

"Fare thee well," Levi said, swallowing back emotion. He

turned away then, from Benjamin and the rest of the people gathered, and took to the Old Waterford Road, heading home. He refused to look back, even once. It would hurt too much.

"Yes, I'm a free man," Lucas said to the Yankee officer.

Tired of being told *no* at every militia muster and Yankee camp he'd found, of being told colored men couldn't fight, that it was against the law for a colored man to take up arms, Lucas was even more tired of having to defend the fact that he was free and not a fugitive slave. He didn't have any papers with him or any certificate of freedom. Damn it, he was born free!

The weeks he'd spent in southern Maryland told him it wasn't any promised land. He'd known that the slave-holding border state only marked the beginning of the trek north to freedom, but he'd mistakenly thought that things would go better for Negroes in Maryland. The law of return governed Maryland: the law that said any caught slaves had to be returned to their owners. Same as Virginia, there were places where Negroes lived in freedom as they did in Baltimore City, but, same as Virginia, there were far more places where Negroes were still enslaved. Bounty hunters combed the countryside, kidnapping colored men, free or not; it didn't matter. If captured, he'd be sold into slavery somewhere in the South. Where Lucas hadn't been able to avoid the bounty hunters, he'd managed to fight them off, sometimes with his fists and sometimes with his pistol.

Every time he had to fend off bounty hunters or bigots, his insides turned and he worried over Surry and her little sister. That he'd set them off on their journey north, through Maryland, weighed heavily on him. Maybe he should have kept Surry with him in Waterford. Maybe he could have kept her hidden and safe, even marrying her, in secret or openly. Maybe that would have been better than sending Surry and her sister across the Potomac right into the mouth of even more danger. Dear God, he hoped Surry had made it all the way north to Canada.

Lucas knew by this time that escaping slaves had to get out of the country to avoid recapture and punishment. North meant Canada and not just states that were a part of the North. If he knew where to find Surry Lion, by God, he just might chase after her. Right now the thought of settling down with her in some nice little town in Canada sounded real good to him. The thought of actually seeing her again sounded even better.

His heart lurched. He felt himself tighten. He wanted her. He wanted to wed her and bed her. That simple. He wanted to protect her and keep her safe, cleaved unto him for the rest of their lives.

But she was on the run, escaping north to find freedom.

He was on the run, trying to join the army to defend freedom.

Kept apart by war and oppression, Lucas knew he'd never see his beautiful, brave runaway slave again. They'd only known each other for a week. That week would have to last him a lifetime.

"Then, yes," the Yankee officer answered abruptly, clearly.

Lucas forced his attention back to the moment, not believing what he'd just heard.

"Mister, if you want to join up, you best say so before I change my mind," the captain said, his expression stony. "If you're free, then we don't have a problem. You can muster in here at Camp Stanton."

"Sure enough?" Lucas needed confirmation, despite knowing he sounded like a kid.

"Sure enough." The captain's face showed a hint of understanding, if not compassion.

Lucas swallowed hard. He couldn't believe this. He'd been turned away so many times from so many camps. "Why?" he heard himself ask. It was stupid to try this sober captain's patience, but Lucas couldn't fathom what had changed to allow free colored men to join the army.

The captain's features stayed hard.

Lucas noticed there were other colored men milling around the set-up tents behind the captain. *Well, I'll be. I'll just doggone be.* He hadn't noticed them when he'd first approached the camp.

"The army needs you," the captain suddenly blurt out. "Lincoln called for three hundred thousand men to enlist for three years, but we don't have three hundred thousand recruits yet. That's by God why," he said with finality. "I'll tell you what." The officer stared past Lucas, his look faraway. "After the bloodbath at Antietam, we turned Lee away, but by damn we lost too many men. . . ." His voice trailed off.

Seeming to catch himself, the captain squared his shoulders and fixed his stare on Lucas again. "The fact is you can muster in here, and you can muster in now. Get over to that tent," he ordered, pointing to a large tent nearby. "They'll sign you up and get you a uniform."

"Yes, sir, I will," Lucas responded, knowing he'd have to get used to saying "sir." He'd have to get used to taking orders, too. He didn't care. He felt good, really good, inside. This captain obviously felt he was good enough to join their ranks. Hell, the Yankee army finally realized he was good enough. Lucas stood tall, all six foot four of him. The fact that other colored troops had already mustered in, well, that set just fine with him. They'd fight together, against slavery and for their country.

Once he put on a Yankee uniform, there'd be no going back. The only way he'd leave the army now was dead. As Lucas walked toward the recruitment tent, his step slowed a little at the thought he might never see his parents again or Waterford . . . or Surry Lion. He stopped short, thinking of his beautiful, brave runaway slave. She was *his*. Somewhere between meeting her and this minute, she'd become his. The thought of never laying eyes on Surry again, of never kissing her for the first time, settled hard.

Lucas continued walking. In a few minutes' time he'd be enlisted in the army of the United States, to fight for freedom. *I'll fight for you, Surry. I'll help set you free. If it's the last thing I do, I'll die for you,* he promised her.

He'd reached the tent flaps.

He opened them without ceremony and went inside, the vow he'd just made to Surry tucked safely next to his heart.

CHAPTER NINE

"Levi, thee must come now. We will be late for meeting," Comfort called out to Levi, who was still in their bedroom.

Making sure of the ties to her bonnet, she scooped up her Bible from the little table by the front door. She glanced around their parlor. Every antimacassar was set just so, the armrest and headrest doilies on their two parlor chairs in good order. All was tidy. Good. She prided herself on a clean, organized home. Levi had built a good house for them. Supplies were scarce, but they still had food on their table. Levi had provided for her despite the calamity of war. Comfort had finally come to terms with the reality of the war. She'd done her best to keep the idea of any fighting and bloodshed, so near to hearth and home, from her thoughts. It was impossible to do so any longer.

Her father had talked of moving west to Ohio. He'd wanted to go before the war, but Comfort had protested. She didn't want her family moving away from her. Marrying Levi meant staying in Waterford and Loudoun County. A twinge of guilt niggled at her insides. Maybe she should have held her tongue. Maybe if they'd moved earlier her family would be safer than they were now, caught in the middle of so much fighting.

Comfort disapproved of Levi's brother Jonah running off to fight. She'd never said it in so many words to Levi, but she thought Jonah's actions were reprehensible, unforgivable. As leader at meeting, she saw it as her job to preach against such actions, to preach against any Quaker choosing to fight. Maybe she'd do just that again this morning at meeting. The Independent Loudoun Guards. Humph. Comfort disdained the idea that a local Quaker, even the esteemed Samuel Means, had organized a group of rangers to fight, some of them Quakers.

Not Levi.

He'd better not. He wouldn't dare go against the peace testimony. She couldn't live with him if he chose such an unforgivable path. She couldn't accept such a change of heart. He still hadn't come into the front room. They'd be late for meeting. Lately she had more and more trouble getting him to listen to her, to do her bidding, to even pay attention to her. She knew the troubles around them weighed heavily on him. They weighed on her, too, but *she* managed to keep her spirits up most times. Why couldn't he? Why couldn't he, just once, show her a smile, show her any sign of affection? It wasn't fair and it wasn't right. She knew the reason, and it wasn't the war.

Willa, love was the reason.

Comfort flopped down into one of the parlor chairs, sending both antimacassars flying off the armrests. Her Bible fell into her lap. She didn't notice. For weeks she'd tried to think of something to distract Levi from thinking of Willa. It turned Comfort's insides every time she remembered how he'd shouted out Willa's name during their lovemaking, and not hers. In the times since then, when she and Levi had been intimate, he'd kept silent, with no name on his lips. She wasn't stupid. She knew who he thought about when he was in bed with her. He thought about Willa.

Comfort bolted up from the chair, sending her Bible to the floor. She began pacing the front room. Levi still hadn't come into the room. "Levi, we are late!" She shouted to no avail. The bedroom door stayed shut. Comfort kept pacing. What on this good earth could she do or say to get her husband to pay her any mind?

An idea struck.

Comfort sat back down in the chair she'd just vacated, and took care to retrieve her Bible from the floor, and then leaned down to retrieve each antimacassar, placing them neatly back on the armrests. It was wrong, what she was about to do and say, but she didn't care. Gaining Levi's attention was all that mattered now.

She leaned against the cushioned seatback, organizing her thoughts. Once she had, she slowly stood, then walked over to the little table by the front door and replaced her Bible carefully atop it. Then she loosened the ties to her bonnet, keeping them tied just enough to stay together. Satisfied they would, she lowered to the planked floor and slowly doubled over.

"Levi!" She screamed as loud as she could. "Levi! Levi!"

The bedroom door opened. Concerned the moment he saw Comfort on the floor, Levi rushed over to her and put his arms around her in worry. "Comfort, what's wrong?"

"I had a pain, husband," Comfort whispered, lifting herself slightly, enough to be clearly heard. "Help me up, please," she said feebly.

Levi kept his arms around her and slowly brought her to a stand. She looked so pale, so fragile, so disquiet. Her appearance concerned him. Comfort was always all right. What could be wrong?

"Please, husband, help me sit," Comfort whispered. "I'll be better when I do," she added.

Levi guided her over to one of the parlor chairs and eased her down. He knelt in front of her. "What kind of pain, Comfort?"

She heard the concern in his voice and saw the worry on his face. "I . . . I didn't want to say anything yet . . . but . . . I have news, husband," she said haltingly.

Levi's insides flinched. He felt uneasy at her words. She was breathing all right and didn't seem in pain anymore. He'd thought she'd come out of whatever spell she just had.

"Levi? My news?" Comfort fought her irritation over his lack of curiosity, even now.

"Yes, of course, your news," he parroted, already trying to think of a reason not to go to meeting with her. He never missed First Day meetings, but he didn't feel like going this morning. He didn't feel like facing his misdeeds. There was no escaping them; he just didn't feel easy about going to meeting.

Comfort made sure of his focus on her and then spoke deliberately, carefully. "Levi, I'm going to have thy child," she said, her lie easily spoken.

Levi shook his head to clear it. Surely he'd heard wrong. "Comfort, thee needs to rest. Let me help thee to the bedroom. Thee can miss meeting. Thee needs to rest." He tried to coax her up.

"Levi Clement!" Comfort shot at him, nestling further in her chair, folding her arms tight in front of her. "Is that all thee can say when I've just told thee that we're going to have a baby? That I can miss meeting and rest this morning?" she fumed.

Dear God, he had heard her right. The heart went out of him in that moment. Frozen in his position before Comfort, this was at once the best and the worst moment of his life. Levi was happy about the baby but unhappy that Willa wasn't giving him this news. God forgive him, he wanted a child with the woman he loved. That woman wasn't his wife. It didn't matter now. Comfort was his wife, not Willa. Comfort was carrying his child, not Willa.

Levi made himself soften toward Comfort. He had to, for the sake of their unborn child. He'd love his child unconditionally, and lay no blame at his child's feet for his own misdeeds. He owed it to his child to love its mother. He'd try to shut Willa out of his thoughts and take good care of Comfort. God willing, he'd be able to.

Comfort watched Levi's face, seeing the changes, knowing she'd won. It was wrong to lie, but it was right to get her husband's attention again. They were man and wife, after all.

Still kneeling, Levi reached for Comfort's hands, easily undoing her arms. "I am happy over this news that we are to have a baby. Thee must take good care and rest. I will take care of thee both," he told her, his mouth hinting of a smile now. "Come, let's get thee up and to bed. Thee must rest," he said, pulling her to stand with him.

"I'm happy thee is pleased about the life growing inside me, dear husband," Comfort cooed. "But I don't want to rest now. I want to go to meeting. It is First Day. I must go. Thee must come with me to meeting. All right, husband?"

Levi sighed heavily. "Yes, all right."

"Good, husband," Comfort said, her smile bright. "Thee get the buggy hitched and I'll just take a sip of water before we leave. I do feel thirsty," she added. "I must think of the baby now in all things."

"I, too," Levi assured her.

Gleeful inside, Comfort started for the kitchen where she kept the water crock. She turned once, thrilled that Levi still watched her. "Hurry, Levi. We mustn't be late. Hurry, now," she said again, knowing he wouldn't hesitate to do her bidding.

Levi had the front door open and shut in the blink of an eye.

Comfort couldn't be happier on this First Day. Levi believed her lie. Levi would be attentive now. Levi would love her again, believing she carried his child. Soon she *would* be. She'd make sure they kept to their weekly schedule of lovemaking. Maybe he'd even cry out her name now. She poured water into her glass and took a slow sip. Suddenly she couldn't wait until the next time he bedded her, imagining him saying, "Comfort, love."

Seven in the morning. Levi had left his farm at sunup to ferret out what supplies he could, and finally arrived in Waterford. He hadn't ridden a horse, always concerned the Yankees would confiscate his mount. No, walking suited him fine. When he heard gunfire coming from the direction of the Baptist meetinghouse, he took off running. The Loudoun Rangers were camped there, Benjamin among them.

Samuel Means was keeping his company in Waterford. It was the reason Benjamin could come home once in a while, leaving his uniform hidden in the woods and wearing his plain clothes, so their parents wouldn't suspect. At first Levi had been pleased the Rangers were ensconced close by. He'd worried that somebody might recognize Benjamin, but so far he didn't think anyone knew his brother had joined the local company.

More gunfire. Levi's heart thudded in his chest. He ran down the street, past the town triangle, past the Arch house, not stopping until he'd reached the Virtz house on High Street, right across from the meetinghouse.

"Get out of the way, Quaker!" a soldier in gray shouted at him.

Levi turned around, watching the soldier come out now from behind the Virtz house. Others stepped out from behind the house, others in gray with their weapons pointed. Except for the soldier shouting, it was quiet, deathly quiet. Scared for Benjamin, Levi looked again at the meetinghouse. The door opened. Soldiers in blue came out, one at first, then a few more. Benjamin wasn't among them. Levi bound across the street, headed for the open door.

"I said get!" The soldier in gray caught up with him.

"My brother's in there. I'm going in," Levi snapped out,

ignoring the soldier and not waiting for any reply. The only thing that would stop him was a bullet from one of White's Comanches. He knew all about Elijah White's Virginia cavalry from the eastern side of the Catoctin Mountains gunning for Means's Loudoun Rangers from the western side. The war had come down now to neighbor against neighbor and brother against brother. What Levi had feared from the outset of the war had come true. Folks who used to get along didn't anymore.

The horses tied close by the meetinghouse whinnied and danced around, doubtless skittish from the earlier firefight. The soldiers in gray brushed past Levi, quickly untying the horses, leading them away. White's Comanches had won. Levi watched them claim the horses, his own step slowed down, each one filled with dread. He had to go inside. He had to find Benjamin, dead or alive. One of White's soldiers lay dead in front of him, his body hidden heretofore by the tethered horses. Two men bumped into Levi, hurrying to retrieve the dead soldier. Each took an arm and dragged the dead man back across the street.

Benjamin. Dear God, Benjamin!

Levi could hear the cries of the wounded coming from inside the meetinghouse. He ran now, praying with everything in him his brother had lived through the fighting.

Met with a chaotic scene the moment he entered, Levi scanned the fallen Rangers littering the floor, looking for Benjamin. The wounded lay in pools of blood, crying for help. Levi didn't see Benjamin among them.

"Over there," a man whispered hard from behind Levi. "There's one dead, over there."

Levi froze. Everything around him stopped. He turned mechanically to look over there. Benjamin lay in a heap in the corner. Dead. Levi rushed over to his brother and crumpled down. He had no words, only tears. In his grief he was vaguely aware of others gathering around him and guiding him to stand upright. He didn't notice the color of their coats; he couldn't take his eyes from Benjamin, watching his brother's body being hoisted onto a litter. Levi followed the litter outside, past men and women from town who'd come to tend to the wounded. He followed the litter to the back of a wagon and remembered someone asking him where to take the remains?

His much-loved brother, who'd been so full of life, was now *remains*. It angered Levi to hear his brother referred to in such a callous way, but he was too bereaved to protest. Telling the driver to take the Old Waterford Road out of town, Levi had to find the words to tell his family they'd lost Benjamin on this day. In his heart, he knew he had to tell his parents and his sisters the truth. Benjamin deserved it. To do otherwise would be disrespectful to his brave, well-intentioned, pure-of-heart brother.

"We commit him into Thy hands now, Oh, Lord, into Thy hands," Levi whispered into the heavy August air, sitting next to his dead brother in the back of the wagon, taking Benjamin home for the last time.

Susan Clement stood out front on the porch, watching the wagon approach as if she'd been waiting for it. She stood straight, her shoulders squared, her features solemn.

She knew.

Levi didn't see his father or his sisters, only his mother, and she knew, despite the fact she couldn't see inside the wagon yet, that he was bringing Benjamin home. Levi could feel her anguish. Connected in life to her son, so was she now connected to Benjamin in death. Levi pulled out his neckerchief and quickly wiped the residual blood from Benjamin's mouth, smoothed out Benjamin's rumpled hair, then pulled the blanket closer over his brother, trying to get Benjamin ready for their

131

mother to see.

He thought then of Jonah. Jonah could already be dead. Levi stared at the empty space in the wagon next to Benjamin, imagining Jonah lying in death next to his twin, praying someone had been there to wipe the blood from Jonah's face and bid him farewell.

It was bad enough for his mother to see her dead son; Levi didn't know what would happen to his father. Even though death had become a fixture to their family what with the war, this was different. This was *their* son and *their* brother. This was Benjamin. Just then Lucretia and Grace came charging out of the house, running down the steps to meet the wagon, their frightened expressions giving way to tears. Not his father. His father had yet to come outside. Levi already grieved for Thomas Clement, for surely his father would not make it through this day. On this night there could well be two people to bury.

Levi climbed out of the wagon the moment it stopped, taking hold of Benjamin and starting to lift him.

"Here," one of the soldiers said, having come around to Levi's side. "Let me help."

With no will to protest, Levi let the soldier assist him in taking Benjamin from the wagon and laying him down on the porch. "Thank thee," he managed to tell the soldier.

Susan Clement still hadn't moved and stood in silence, as if at meeting. Levi's sisters both knelt down next to Benjamin, dissolving into tears over him. His father had yet to come outside. Levi dreaded the moment.

The Yankee soldiers touched their caps and nodded to Levi and his family, then turned their wagon and pulled away. Levi watched them, afraid to look at his mother again. He'd seen that look of horror on her face before when he'd spoken his vows to Comfort, when she recognized her son was marrying a woman he didn't love before God and everyone at meeting. His mother had that same horror-stricken look on her face now, only worse, much worse.

Unsure what to do to help bring her ease, Levi stepped close and pulled her into his arms. At first she tried to pull away, but then dissolved into tears against him, at last allowing herself to cry. His sisters still cried, too. There were no questions about what had happened, about why Benjamin lay dead on their front porch, only tears.

The front door unexpectedly pushed open.

Thomas Clement stepped outside, past his dead son's body, past all of them, and headed for the barn. He didn't say a word. He didn't look at Benjamin. He didn't look at any of them, but just kept walking.

Levi kept hold of his mother, worrying about his father at the same time. What if the unthinkable was about to happen? What if . . . what if his father meant to. . . .

"Mother," Levi said, keeping his voice as steady as he could. He gently put her at arm's length from him. "Thee must go inside now. Take Lucretia and Grace with thee. I will be in soon, and then we'll talk of what we need do for Benjamin."

Susan Clement looked first at one son and then the other, one dead and the other alive. "Yes. Yes, Levi," she said weakly; then she turned mechanically to go inside, not waiting for her daughters to follow.

Lucretia stood. So did Grace.

"Go with thy mother," Levi quietly commanded.

Lucretia nodded and then quickly went inside.

Grace hesitated, bending back down to her brother, and then slowly straightened. She shot Levi a rebellious look, yet went inside all the same.

Levi took off for the barn. As scared as he'd been to go inside the Baptist meetinghouse to find Benjamin, he was as scared now to go inside the barn to find his father. It would be too much for his mother and his sisters, losing their father on this day as well. He ran now. He ran until he'd reached the heavy barn doors, and flung them open.

"What is the meaning of this?" his father gruffly greeted him.

Levi had expected just about anything, but not this, not seeing his father bent over his workbench, crafting a coffin. Thank God his father appeared to be all right, at least physically.

"Keep the doors open. The light's better," Thomas Clement clipped out, and turned back to his work.

"Yes, Father." Levi warily approached.

"Hand up that board, Levi," Thomas ordered, keeping his eyes trained on his work.

Levi took up the board and passed it to his father.

Thomas nodded in acknowledgement, still not looking at Levi.

The barn was silent, but for the hammering and fitting of the coffin Thomas was crafting. The dairy cows and horses once stabled there were long gone, taken by troops moving through the area. One horse stomped around in the corral outside, the only one left. And one hog, a pet to Lucretia and Grace. Soon, Levi knew, they'd need to slaughter the hog for food. It wasn't going to be an easy day. Not unlike this day. Levi couldn't get a clean breath. It hurt too much, knowing Benjamin was dead. He thought of Willa, envisioning her body lying next to Benjamin's on the front porch. She could be dead now, too. How could he ever bid her farewell? His heart wrenched, yet again, imagining his Willa, love dead and gone from him, too.

The loud hammering of nails pulled his mournful thoughts back to the moment. He must think of his father, and his mother and his sisters. He must think of the living and not the—. . . Levi refused to think the word.

"We will not call a memorial meeting," Thomas announced, his eyes still on his work. "These times don't allow for it. We will bury Benjamin on this day, on our land. We will keep him with the family." Thomas hammered another nail.

Although he'd become used to his father's silence over the past months, Levi was incredulous at his words, and especially at what he said. Here Levi had thought his father oblivious to everything around him since Jonah had left, when all the while maybe his father had not been.

"Does thee agree?" Thomas looked at Levi now.

"Yes, Father." Levi studied his father's drawn, aged face, made more so over the past months. Gray hair peeked out from the sides of his hat, his beard a match. Lids drooped over his watery brown eyes. He'd lost some of his weight and height. But right now, Thomas stood tall, his shoulders no longer stooped.

Levi thought of days gone by, before the war, when he did his father's bidding at the mill. This felt like such a time. It eased him a little, feeling like he could lean on his father, sharing the impossible burden of Benjamin's death.

"Son." Thomas spoke low and quiet, his attention back on the task at hand.

Levi set another board in place and held it fast for his father. It was like manna from heaven, hearing his father call him son again.

"I have been wrong to condemn Jonah. I have been wrong." Thomas's voice took a wistful turn. "Benjamin is dead. Jonah might be, too."

Levi thought the same thing.

"I love my sons. Death cannot destroy that love. This war cannot destroy that love. I was wrong to deny Jonah, in this life or the next. He is no longer shunned," he finished, his words hoarse with emotion.

Despite this wretched day, despite the fact that one brother was dead, Levi took heart that his father breathed new life into the other brother by accepting Jonah back into the fold and into his heart. By some miracle, maybe Jonah didn't lie dead somewhere and would come home. If only Jonah knew that he'd be welcome, if he did return. Levi remembered the anguished look on Jonah's face the day he was banished from home and the Friends. He'd give anything now to see Jonah come up their lane, returning home from the war. And Willa with him. Coming home to Levi.

For now, thinking of the possibility of miracles coming true, Levi forgot that he already had a wife at home and a baby on the way.

CHAPTER TEN

August 30, 1862

The three-day battle at Manassas—the same ground fought on in 1861—had just ended, with the Yankees withdrawing.

Losses had been heavy on both sides. Major General Jackson and Major General Longstreet's divisions of Lee's Army of Northern Virginia, 50,000 men, had fought together against the joined corps of the Union Army of Virginia, 62,000 men, under Major General Pope. Lee's Army had won, but at what price? They hadn't destroyed Pope's Army. Pope hadn't gotten Stonewall Jackson, either. Now the Yankees were withdrawing quietly, in an orderly manner, down the turnpike to Centreville. Weary from battle and low on ammunition, the Confederates didn't pursue in the darkness. Thirteen hundred in their ranks had been killed with 7,000 wounded, while the Yankees suffered 10,000 killed and wounded.

"The Lord is my Shepherd, I sha-shall not want. He mak-maketh me to lie down in green pastures. . . ."

"Finish him off, soldier. He's done for anyway," the Confederate corporal told Willa, then kept on walking past the fallen Yankee soldier.

Exhausted and melancholy and worried over the baby she carried in her womb, Willa didn't realize she'd actually passed the Stone House where Walter and Henry had died. Then her corporal had told her to finish off the wounded Yankee. She stopped at the back of the Stone House, seeing the wounded soldier now, propped up against the outside wall. She vaguely heard him muttering, only now trying to make out his words.

"Yea, though I walk through the val-valley of the sha-shadow of death. . . ."

She recognized what he repeated. It was the twenty-third psalm. She'd repeated it to herself many times during the past months, praying she wouldn't die, all the time believing she would. Right away, she felt a bond with the soldier, despite him being the enemy. Evening was coming on. It would be dark soon. Thunderstorms threatened overhead.

Willa blinked hard, trying to stay awake. She'd never been so tired. What was she supposed to do? Oh, yes, finish off the wounded enemy soldier. Other soldiers, her comrades, passed by now, all doubtless too tired to notice her or hear the prayers of the dying Yankee. She wanted to join the throng and move out, too, and find a place to put her head down. But she was a good soldier accustomed now to following orders. Before she could sleep, she had to see to the enemy soldier.

Intent on helping the soldier, rather than hurting him, she thought of Walter and Henry. They'd died on this same hallowed ground. They'd never taught her to hurt anyone or anything that was down, except to put them out of their misery. Maybe it would be the right thing to do now, to put this soldier out of his misery. As she approached him, she wondered if she could do that to this poor fellow.

"Go ahead and fin-finish me off," the soldier told her, his words spoken with effort.

Willa knelt down next to him. Why, he wasn't much older than she was. Her heart went out to him, wishing he wasn't so young and wishing he wasn't dying. He was bloody all over, but she noticed that his leg wound must have been the killing hit.

Blood gushed from it. He'd be dead in minutes if she didn't do something. But what? She didn't have any kind of tourniquet on her?

Wait. Immediately, she unbuttoned part of her heavy jacket and reached inside, past her long underwear, and put her fingers inside her breast bindings, at last pulling out her wound-up, green grosgrain ribbon. Without another thought, she bound the ribbon tightly around the soldier's thigh, just above the bullet's entry.

"Who-who art thou?" the soldier managed.

"I'm nobody," she answered, focused on making sure the ribbon would do its job, not hearing that he'd said the word thou.

The soldier coughed.

Willa waited, knowing his life's blood could be drained at any time now.

He tried to push himself up to sit straighter.

Willa thought him handsome. In fact, he reminded her of someone. Too tired to think much on it, she kept her focus on stopping the bleeding from his leg.

Thunder boomed overhead.

"Thee didn't Mi-Mind the Light," he whispered. "Thee didn't finish me."

Willa jerked her gaze to his. He was Quaker! Dumbfounded, she stared into his eyes. He reminded her of someone. *Levi!*

"Will thee . . . will thee stay?" the soldier pled. "I'd just as soon not die a-alone." He coughed again.

"What's your name?" Willa demanded, before she could stop herself. It was crazy to ask the fallen soldier at such a time, yet still, she had to know.

The soldier tried to smile through his pain. "Jo-Jonah."

"Jonah what?" Willa pressed, desperate to know.

"Cle-Clement," he answered her, his eyes closing.

The baby suddenly moved. She immediately put her hands

over her belly, stunned at the impossible coincidence that she'd just come upon Levi's brother. So many on the battlefield, so many killed and wounded, and she'd encountered Levi's kin. A Quaker, fighting. It pushed the bounds of reality. The baby quieted. Willa took her hands from her belly and automatically took up Jonah's, her fingers bloody again.

Close to losing consciousness, Jonah forced his eyes open at Willa's touch.

Fighting tears, knowing Jonah was near death, Willa knew the reason she'd been led to him on this awful day. He wouldn't die alone. She'd be with him and so would his nephew Adam. She'd little time to do what she could to bring ease to Jonah, helping him leave this life for the next.

"Jonah, Jonah," she said, squeezing his hands, trying to keep him conscious.

He looked at her through heavy lids.

"Jonah, you must listen to me." Willa bent closer to him.

He coughed again.

Willa quickly scanned his chest and gut area, checking for more wounds. He must be bleeding internally, to cough so. It grew darker by the second. She couldn't see well. With the storm brewing overhead, she knew there wouldn't be a moon tonight. Suddenly she felt Jonah's fingers tighten around hers. He was still with her. There was still time to tell him what she must.

"Jonah, I know your brother Levi, Jonah," Willa urged.

Jonah opened his eyes wide.

Despite the dimming light, Willa could see that he listened.

"Le-Levi?" he managed to whisper.

"Yes, Jonah, your brother Levi. You must hear me out, dear Jonah. You must stay with me and hear me out."

"Yes . . . ," his voice trailed off, his eyes shutting again.

Willa leaned even closer, wanting him to hear her words,

hoping they would help carry him peacefully into the hereafter. She kept hold of his hands, making sure he could feel her touch so he'd know he wasn't alone. "Jonah." She spoke close to his ear. "I'm really a woman, a woman-soldier. Most folks don't know. But when I met Levi in Waterford, he knew right away. We fell in love, Jonah." Willa's insides clenched at having to say the word *love*. Levi didn't love her. He loved another. "Levi and I slept together, Jonah. Your brother doesn't know it, but I'm carrying his child. It's a boy, Jonah. I'm sure of it. I'm going to call him Adam. Adam is your nephew, Jonah." Willa put Jonah's hands over her belly now. "Feel him, Jonah. He's kicking now. Your nephew, Jonah."

"Adam . . . ," Jonah repeated, trying to open his eyes.

"I am with you now and so is Adam. We are with you, Jonah. We are with you." Willa choked back her tears. She closed her eyes in prayer, knowing Jonah's pain in this life would soon be over.

Jonah lay still now, his eyes shut.

Willa started to pull away.

"Marry? Are you mar-married?" Jonah suddenly whispered.

Willa bent back to him. She wanted to lie to Jonah but somehow, in death, it didn't seem right. "No. Levi is married to another."

"Comfort," he volunteered.

"Yes. Comfort," Willa repeated, incredulous that Jonah still had the strength to carry on any kind of conversation.

"Tell him, Willa."

Jonah spoke so clearly, it sent a chill down Willa's spine. She automatically backed away.

Jonah forced his eyes open. "*Tell* him."

"Levi is married, Jonah." Willa leaned closer again.

"I know my brother. Thee *must* tell him. Promise me thee

141

will. . . ." Jonah couldn't finish, suddenly gripped with a coughing spasm.

She'd no intention of ever telling Levi about Adam. But Jonah was dying. What was the right thing to say to him? Should she lie? Thunder clapped overhead, as if signaling the answer she must give. "Yes, I promise thee," she whispered, unaware she'd used plain speech.

Jonah heaved in a deep breath, let it go, and then lay still.

Had he died? Willa felt his hands still in hers. No, he wasn't dead yet, but unconscious.

"Soldier! Leave that enemy vermin and get going! If you don't, I'll get General Jackson after you myself!"

Willa quickly stood and pivoted to face the passing Confederate officer.

"You best follow orders, son." The officer's harsh tone softened.

"Sir." Willa automatically saluted and bent down to get her gear, quickly eyeing Jonah. Good. He still slept. Was it the sleep of death? She didn't know.

The officer turned away and kept on up the hill behind the Matthews' house.

Quick as she could, Willa set her pack back down and took out her gum blanket. Before anyone else passed and could notice, she placed the rubber blanket over Jonah to protect him from the rain that was coming.

"Surely goodness and mercy shall follow me all the days of my life, and I will dwell in the House of the Lord forever," Willa whispered, finishing the twenty-third psalm for Jonah. She turned from him and started up the hill behind the Stone House. Two loved ones died here, and there was soon to be a third on this hallowed ground. Walter and Henry and Jonah. Her heart had never weighed more heavily.

"Come breathe in this magic evening air, Penny," Surry bade her sister, knowing Penny had just come out the door of Saxonia Shadd's house. Surry took another deep breath and closed her eyes, content and happy to be doing so after months of being on the run.

"What's so magic about it?" Penny came up to Surry, and they both stood just behind the neat, white picket fence out front.

Surry took in another deep breath, and then slowly let it out. She opened her eyes and turned to her sister. "It's *free* air, Penny. That's why. It's *free.*"

Penny's smile brightened. She hugged Surry as tightly as she could around the waist.

The two sisters stood for long moments, holding on to each other, and holding on to the fact that they were no longer fugitive slaves but free Negroes. Here in the Elgin Settlement, in Canada West, Ontario, they lived with hundreds of their own people, all free. No bounty hunters laid chase to them. No one tried to catch them and send them back to America, selling them back into slavery. They'd followed the North Star to Canaan Land. Free at last.

After they'd been put ashore in Toronto, a conductor on the Underground Railroad met them, guiding them away from the city to the Elgin Settlement, an all-colored community situated between the Great Western Railway and Lake Erie. Elgin marked the end of the Underground Railroad. It wasn't the only end point for fugitive slaves from America, but certainly one of them. Yes, it would have been possible for Surry and Penny to try to live in one of the cities in Ontario, but their guide told them Elgin would be better. Even though they'd made it to Canada, to freedom, there was still bigotry and prejudice, still bounty hunters, and it was very hard for runaway slaves to secure decent jobs. They'd fare much better in Elgin, their guide reassured them. In Elgin they would be protected and more secure. In Elgin, families would take them in.

Started by Reverend King, a Presbyterian minister from Scotland, the twelve-year-old settlement was successful and growing. Every resident—most of them former slaves—had to buy their own property at two dollars and fifty cents an acre, build their homes according to regulation, work their land, and meet other requirements for life inside the community. Liquor was forbidden in the settlement. If a resident sold his land, it must be to one of his own people. The settlement could boast of a potash factory, a brickyard, and a saw-and-grist-mill. Elgin produced lumber and barrel staves, and its farms produced corn, wheat, oats and tobacco to be sold at market.

A truly unique characteristic of Elgin was that the residents shared responsibilities. Common events included logging bees, chopping bees, and house-raising bees. Out from under white control, residents enjoyed economic freedom and a strong sense of community and solidarity. Yes, it was important at last to be free and in their own community, but even more important to the escaped slaves who made up the population of Elgin was the fact they had control over their own families and their own destinies. No one could sell part of their family to another master. Men could be husbands and fathers. Women could be wives and mothers, a new experience to former slaves.

Families could stay together and attend church together and their children could attend schools, their own schools. No laws forbade them from learning. In fact, Elgin soon became known for its quality education, with some of the white folks from surrounding areas sending their children to the now-integrated schools in the Elgin Settlement. Besides the noted Mission School, parents paid for the building of a new school, wanting to keep educational standards high. Curricula included the subjects of Latin, geography, English grammar and history. Graduates went on to college in cities like Toronto, becoming physicians, ministers, lawyers, and teachers.

Surry wanted to be a teacher, especially now that she could legally do so. She and Penny both attended the Mission School, and were ahead of some of the students—because they could read and write and knew basic ciphering—but were behind others. Surry loved her classes and wanted to get her teaching certificate from King's School, and maybe even go on to college. Imagine. College. It was a pure wonder to Surry. Only yesterday it seemed, she'd been a fugitive slave on the run. Today she was Surry Lion, a student at King's Mission School in Ontario, Canada.

"Surry," Penny said, pulling her arms from around her sister.

"What's that frown about?" Surry had hoped never to see Penny sad again once they'd crossed the border into Canada.

"Surry, Mrs. Shadd is real nice. I like her a lot but. . . ."

Surry knew what was coming. She thought the same thing.

"She's not Mama." Penny bit her lower lip. "I miss Mama, Surry."

"Me, too," Surry said quietly. Not a day went by that she didn't miss their mother and their brothers and their sisters and Willa . . . and Lucas, who were all back home. Surry's insides caught. If only she knew they were safe. It wouldn't be so bad being so far away from home, if she knew. Maybe her brothers who'd run away from the plantation were safe. Maybe Sam and Pitty Pat hadn't been sent to some awful prison, but were back home in their mother's arms. Maybe her mother stayed safe at the plantation, somehow protected from the murdering overseer's son.

Surry's heart turned to steel.

Maybe Boyd Blankenship is dead and gone to hell where he belongs.

Her thoughts eased. She thought of Willa. Maybe Willa would find a way to stay alive. Surry believed in miracles. She had to, for Willa's sake and her own. Was it too much, asking God for such a miracle? Was it too much, asking God to keep alive her one true friend who'd loved her unconditionally. When others had turned from her when she was a slave, Willa had not. Willa had never shunned her and was always there, waiting on the banks of the James for her, waiting to listen, to talk, to laugh, to cry, to lean on. Surry closed her eyes and imagined Willa waiting there now, on the banks of the James, fishing pole in hand, waiting for her.

"Are you sad 'cause of Mama?" Penny broke into Surry's wishful, melancholy thoughts.

Surry nodded her head yes, afraid to say anything for fear she'd start crying. She didn't want to upset Penny any more than she was, about missing family and home.

"I think you're missing somebody besides Mama," Penny teased, a slow grin coming over her face.

"You're right, Penny girl. I miss my friend Willa." Surry tried to keep her voice even, realizing yet again how very smart Penny was.

"No, not Willa. Lucas Minor, that's who," Penny corrected, her tone mischievous.

Shocked and feeling found out, Surry turned toward Penny. "That's not true, and besides, how do you even know who Lucas is?" Surry felt like the younger sister now.

"Don't get mad, Surry." Penny lost her smile. "I'm sorry."

"Oh, Penny, I'm the one who's sorry," Surry apologized; upset that she'd upset her little sister. For pity's sake, they weren't home in Virginia arguing as sisters sometimes did. That wasn't a luxury either of them could enjoy now. Surry needed to be more careful of what she said and did around Penny. "What do you think you know about Lucas Minor, young lady,"

146

Surry teased, suddenly curious.

Penny smiled again. "Well, I know that you like him."

Surry smiled back. "You're too smart for your own good, you know," she joked, tugging on one of Penny's braids.

"I know," Penny agreed, starting to laugh.

Hearing her little sister laugh again was music to Surry's ears.

"Surry's got a boyfriend," Penny gleefully taunted. "Surry's got a boyfriend," she teased her big sister, and then took off for the house.

Surry was right behind her. "Penny Lion. You just stop right now," she called out, laughing as she did so. It felt good to laugh. It felt good to chase her little sister as if they were back home again, with nothing more to worry about than a sister's teasing. For the moment, Surry let herself forget all the pain and worry over the war and who would live and who would die, and ran after Penny like it was an ordinary, late summer evening back in Virginia, when the family had gathered together after an exhausting day's work. For the moment, too, she let herself forget all the pain and worry over plantation life, worry over who would get whipped and who would survive.

A little taste of freedom can do that, make you forget.

"I'm not gonna fool with you, here, Private Minor. This is dangerous business. If you get caught, you don't say anything about anything, you hear me?"

Lucas listened carefully to his captain. He'd been called to the officer's tent, hoping for some kind of assignment taking him to the fight. So far, the colored troops gathered at Camp Stanton had done just that: gathered, and that's all. Lucas had the feeling it was still secret for men of his color to join Yankee forces, since they'd not been sent into any action so far. What was everyone waiting for? What was President Lincoln waiting for? Hell, the war would likely be over before he could even get in it.

"Time's coming soon for you to fight, you and the rest of your unit, but not yet." The captain kept his voice quiet, as if not wanting anyone to overhear. "I've caught wind of what's going on in Washington, and things are gonna change real soon for your people."

Lucas listened so hard, his ears rang.

"Can I trust you?" The captain leveled his question.

"Yes, sir," Lucas didn't hesitate in answering.

"All right then." The captain looked past Lucas to the closed tent flaps. Seeing no sign of anyone around, he looked at Lucas again. "I suspect that soon President Lincoln is gonna free your people in the South. Only in the South."

Lucas must have heard wrong. He shook his head a little to clear it. The captain still looked him right in the eye, man to man. It was always in the eyes. Shades of glory! The captain spoke the truth.

"Did you hear me, son?"

"Yes, sir," Lucas said, trying to keep his emotions in check.

"Your people in the South—in the enemy states—will be free, but not in the North, and not here, in Maryland. We're a border state and the slaves here won't be set free."

Lucas understood. This was more about winning the war than freeing his people. Yet it was a start. Thank God Almighty, it was a start.

"The word will come soon, but not yet. Right now, we have to keep this under our hats. All right, Private Minor?"

Lucas nodded his agreement. He thought of Surry Lion. Wherever she'd run, she and her little sister, they might be able to return. His heart filled at such hope for her—and for him. Maybe they could have a life together after all, if they both survived the next years. Lucas believed that the war would go on much longer than even he had first thought. There was too much fighting and too much ground to take and then hold. Since he'd been at Camp Stanton, he hadn't heard anything about an early victory. But if the captain spoke the truth and if Mr. Lincoln was going to free his people in the South, there was victory in that. Indeed, there was.

"Right after all this is made public, it's gonna be official to recruit your people to fight on our side. You probably know by now, Private Minor, that I don't exactly go by the book. I've already recruited you," he quipped, the corners of his mouth hinting of a smile.

Lucas didn't feel like smiling, yet he was grateful to be thought of as capable of fighting, at least by the captain.

"You were with the Underground Railroad. I know about the route to free runaway slaves. I might be cussed and getting older, but I'm not stupid. You were in intelligence with the Underground Railroad as I see it. That's the duty I'm ordering you into for your country now: intelligence."

Lucas waited to hear the rest.

"I don't want to wait for any official word to come from Washington. I want to muster in as many coloreds as I can right now. There's no official United States Colored Troops for me to draw from as yet. No, sir, I need recruits now. I'm gonna get my own men together. There are some gathered here, but not near enough. That's where you come in, Private."

Lucas kept listening, keen on what he was hearing.

"I need you to dress in civilian clothes and infiltrate plantations here in Maryland, and recruit men for our cause. I don't have to tell you that Washington wouldn't approve. We have some runaways in our ranks, but not nearly enough. You get me, Private?"

"Yes, sir."

"Fair enough. It's a dangerous job, but you're the best one

for it, as I see it. Fighting will come soon enough for us all, but for now, we have to win *this* fight. We have to get more troops gathered and be ready."

"Yes, sir. Understand, sir," Lucas spoke loud and clear, his spine straight, standing his full six foot four.

He took immediate pride in the captain's confidence. The captain knew he had fight in him. The captain didn't think that just because his skin was dark he wasn't an able soldier. Lucas felt even more proud that the captain thought him intelligent. All white folks didn't think people of color were smart. The captain did, though, and the knowledge made Lucas stand even taller.

"At ease, son." The captain pushed back his hat and then reset it. "I've got a list of the plantations and their locations." He reached for a paper on the makeshift table behind him, and then handed it to Lucas. "I want you to study this and then destroy it."

Lucas took the outstretched list.

"Like I said," the captain continued. "Look it over, remember it, then burn it. It will go better for the both of us if there's no evidence of your movements. Just like you guided folks on the Underground Railroad, I want you to guide recruits here. Keep 'em coming for as long as you can."

His meaning wasn't lost on Lucas. Anything could happen to him on this mission. He could be caught. Hell, he could be caught by goddamn bounty hunters and sold into slavery if he wasn't careful. He could be caught by the law, too. If lucky, he might only be imprisoned. If unlucky . . . well, he wouldn't have to worry about much else.

"I want you to set out at first light."

"Yes, sir." Lucas folded the list and shoved it in a pocket.

"Good luck, son."

"Thank you, sir."

"God go with you," the captain said, his tone fatherly.

"Yes, thank you, sir." Lucas saluted, then turned and passed through the tent flaps back outside, happy to at last see some kind of action. He was a soldier and wanted to do a soldier's job and see to his duty for God and country. He owed it to himself and to his people . . . and to Surry.

CHAPTER ELEVEN

"Levi, it's my letter and my private business," Lucretia huffed, quickly turning and walking out of the mercantile in Waterford, her letter safe in hand. The post had been getting through, hit and miss. Ever since Private Caleb Ryan had left town and gone off to fight, Lucretia made sure to write him every week and hoped her letters made it to his unit. This was the first letter she'd received from him. Anxious to read it, she didn't care if Levi found out.

Levi followed his sister outside. He didn't want to pry. Curious as he was about who was writing to her, he'd leave it be. "Lucretia!" he called after her.

She finally stopped walking and let him catch up to her. "I said it's my—"

"I know. It's thy letter," he quickly reassured her. "I just wanted to say . . . I wanted to ask thee to come over sometime. Thee doesn't visit us much and I . . . well. . . ." Embarrassed by what he'd just said, he stared down at the ground rather than at his sister.

"Yes, Levi, of course I'll come over," Lucretia was quick to answer. Too quick, perhaps. She really didn't care for Comfort, even with the news that Comfort was going to have a baby. Comfort seemed cold to her. It wasn't right for her brother to have such a cold wife. But Lucretia didn't realize until just now that she'd been hurting her brother by staying away. The family still grieved over Benjamin's death, Levi especially. She wasn't being a good sister by leaving him alone.

"Well, good, then." Levi brightened, tossing Lucretia a smile. "Maybe Grace will come, too."

"Of course, Levi. Grace will come, too," Lucretia promised, knowing she'd have to talk her little sister into it. Accustomed to Levi visiting them, and coming alone, Lucretia and Grace hadn't seen the need to visit their brother at his house. Really, they were avoiding Comfort. It would hurt Levi if he knew. Lucretia felt guilty for yelling at Levi earlier about her letter and for having neglected to visit him at his house. "We'll be along this evening before candle-lighting. Does that suit, Levi?"

"Come for supper," he offered right away. He had no idea what they were going to eat tonight. The meat was gone; chickens, too. There were some vegetables. Comfort could make a nice soup for them all. She'd been in such a mood of late; he hoped she wouldn't mind company. Her mood must be because of the baby and not feeling well. She complained all the time of being tired. Heck, he'd make the soup. Biscuits, too. There was a little flour left, a very little. It didn't matter. His mood improved at the idea that his sisters would join them for supper.

Lucretia gave Levi a hug, and then hurried off.

He knew why. She wanted to read that letter of hers.

Dearest Lucretia, her letter from Private Ryan began:

> *I can't tell you where I am, but to say I'm still in Virginia with my company. We're not close to Waterford anymore. If I was, I'd be there with you now. The past weeks have been rough but not so much for me. Your letters have found me. I hold them close to my heart.*
>
> *I hope you are well and free from harm. I've written to you before but kept tearing the letters up, losing my courage. I shouldn't have doubted that you'd write me. I've been alone most all my life, and I've never had the companionship of*

anybody I can trust. But now I do. I have you.

I have your letters. They see me through my days and nights. They see me through the fight. They give me reason to stay alive and to see you again.

I'm sorry this has to be short. I've got to hurry and get this to the company post. We've been on the move, not stopping for much of anything but to sleep and re-supply. I'll write you every chance I get from now on.

I won't lie and say that all of us who came to your brother's wedding celebration are still alive. I won't lie and say that this war isn't ugly and mean. But I believe in my heart I'm fighting for my country, for a cause that's true.

You're the prettiest gal I ever saw, Lucretia Clement. I get all tied up inside thinking of you. You're my angel, my guardian angel. I know I'll stay safe with your letters close.

From my heart to yours,
Private Caleb Ryan
US Army of the Potomac

Lucretia read the letter again, her insides all tied, up, too, as she thought of Caleb. Nothing in the whole of her life had made her feel this good. She tingled from head to foot. It was wrong to feel so much for someone she'd barely met, but she did. It was wrong to exchange letters with an outsider, but she did. She'd pray every day and every night for Caleb to stay safe. From her heart to his.

It was early morning. It took all Willa's strength to keep on her feet and keep up with her unit. Exhausted, hungry, and having more pains in her belly of late, she questioned whether or not she should slip away from the army and head back to Bedford County before her baby was born. Surprisingly, she'd kept her swollen belly hidden under her baggy uniform. Other than a few of her comrades poking fun at her for putting on weight when everyone else was losing it, no one had noticed or said much to her about her changing shape. She knew why. In war, nobody was looking for any woman to be in their ranks; they were all too busy looking for the enemy. Another pain hit her. She'd thought she'd have more time, but right now, with her pains coming one after the other, she wasn't so sure.

Everyone who'd found out about her true sex was dead by this time, killed in battle. Everyone but Levi. Much as she didn't want to think of Levi, she did, especially since she'd encountered his brother Jonah on the Manassas battlefield, at the Stone House. Jonah must have died there. His family should know. She'd wondered if they'd been officially informed. Guilt-ridden that she hadn't written to Levi and told him about Jonah, Willa couldn't bring herself to face him, not even in a letter.

She let out a gasp. She was close to him now. Levi was only twenty miles away from Harper's Ferry! Maybe she should slip away to tell him about Jonah.

New pains shot through her. She doubled over, dropping her musket and her gear. The soldiers around her kept going. Their marching pace to Harper's Ferry had been fast. With Jackson's brigade, there was no other way to move but fast.

"You all right, Taylor?" One soldier, a private, did stop.

"Ye-yes," Willa answered and pulled to a stand. "I just had a pain in my gut. I'm good now." She knew what the soldier would think: that she'd gotten dysentery. The dreaded bowel ailment killed more men than enemy bullets.

The private patted her on the shoulder then turned and kept going. They were on orders to take the garrison at Harper's Ferry, with all its valuable stores of cannon, small-arms, wagons, tents, and camp equipage. They'd crossed the Potomac at Williamsport and were now in the rear of Harper's Ferry, having already taken London Heights and Maryland Heights. With Confederate troops commanding the high ground after a day's fighting, Willa suspected the garrison would fall soon.

Shaky on her feet, she didn't think she could make it up the rest of the hill in time to be out of harm's way. Artillery fire rained down on the garrison. She could easily be killed by friendly fire. She squatted back down to protect herself from gunfire and to defend against the pains she experienced. Refusing to let herself think the unthinkable—that her baby wanted to be born now—she prayed for the strength to get up and move. Instead of standing, she started to crawl, dragging her musket and her gear as best she could.

The terrain was rocky and hard to ascend. Willa climbed anyway, looking for shelter. She didn't have time to be scared about having her son right here on this mountainside, in the middle of a war, under fire from friend and foe. She didn't have time to think about the fact that she knew absolutely nothing about having this baby all by herself. All she could focus on was keeping Adam safe. She was going to be a mother. That instinct instantly took hold of her. Willa'd never expected this. In all these months, she'd never prepared for the impact of a mother's love. It was the only thing that drove her now. Fiercely protective of her unborn child, nothing else mattered but him. She'd been a fool to stay in the army all these months when she should have left to better take care of her son.

Now, he might die because of her stubbornness. Dear God, he might.

Just then she felt a warm wetness between her legs, as if someone poured water on her there. What on earth? *The baby's coming!* Spurred on by her birthing pains, Willa crawled until she couldn't crawl anymore. She'd made it to a cropping of boulders. Propelled on by her urgent need to push, she managed to get behind the boulders. *Please God. Please show me how to have Adam. I don't know how. Please help me.*

Fighting for calm, trying to get ahead of her pains, Willa

unfastened her heavy jacket and managed to pull it off. Her hat fell off at the same time. Struggling to reach her pants buttons, she undid them and tried to slide her pants off her. Dang it! Dang it! Dang it! She couldn't bend enough to get them off.

"What in blazes?"

She heard a man's voice. Too worried about getting her pants off to care, she kept up her struggle to get her clothes off.

"Soldier, what are you doin'?"

Irritated with such a stupid question, Willa was desperate to prepare herself to have her baby.

"Here, now, I'll get the medic." The soldier put a hand to her shoulder then started to leave.

"No!" she shouted, clutching his hand to keep him there. Thank God he was dressed in gray. "Don't leave me. Help me, please."

"Listen, I don't know what you're tryin' to do here. I gotta get the medic." He started to pull away again.

"I-I'm trying to ha-have a baby!" she gritted out, seized with another pain. They were coming one after the other now.

"What in tarnation? A ba—"

"Yes, a baby! Do you kn-know about birth-birthing?" she managed to ask.

The soldier said nothing, but stared at her, dumbfounded, as if he couldn't believe what he was seeing and hearing.

Willa didn't recognize him. Nothing unusual about that. There were so many thousands of soldiers gathering here and in Maryland. "Pl-please help me," she begged, grabbing harder on his arm. Covered in perspiration, she felt that any moment she could pass out. She couldn't. She had to stay on top of the pain and deliver Adam! "Please," she feebly managed a second time.

"I'll be doggoned! You're a woman!" he whispered in disbelief while kneeling down to help her. "Don't you worry none, ma'am. I know about birthing. Helped my wife deliver our first young-un, I did."

"Th-thank you," she whispered, then fell back against the rock and tried to calm down. She automatically slid down to lie more flat, preparing to give birth.

"Let's get all this off," the soldier said, taking immediate charge.

Gunfire roared past. Tucked away behind the large boulder, they had some cover, temporarily out of harm's way.

"When I tell you, I want you to push, all right?"

"Ye-yes," she acknowledged, seeing now that he had her bottoms off. She wanted to push. She watched as he pulled a blanket from his pack and put it partially under her, then took off his jacket and draped it over her for some measure of privacy. She bent her knees slightly, as if it were the natural thing to do. Lord, she wanted to push.

"It's a comin'," the solider announced. "Push, now!"

Willa screamed in that moment, her cries soon matching those of her baby, heralding his birth into the world. She quieted the instant she heard him. Her son's strong cries eclipsed the gunfire thundering all around then. He sounded angry. She wanted to laugh, she was so relieved to hear his little lungs fill with air for the first time.

"You got a healthy boy," the soldier told her, his voice heavy with emotion.

Willa lifted herself enough to see her son. At first she couldn't see him through her tears, but then she could. She didn't speak. She couldn't, but she held out her arms to her son instead. Another pain hit her, this one pushing out the afterbirth. Still, she kept her arms outstretched to hold her son.

"Easy, now, ma'am. He's almost ready," the soldier said gently.

Forced to lower her arms, too weak to keep them outstretched, she watched the private minister to her baby, cutting the cord, and then tying it off. He pulled his own shirt off then and wrapped her baby in it. Adam cried the whole time. Willa laughed through her tears, listening with all the love in her.

"Here's your son, ma'am." The soldier brought Adam close and laid him on her chest.

Willa managed to pull herself up to sit against the rock, taking hold of her child for the first time. The moment Adam opened his little eyes and looked into hers, he stopped crying. She did, too. Everything went quiet. The battle scene around her faded from sight. The soldier who'd just helped her went out of her focus. No one existed in the world at all, but her and little Adam. He was beautiful, so beautiful, so handsome with his full head of dark hair, just like his father. Just like Levi. Willa hugged Adam closer to her, thinking of Levi. It wasn't right that Levi wasn't here with them now. Levi should see his son. Just as Jonah had said. *I should tell him.* "I should, little man," she whispered to her son.

"I'll be back with help, ma'am."

Willa looked up at the soldier then. "What's your name?"

He smiled at her. "David. David King."

"Like King David in the Bible," she said, smiling up at him. He laughed.

"I'm naming my son Adam David, after you. Is that all right?"

He didn't laugh now, but seemed to have trouble finding his voice. "Th-that would be real nice."

"Willa. My name is Willa. Willa Mae Tyler." Only then did Willa notice that the fighting around them had ceased. Adam started to cry again. She cradled him closer. "I love you, Adam David. I love you so much," she whispered. "So much."

"Well, Willa Mae Tyler," Private King said. "I'm goin' for the medic or surgeon or whoever I can find. It's gonna be somethin' when everybody finds out about you. You and the little fella. Yes, ma'am, really somethin'," he repeated, and then hurried to spread the word.

Willa dared not close her eyes for fear she'd miss one moment with Adam. Exhausted and in some pain, she tried to ignore it.

Content at last, Adam didn't cry but looked up at her and yawned, and then his lids closed in sleep.

Willa pulled the edge of her blanket up over her son. She hoped to find shelter somewhere inside at Harper's Ferry. She needed a more private place to try and feed him. Having a baby out in the open was one thing, but letting him suckle in front of half the Confederate army was another thing entirely.

Two men approached her, two Confederate soldiers. Then three, then four, then more. Some bloodied, some not. Some with weapons still in hand, some with hats in hand. Some looked surprised, but they all looked shocked. Willa clutched Adam closer to her, suddenly afraid of what the army might do to her. She didn't want to be sent to prison and be separated from her child.

Willa tensed.

Adam woke up and began crying.

Everyone was hushed, as if in church.

Willa's nerves began to ease. These men meant her and Adam no harm. She could tell from the tears welling in their eyes and the looks of wonder on their faces.

One soldier knelt down and quickly removed his hat. Another followed. Then another.

Adam settled.

"Is it a boy?" one of the men asked.

"Yes." Willa smiled.

"And you're a . . . a girl?" another of the men said in surprise.

"Yes." Willa laughed. "Yes, I'm a girl."

"It's a miracle," another soldier muttered, as if in prayer.

"Sure is." More soldiers echoed the sentiment.

Humbled by the moment herself, Willa felt blessed that these brave soldiers didn't shun her and revile her for being a woman in their ranks. They didn't shun her as a woman of immoral character, having a baby on a battlefield with no husband to hold her hand. Quite the contrary, she felt showered with their blessings, as if this were a stable in Bethlehem instead of a hilltop above Harper's Ferry.

This could be Christmas morning in all of their homes. Willa could see it in their faces; all filled with longing, doubtless thinking of the loved ones they'd left behind. Some of them would never again see their sweethearts or their wives or their children. Her heart broke for them all, knowing she and Adam reminded them of home. They'd forgotten about home, they were so caught up in the business of war. They'd forgotten because they had to. It was the only way to get through the next day, the next battle. But for now, in this moment, seeing her and her newborn child, she could tell they remembered. They remembered their families and they cried. She cried, too. She cried for them all.

"General Jackson, *sir!*"

To a man, every soldier around Willa abruptly stood at attention. Her first instinct was to do the same thing. General "Stonewall" Jackson, himself, had approached. Willa's heart went to her throat. This was do or die time. At least she was covered up properly, as any lady should be, in this most improper of situations.

The general, in full gray coat and saber, his bearded face hard, stared down at her, saying nothing.

Willa wondered if she should speak but decided against it. What could she possibly say that would explain the impossible? Adam began to fuss. Glad for this distraction from the imposing general, she cradled Adam closer, gently rocking him. When she looked up again, she noticed Private David King stood behind the general. He'd brought help, all right.

General Jackson kept up his stare.

Willa swallowed hard, waiting for the inevitable.

"Men, in case you don't know, there's a garrison of thirteen thousand enemy soldiers surrendering down the hill that could do with your attention. Best get to it." The general snapped out his order.

The group around him immediately cleared. Private King stayed, along with the surgeon he'd found.

"Ma'am." General Jackson spoke directly to Willa. "You all right? You and your little 'un?"

Willa nodded, afraid to say something that might get her into more trouble than she was in already.

"When and where did you muster in?"

"Last fall, sir, outside Fairfax Courthouse," Willa heard herself answer.

"How long have you been in *my* army?" General Jackson pressed.

"Six months." And that's at least how long she'd likely be in prison for her misdeeds, she thought dismally. The next thought hit worse. What about Adam? Dear God, what would happen to Adam? Willa shut her eyes, refusing to look at the general when he made his fateful decree that would destroy her hopes and dreams for her innocent child. Adam hadn't asked for this. Adam hadn't asked to be born and then banished. It was her fault, all of this. It wasn't even Levi's fault. It was her fault entirely for staying in the army and not leaving sooner to have her baby in a less dangerous place. If she hadn't stubbornly stayed, none of this would be happening, and Adam's life wouldn't be in such danger now.

General Jackson started to laugh.

Willa's eyes flew open. She'd expected just about anything but this.

Little Adam started to fuss again.

Willa tried to soothe her son, overcome with relief at the general's lightheartedness in this anything-but-lighthearted situation.

"Ma'am," General Jackson said. "You've put a real good one over on us all." He kept up his smile. "I don't know if you followed your sweetheart or your husband or joined up for another reason. That's not my business." His smile faded. "But what is my business is to see that you're out of this man's army as of now."

Her heart thudded in her chest, afraid of his pronouncement.

"After things get sorted out down the hill yonder, we'll get you and your little 'un out of this war. I don't care if it's on a wagon or a train or a boat, but you two are heading home," the general said with finality.

"Yes, sir." Willa would have put her arms around the general and hugged him now, rules and convention be damned, if she could. She surely would.

General Jackson started to leave, but then turned back to Willa. "What's your name, soldier?"

"Willa Mae Tyler."

"No, your army name?"

"Private Will Taylor," she answered uneasily.

His smile turned into roaring laughter, echoing along the mountainside as he started down the hill toward the Harper's Ferry garrison.

Willa couldn't believe it. She and Adam could head home now.

Home.

Thoughts of seeing her parents again warmed her through and through. Unbidden thoughts of Levi did the same thing. She'd let go of all her anger and upset at him for marrying someone else the moment Adam was born. Now she warmed to thoughts of Levi, remembering his touch, the sound of his voice, his male essence, his nearness, *him*. Then she thought of Jonah Clement's dying wish that she should tell Levi he had a son, and she didn't know where to call home.

Was home with her parents or with Levi?

CHAPTER TWELVE

It had been an exhausting journey for mother and child. After traveling by wagon out of Harper's Ferry, Willa managed to find train passage to Roanoke through the Shenandoah Valley and western Virginia. The tracks had been spared by the war, at least so far. The route must not be a prime supply path. No soldiers, blue coat or gray, boarded the train during the entire passage, which was a miracle indeed. Willa felt like the Red Sea had parted for her and Adam, allowing them to arrive safely in Bedford County unharmed. The trip had taken long days and even longer nights, but they'd made it home.

Home, she'd decided, was with her parents.

Home could never be with Levi. He was married. Worse, he didn't love her. She couldn't follow her heart and return to Waterford and tell Levi he had a son. Jonah had said she must tell him, but she didn't know how to, not yet. Her heart wrenched, thinking about Jonah dying at the Stone House in Manassas. She should tell Levi about his brother. She'd no way of knowing if the army had done so. Maybe she should try to post a letter to him. But, then, how should she say it? How could she tell him about Jonah? She remembered only too well the day the letter came about Walter and Henry. Her heart wrenched again, this time more painfully. No, she wouldn't post a letter to Levi about Jonah yet. The sad news could wait. She'd post the letter in time. All in good time.

"Ma'am."

"Thank you." Willa smiled at the conductor as she stepped off the train and onto the platform. Adam slept in her arms, despite the cold breezes.

The silver-haired conductor turned to leave.

"Excuse me," she called after him.

"Yes, ma'am?" He stopped and faced her.

"Do you know how I might best get to Liberty?" Adam started to fuss a little. She cradled him closer.

"Yonder to Liberty? Yeah, I know the town. There's a wagon going that way taking mail from this here train. Wagon's going all the way to Lynchburg. I'm sure you and the little 'un can hitch a ride," the conductor offered. "I'll go arrange it." His wrinkled smile faded. "Ma'am, you know it ain't any too safe anywheres now. Might be soldiers, blue coat or gray, could stop you along the way. Sure don't want you and the little 'un to be harmed. I sure don't."

"You're very kind," Willa said, and meant it. She was grateful he hadn't asked her questions about why she traveled, a woman alone, with a baby. She'd run into more kindness than she'd expected in the civilian world. Fighting as a soldier for more than a year, seeing all the death and dying, witnessing one bloody melee after another, kindness and caring had been luxuries she couldn't afford on a battlefield. Hardened and tougher than she'd been before the war, it would take Willa time to adjust to non-military life. It would take time for her not to instinctively reach for her musket the moment she awakened every day. Accustomed to doing her duty as a soldier, it would take time for her to adjust to doing her duty as a woman and as a mother.

Willa had on the same dress she'd borrowed from the store in Centreville, the green plaid. The wool wrap, too. She used it to cover Adam. The soldiers in Harper's Ferry had found him some baby clothes and cloths for diapers, donated by some of the women in the garrison. The women had also donated undergarments for her. Ever appreciative, Willa hoped to return their kindness one day, and to return the dress to the mercantile in Centreville. Her insides caught. She thought of the reason she'd borrowed the dress in the first place: to find Levi and tell him about their unborn child. Well, her life and Adam's had taken a very different turn, a turn away from Levi.

It was just the way of it, Willa thought.

"Ma'am?"

The conductor interrupted her melancholy thoughts.

"Come on with me inside the stationhouse. It's too cold out here for you both," he instructed, motioning for her to follow him. "I'll see to your ride. You shouldn't have to wait long."

"Thank you." Willa held Adam close. He fretted in earnest now. She knew he was hungry. Hurrying behind the conductor, she hoped to find a private place to feed Adam before the wagon was set to leave. She hoped for something else: that she could calm down enough to feed her son. She had no idea what her parents would say or do when they saw Adam. God in heaven! Another more dire thought struck. What if her parents weren't there? The war had harmed civilians, too. What if . . . if the unspeakable had happened? Filled with dread, Willa forced her troubled thoughts to quiet. She had to, for Adam's sake.

"I have a stopping in the mind, Comfort." Levi sat down across from her at their breakfast table. He didn't like the dark turn his thoughts had taken of late about Comfort and their unborn child. He felt uneasy about things and determined to find out why this very morning, this very moment.

"What is it, Levi?" Comfort struggled to keep the worry out of her voice. She sensed something about her husband this morning, and she didn't like it. He studied her too closely in the lamplight. Used to his more careful attention after she'd told him they were going to have a child, she wasn't accustomed to this kind of scrutiny. This kind made her uncomfortable. This kind made her think of her lie and the sin she committed by doing so.

Levi took another sip of his coffee, peering over his mug at his wife. Despite the early hour and the fact she'd tossed and turned all night, she was the picture of beauty. Her pristine face shone in the flickering lamplight. Her bonnet was tied just so, not one blond hair peeking out from under it. Her collar was fastidiously buttoned, her apron neat and clean. She always looked perfect. She always behaved perfectly, as if there wasn't a woman with any feelings left inside.

Where was the Comfort he'd once known? Despite her role as leader at meeting, she used to laugh, to cry, to tease, to show signs of life. Not anymore. This shell of a woman seemed distant and cold now. Levi set down his mug. They were his fault, the changes in Comfort. He'd killed her zest for life because he didn't love her. But he knew she didn't love him, either. More and more, even with the baby coming, he was sure of it.

That was the question nagging at him now.

The baby.

He didn't see any signs that Comfort was expecting. Her stomach hadn't swelled, even a little. He knew enough about babies to know that she should be showing by now. She wasn't, and this gave him a stopping in the mind. He'd hesitated to raise the subject before, because he hadn't wanted to upset his wife, but he felt he had to now.

Comfort squirmed in her seat. A sick feeling crept over her, telling her Levi might know she wasn't pregnant. Upset with herself, she realized, too late, she should have insisted Levi keep bedding her once a week. He'd been reluctant to touch her after news of the baby. She'd coaxed him to bed on occasion, but obviously not often enough. Maybe she was barren! Oh, dear. Oh, dear. Her heart began to pound in her chest. Lies coiled inside her, tying her stomach in knots. Nothing had gone as she'd planned.

Levi was supposed to fall in love with her again.

Levi was supposed to have forgotten his Willa, love.

Levi was supposed to be a father, in truth, by now.

Truth. The word settled hard in Comfort's stomach, as if she'd swallowed hemlock. She'd strayed from the truth and from her faith, all for Levi. She'd done it to keep him as her husband, to keep him from leaving her for another, all to save face before the Friends. Comfort's insides churned. It took everything in her to sit still and not run outside and empty the bitter contents of her stomach. She was a leader at meeting. She was supposed to speak the Truth. Not this.

"Comfort," Levi said, breaking the uncomfortable silence.

She couldn't look at him. She wasn't ready to hear what he might say. She wasn't ready to answer for her lies. A part of her did love Levi. That's what had made her do this. That's what had made her so jealous that she had to lie to keep him. He was her husband, not Willa's!

"Comfort, thee must look at me. Thee must tell me what is wrong," Levi quietly demanded.

Comfort brightened. Maybe he was just worried about her and their baby. Yes, maybe just that. She raised her chin, her eyes even with his. Unable to read his handsome features, still, she breathed a little easier.

"Comfort," Levi demanded a second time.

"What makes thee think something is wrong, husband?" she asked innocently.

Levi scraped his chair back and stood. His jaw tensed. He ran his fingers through his thick, cropped hair, mindless that he'd forgotten to put on his hat after dressing. He'd never felt more uneasy.

"Husband?" She pushed her chair back now and got up. "I must ask thee what is wrong. Thee seems troubled. Thee must tell me what is wrong." She feigned concern, all the while pleased she'd been able to turn his question back on him.

"Enough!" Levi suddenly raised his voice.

Shocked and alarmed, Comfort eased back down in her chair. He'd never shouted at her before.

Levi didn't sit. "Comfort, things have been wrong between us for a long time. Thee and I both know we should not have spoken wedding vows. Thee and I will have to live with this lie of a marriage for the rest of our days," he said solemnly, evenly, as if at a funeral.

Comfort stared down at the plate in front of her, squirming in her seat.

"But by all that's holy, Comfort Clarke, thee must tell me about the baby. Something is wrong. Thee is not swelling as a mother should," Levi said.

Comfort bristled, unnerved and angry. How dared he say Comfort Clarke and not Comfort Clement. How dared he!

"I said—"

"How dare thee!" She abruptly stood, interrupting Levi, furious at him. "How dare thee speak to me so? I am thy wife. I am a leader at meeting. I am . . . I am carrying thy child—"

"No." Levi coolly stopped her in mid-sentence. "No, thee is not. Thee would have a swollen belly by now and thee does not. Thee is not speaking the truth."

Silenced by that one word—truth—Comfort dropped back down in her chair. Momentarily hesitant to say anything further less she damn herself even more, her thoughts took a slow, jagged turn. To her, this wasn't about the truth anymore. This was about Levi loving another woman. She wanted to punish him for it!

"Speak the truth," Levi insisted, his tone still sharp and accusing.

Comfort abruptly stood. The plates and tin cups rattled on the table. She swallowed hard, struggling to contain her fury. "I'll speak the truth, Levi Clement," she announced, locking stares with him. "I'll speak the truth when *thee* speaks the truth."

Levi said nothing.

His silence made Comfort even angrier. She fumed inside that he wasn't even curious about her demand that he speak the truth. That he cared so little for her.

Levi gave her his back, not wanting to look at her. Her once-beautiful face didn't look so beautiful now. She'd turned cold on him, cold as the grave. His uneasiness with the situation and the conversation increased tenfold.

"Who is Willa, love?" Comfort asked, as cruelly as she could. She'd hurt him to the quick for giving her his back.

Levi wheeled around so fast he bumped his chair and the table, setting the plates and cups to rattling yet again. He'd expected almost anything to come out of Comfort's mouth, but not. . . . "What art thou saying, woman?" he whispered hoarsely, almost as cruelly as she'd just spoken to him.

"Thee heard me. Willa, love. I said, Willa, love," Comfort spat out.

"Where did thee hear her name?" he demanded, sure that Comfort and Willa had never met.

"From thy lips, Levi Clement, when thee first bedded me. That's why I lied about a baby. That's why!" Comfort refused to cry.

Gut-punched, Levi pulled out his chair and slumped into it. This—all of it—was his fault. There was no taking it back. No denying the truth of it. No denying that now Comfort knew he loved another. He'd said *Willa, love*. Drained of any upset at Comfort, he understood her lie about the baby.

"So." Comfort sat back down, a strange calm coming over her. She felt good that she'd spoken the truth, didn't she? It was right to see Levi so forlorn now, wasn't it?

"So." Levi picked up where she'd left off. "So, where does this leave us?" he quietly asked, looking her straight in the eye.

Unprepared for his directness, caught off guard, she didn't know how to answer.

"What does thee want me to do?" Levi whispered. "Does thee want me to leave?"

"Leave? No." She reached her hand out to him. "No, husband, I don't want that," she whispered back, surprised at her own words, frightened she might actually lose him.

Levi took her hand in his, staring long moments at their handfasting.

"I want thee to stay," Comfort softly pleaded.

Levi nodded his agreement.

"I must speak the whole tr-truth to thee," she said haltingly.

Levi let go of her hand and sat back against his chair.

"I lied to thee about the baby, but I told another lie," Comfort confessed. "I told thee that no one came to our door all those months ago when thee asked me, but someone did, looking for thee. It was Willa Mae Tyler. She told me her name."

Levi's gut turned. Dear God!

"I-I told her my name, too. I told her I was Comfort Clement, thy wife, and then I shut the door in her face. I did, Levi. I surely did." Comfort couldn't look at him anymore. She'd hurt him to the quick, all right. She'd had to speak the truth and turn her face back to God and what was right.

Willa knew! Dread settled deep over Levi's broken heart. Willa knew what he'd gone and done. Levi had never hated himself more than he did at this moment of truth. There was no taking it back. In this awful moment, he knew he'd take to the grave this oppressive agony over hurting Willa and Comfort.

Until then, he'd pray every sunrise that God in His mercy might spare these two women any more pain. Levi felt dead already in this moment, killed by the knowledge that Willa knew what he'd gone and done.

The November afternoon was cold. Willa shuddered in her wool cape, pulling most of it around Adam to keep him warm. They rode in the mail wagon, in the bed just behind the driver's seat. It had no covering. Willa wished the transport had some kind of canvas or tarp. She feared it would rain, even sleet, the temperature was so cold. She feared far more than the weather, though. The wagon had already made its delivery in Liberty and was on its way to Lynchburg. Her home was in between. Her home as she remembered it.

Would her parents be there? Were they all right?

Adam started to cry. He was hungry. With her back to the driver, seeing that his concentration was on the road ahead and not her, Willa opened her dress front enough to feed the baby. She pulled her cape over him for cover. At least she wasn't so tense about coming home that she couldn't feed her son. Funny, but just now she couldn't remember when she'd last eaten. She'd taken a bit of water here and there, and maybe a piece of biscuit. Right now, so focused was she on her parents' welfare, she couldn't remember. Her haversack. Where was it? Oh, yes, there; now she saw it. It held her uniform; really, just her coat. For some reason she wanted to keep it. Maybe as a reminder of everything she'd experienced in the past year. Maybe for warmth should she and Adam need it, or maybe for a tie to Walter and Henry—and Jonah Clement. She just wanted to keep it close. The gray coat had been a part of her for so long, she didn't want to let go. Not yet. Besides, Levi knew her in that coat. He'd wanted her, uniform and all, in that coat.

The wagon pulled up short.

"Is this good enough?" the driver asked, inclining his head toward Willa.

Adam had finished feeding. Willa quickly closed her dress front; then looked around. Home. She was home. She recognized every tree, every field, every distant view. The wagon had stopped at the end of the very road leading to her family farm. Just over the hill was home.

"Yes, this is good," she finally answered the driver while inching toward the open end of the mail transport. Holding Adam securely, she caught up her haversack and slid off the back of the wagon. The driver had come around to help catch her by the time her feet hit the ground.

"You all right, ma'am? You and the little 'un?"

"We're fine, thank you," she said, smiling at the older man's concern, though she didn't feel like smiling. She didn't know what awaited her over the hill. Would her parents be all right? Would they welcome her or would they revile her? Would they accept her son? *Oh, please, dear God,* Willa prayed in earnest. *Please let my parents be all right and please let them love my son.*

"Good luck to you, ma'am," the burly driver called out, already starting up his team and heading down the Lynchburg road.

Willa watched the driver and team for long moments, wondering if she should yell out for him to come back and fetch her and her son. Maybe tomorrow would be a better day for a homecoming. Maybe tomorrow she'd have the courage she needed for the way ahead—the way home. Drops of rain started to fall. She pulled her cape over Adam, making sure to keep him dry.

Hurried by the coming weather, despite her nerves about returning home after so long, she made her way along the familiar rutted, wagon road. She dreaded this homecoming, afraid her parents would be gone, just like Walter and Henry:

killed by an enemy bullet. As if she were a soldier again, and as she'd done in many a firefight, she pushed forward. Used to turning off her feelings when going into battle, she could hardly do that now. Suddenly she thought of Surry, remembering when Surry talked of bein' scared . . . really scared.

I am scared, Surry. I surely am.

It began to rain in earnest. Willa picked up her step. She hardly noticed the landscape around her, except to realize there were no animals anywhere. No neighbor cattle grazing. No horses roaming the open fields. And the fields . . . they looked dead, too. Everything looked dead.

Her nerves even more on edge, she didn't need the rain to urge her on. At the top of the rise, she spotted their farmhouse. No one was outside. "Of course. The weather," she lectured herself to allay her increasing fear. The barn and other outbuildings were still there. Nothing had been burned to the ground. Relieved to see everything still standing, hopeful all would be well and her prayers answered, she hugged Adam closer and made sure of her step down the now-slippery, muddy, wagon way.

The front door opened. Two dogs ran outside.

Skipper and Roscoe! Willa held her breath.

James Tyler stepped onto the covered porch, rifle in hand.

"Daddy! Daddy!"

The rifle slid from James's hand.

"Daddy!" Willa yelled through the pouring rain. Skipper and Roscoe circled and jumped, tails wagging and barking wildly. Adam started to cry. Willa hugged him closer. "It's your grampa. Your grampa," she whispered reverently, her heart full to bursting, hurrying to meet her father.

James had no sooner stepped off the porch, than Willa was there. His arms went around her. "My precious girl," he managed to whisper, his throat tight with emotion. "My precious girl." He hugged her closer, his tears blending with the rain.

Adam protested and screamed at the top of his lungs.

James broke his hold on his daughter, only now realizing she hadn't come home alone.

Willa smiled at her bewildered father and then hurried under cover of the porch, the dogs with her.

Other than pivoting to follow his daughter's movements, James didn't budge, seemingly mindless of the driving rain.

Just then the door opened behind Willa.

"Whatever is this fuss? Skipper! Ros—"

Willa turned toward her mother.

Litha Mae stood frozen, much as her husband had done.

"Mama, it's me," Willa said as gently as she could, over the loud squalls of her son and Skipper and Roscoe yapping.

Litha's hands went to her mouth, her eyes wide with emotion. "Truly, Willa? Is it truly you," she murmured in disbelief.

"It truly is, Mama. It's me and your grandson. His name is Adam." Willa uncovered her son for the first time, now that she was safe under the protection of the porch.

"Adam?" Her mother's voice held no censure, only love. "Welcome home, children," she choked out, pulling Willa and her grandson inside the house.

The dogs followed them in, mud and all. James followed, too, closing the door behind him, also to close the door on his ever-present, oppressive fear for his daughter's welfare. She was alive and didn't lie dead on some battlefield like Walter and Henry. She'd come home to them . . . with their grandson. The house would be full of life again. He might even take out his fiddle for such an occasion. When James stepped inside and closed the door, he left the war outside. For this day, for this homecoming, he could do that.

Thank the Good Lord, he *would* do that!

CHAPTER THIRTEEN

"Shush me up!" Surry couldn't believe what Saxonia Shadd had just told her, no matter that one of the Elgin Settlement's most trusted citizens read to her straight from the *Ontario News*.

"It's true, child," Saxonia reassured. "Sure as I am that today is the first day of the new year, eighteen sixty-three, it says right here that 'slavery is ended in any area still in rebellion against the United States.' "

Virginia. Surry's heart thudded in her chest. Virginia's in rebellion against the United States. "What else does the paper say, Saxonia?" Surry asked, suddenly frantic for every detail. In Virginia slaves were free now. Her mama was free! Halleluiah! Halleluiah! Praise Be to God!

" 'The Emancipation Proclamation does not end slavery in the border states of Maryland, Kentucky and Missouri. It also doesn't end slavery in areas in the South that Union forces have conquered or in Tennessee, Louisiana, and parts of northern Virginia.' " Saxonia put the paper down a moment and peered over her spectacles at Surry. "You listening to all of this, child?" she asked, her ever-kind expression a picture of joy and light.

Surry's smile matched Saxonia's. The Shelby Plantation wasn't in northern Virginia. Her mama was free; indeed she was. Her mama and her two youngest sisters who'd stayed at the plantation. As for the rest of her family, Surry didn't know where they were. It broke her heart that she didn't know. Sam and Pitty Pat could be in prison or worse, and her runaway brothers . . . she'd no idea if they were imprisoned or returned to slavery or. . . .

" 'Emancipation celebrations are going on all over the South where slaves are now free,' " Saxonia continued to read, rescuing Surry from the unhappy turn of her thoughts. " 'It appears that the war to preserve the Union of the United States is now a war to end slavery,' this reporter writes." Saxonia bristled at what she'd just read. "I know how it all appears to me, Surry. It *appears* that slavery is ended in some places just to make it harder for enemy states in rebellion of the United States, and not because it's the right and just thing to do. It's political, if you ask me 'cause all the slaves in all the states should be set free now. Humph."

Surry pulled the paper out of Saxonia's hands and hugged her as tightly as she could.

"Land sakes, child." Saxonia tried to feign upset, when in truth the news in the paper was manna from heaven. The road to freedom for her people had at last begun to open up in America. Thank God Almighty.

"I must find Penny!" Bursting with excitement, Surry suddenly let go of Saxonia. "I must tell her this news!" Tears welled in Surry's eyes and streaked down her cheeks. She didn't wipe them away. She wanted to remember each tear, each surge of pride she felt, at long last bein' free in her native state of Virginia. How she wished Willa was with her now, sharing in this moment. Her heart ached to see Willa as much as to see her family and Lucas. He was already free, but was he all right still? He could have been captured and sold somewhere into slavery. Surry had seen and heard so many horror stories by now that she worried for Lucas.

If she only knew for sure about those she loved.

If only she knew who lived and who did not.

If only . . . if only. . . .

"Child, do you have lead in your feet? I thought you wanted to find Penny," Saxonia chastised good-naturedly.

Surry took up Saxonia's hands. "Yes, but I want something else now, too. I want . . . I want to go home."

"Dear, sweet child, I understand. I truly do." Saxonia patted the top of Surry's hands. "You go find your sister and then come back. We'll talk of how to get you home, all right?"

"Yes, ma'am, thank you." Surry brightened inside and out. Her heart had never been so full. She stood taller, bein' free in her own country.

The wind whistled outside, the January day bitter cold. Levi put another piece of wood on the fire. Their store of wood was low, but not Levi's spirits . . . not entirely anyway. The slaves in the South had been freed by President Lincoln. Levi's flagging spirits over his empty marriage had been buoyed by this welcome news.

The slaves in the northern slave-holding states were not free yet. After the war, if the Union won, they would be, Levi believed. He was unsure about his own county in Virginia, since slaves were not freed in areas the Union had invaded and conquered. Did that mean parts of Loudoun? He reached for his heavy coat from its peg by the front door. It now made sense to him why he hadn't been needed to help along the Underground Railroad or to carry any secret messages across the border into Maryland of late. Union troops held the area now, making it a little easier for residents in Waterford to try to secure supplies. Partisans roamed the countryside, with skirmishes not uncommon. Loudoun County still had cattle and horses and grain left to be taken.

Levi's thoughts took a more downward turn. Conscription was law in the South now, and soldiers were needed. He refused to be one of them, knowing the day might come when some might try to force him to fight. Things had been said behind his back. He wasn't immune to comments from some folks when he ventured into town or heard passersby on the Old Waterford Road. Every day was still a dangerous day. Every day was still a day when folks went hungry. Frustrated and a little angry at himself for his inaction of late, he pulled the front door open.

He needed to down more trees and split wood. He needed to keep busy, especially since he and Comfort had settled on an agreement to stay together, yet live separately and not as man and wife. She'd taken the bedroom and he slept on a palate in the loft. Though he didn't feel easy about their arrangement because it was a daily reminder of their failings, he agreed to stick to it. It was best for Comfort and for him.

To everyone at meeting, nothing in their marriage was amiss. No elders needed to come and counsel them to mend their problems. He'd said nothing to his parents or his sisters, either. He was certain that Comfort had said nothing to her family other than she'd miscarried. It was a lie, but Levi had agreed to it, thinking it best for all involved.

He was about to step outside when Comfort stopped him.

"Levi, wait. We need to talk." She was behind him, her hand touching his arm.

There was a time when she'd touched him that he'd felt it through his clothes, right down to his toes. No more. That was long ago, in his youth. He was a man of twenty-two now, and her touch didn't faze him. His heart heavy, he pulled the door shut and turned around.

"Please, Levi. Come and sit." Comfort took one of their two parlor chairs and gestured for him to take the other.

He shrugged off his coat and rehung it on its familiar peg. His hat, too. Uneasy about what she wanted, he folded his tall frame into the chair. Worn out from living with a woman he didn't love, his thoughts weighed on him like an albatross. He'd definitely rather be outside chopping wood. That had purpose. That was God's work. Not this.

"Levi," Comfort spoke up. "Please look at me."

He did.

"Thee looks unhappy," she observed.

He straightened his spine, his jaw tight. What was there to say? She was right. Should he compound all his other lies that bound them together now, by telling another?

"I am unhappy, too, Levi," Comfort confessed, her beautiful face serene, almost peaceful.

Levi noticed the change in her expression, alerting to it more than her words. She hadn't looked this pretty in a very long time. He sensed the Comfort of old, the Comfort of his youth, the Comfort who was leader at meeting, talking now.

"Levi, we must part. We must divorce."

Levi scraped out his chair and stood.

"Please, Levi, sit back down. Please." She held herself composed.

Shocked at her pronouncement, he obediently fell back into his seat. Quakers didn't divorce. Quakers didn't go against God and break faith in their marriage.

"I have thought about this and prayed about this for weeks. I have thought about it ever since we agreed to this arrangement in our marriage to live together but apart, not as man and wife. At first I believed the arrangement would work and that we could go on and keep up this ruse, this pretense of being happy when neither of us are."

Levi had never listened to anyone so intently in the whole of his life as he listened to Comfort now. Maybe this was the Word he'd been waiting for. Maybe this was the Word to ease his stopping in the mind over their loveless marriage. Maybe this was the Word they'd both waited for.

"When we live together, we do not Mind the Light, dear

181

Levi," Comfort said quietly, calmly, and with conviction. "In my heart, after much prayer for guidance, I believe we must divorce. The Way has opened for me to proceed with this decision. I realize divorce is unknown to us and must sound wrong, but it is the right thing for us to do, Levi. I cannot stay in this empty marriage. It would be wrong, Levi. I hope thee understands. Please tell me thee understands," she pled, her voice trembling now.

In that instant Levi felt his heart lift up to the heavens. It was the first time since they'd spoken their vows that he'd felt so unburdened. Yes, Comfort had brought the Word, unburdening them both. "Comfort," he said at last, getting up and guiding her to stand with him. He took her hands in his. "I understand. I agree. I believe this is the right thing to do. I believe this helps us both right the wrong we've done unto God and unto one another," he said, his voice tender.

"Thank thee, Levi," she whispered, falling into his arms.

He held her for long moments, each one of them receiving succor from the other in this life-changing moment.

Comfort was the first to break free. "I must tell thee something else."

Levi waited, noting the tears in her eyes. His heart wrenched for them both.

"I cannot stay in Waterford. I feel I must leave Fairfax Meeting and begin anew. I'm going to talk to my father and see if he thinks it's not too late for us to go west to Ohio. The land there is good. There are many Quakers who've already settled there, leaving this awful war behind," Comfort explained, her tone eager.

Levi took heart, seeing the sparkle return to Comfort's beautiful, robin's-egg-blue eyes. It had been a long time since she'd looked happy like this. She had her spirit, her Inner Light, back. He smiled down at her.

"Thee is a good woman, a good person, a good Quakeress. I want thee to be ever happy in life from this day forward. If that means leaving for Ohio, then leave for Ohio with my blessing," he reassured her.

"Thank thee, Levi. Dear, dear Levi," she whispered, choking back new tears.

Levi held out his arms for her to console her.

"No," she gently protested, regaining her composure. "I will go tomorrow and talk with the elders. I will present our wish to them, to divorce. They will be shocked. No one at Fairfax Meeting has ever queried for divorce. They will not want to hear our query, but they will listen. They *must* listen. I will explain why the dissolution of our marriage is the right thing to do, the right decision for us. The elders will take this hard, but I believe they will agree to seek counsel and approval from Yearly Meeting in Baltimore," Comfort said, carefully laying out her plan.

"I will go with thee."

"Yes, of course." She smiled now.

"Thee best hide that smile tomorrow with the elders," he joked. "They will not be in the mood for thy smile, no matter how lovely it is."

Comfort kept up her smile.

Levi's brow furrowed. She was up to something.

"Levi, there's a certain young lady out there who will no doubt be happy at the news of our divorce," she teased.

"Wh—?"

"Thee need not play the innocent with me anymore, Levi Clement. Thee can find thy Willa, love with my blessing," she said, her tone earnest and heartfelt.

Stirred by the mention of Willa's name, he hadn't thought about being free to marry Willa until now, until Comfort said as much. Levi's heart sank at the realization he had no idea where to find Willa. She might already be dead. The thought struck him hard.

"Good work, son. You're a credit to the 19th Maryland."

"Thank you, sir." Lucas saluted his captain. Lucas was exhausted from his exploits over the past month, but his heart was brim-full, knowing it was official now: slaves in the South were free. He'd known about the preliminary Emancipation Proclamation—his captain had told him as much—but now, to have it official . . . thank God Almighty. In the next second he thought of Surry.

"At ease, son," the captain ordered.

At liberty to do so, Lucas returned his hand to his side and relaxed his stance. If Surry were home now, she'd be free. The realization tugged at his chest . . . that, and worry over her safety. He'd give anything to see her, just for a day, just for a moment.

"Private Minor."

Lucas forced his attention to his captain.

"I'm not changing your orders, son. I know you want to see action on the battlefield, but I need you for intelligence work," he explained. "With the Emancipation Proclamation law, it doesn't affect our state in the least. Free Negroes can join up, but not slaves. You, son, have managed to recruit a goodly number of runaways for our regiment. You've also managed not to be killed or captured. Like I said before, good work," the captain repeated, the corners of his thick moustache hinting of a smile.

Lucas listened. He wanted to be sent into action. He knew the United States Colored Troops were forming regiments now under white commanders. He'd heard about the 54th Massachusetts, especially, that had formed up under a white commander, heading south to fight. There had already been units fighting like the 1st Kansas and units in Louisiana. Lucas made it his business to find out where colored troops, volunteer or regular, were forming up and fighting.

"It's a sticky wicket, this Emancipation Proclamation. It's a sticky wicket here in the border-slave-state of Maryland and in the northern states where slavery is still law. Even though it's approved to recruit colored troops in the Union army, it's a problem that slavery is still in place and that, if caught, slaves have to be returned to their masters. I need you to keep doing what you're doing for the time being."

Lucas didn't like this one little bit.

"Our ranks are increasing. Washington has noticed," the captain revealed. "They want us to keep doing what we're doing, however we're doing it, Private Minor."

"Yes, sir," Lucas said, getting the point.

"Some of our generals are going their own way on how they treat colored recruits. Some escaped slaves are considered contrabands of war and not to be returned to their masters. Some are considered free, since they ran away from their masters in rebellion against the Union. I don't have an opinion one way or the other. I call all of my recruits United States soldiers, I do," he firmly attested.

Heartened to hear what he already knew about the captain, Lucas stood tall.

The captain stared hard at Lucas, scrutinizing him carefully. "Son, I promise you that we're going to form up the best and the brightest United States Colored Troop regiments in the whole goddamn army, thanks to the help of good soldiers like you."

"Yes, sir."

The captain seemed to be pondering his next words.

Lucas kept himself at attention.

"Bad things could happen to you if you're captured, son. I'm sure you know that. It's not easy, what I'm asking you to do. Things are stirred up enough between whites and coloreds. Now, with your people let in the fight . . . well, I think you know what I'm saying."

"Yes, sir," Lucas said.

"I don't think things are going to be equal at first for colored troops, Private," the captain gritted out. "I think it might go rough for a spell. Pay won't be the same, either. Its thirteen dollars a month now for white troops and won't be more than seven for coloreds by the time money is taken out for uniforms."

Lucas's gut turned. It wasn't fair, but it was the way of it.

"Duty won't be the same for a while yet. Sure, there are some colored ranks under white commanders that will see fighting." Here the captain stopped. "They sure as hell won't be paid the same for dying, shedding their life's blood for this country, will they, Private?"

"No, sir," Lucas agreed, his jaw set hard.

The captain's shoulders sank.

Lucas noticed. He understood. It was one of the reasons he liked his captain so much: his captain liked colored folks. His captain believed colored folks could fight just as hard and just as long as white folks. His captain believed colored folks were just as smart as white folks. His captain would never have owned slaves, Lucas decided.

"What with Union conscription in effect soon, for whites and coloreds, it's not going to go easy for any conscripts, no matter their skin color. Soldiers who mustered into the army aren't going to take to soldiers conscripted in. I just want to warn you that this is a fact, son. I'm sorry to say it, but it's a fact."

"Yes, sir," Lucas said. Lucas got it. He knew that most Negroes in the country, free or slave, got it, too. Negroes were used to the unfairness of life in the country. It was just the way of it.

Not anymore.

By God and by all that's holy, not anymore!

Change was coming to America. Lucas was proud to be a part of this long-awaited moment for his race. He'd proudly die for his race, for his country. But if God spared him in this fight, if God allowed him to live to see the end of slavery in America, the first thing he'd do would be to find Surry Lion, no matter if she was in Canada or the Caribbean, and wed her and bed her!

"Yes, sir, and amen to that!" Lucas unwittingly spoke aloud.

"Good then," the captain said, seemingly puzzled at Lucas's sudden exuberance over his sobering words about conscription.

Embarrassed, Lucas didn't look the captain in the eye.

"Private, after you've cleaned up and had a rest, I want you on the job at first light tomorrow."

"Yes, sir." Lucas saluted, then quickly pivoted and left the captain's tent. No matter that he was exhausted; it would be hard to sleep tonight, thinking about Surry Lion.

"I'd surely love to meet the young man who finally got you to wear a dress," Litha Mae quipped innocently while helping her daughter bathe little Adam.

Willa suddenly dropped her bar of soap in the washtub.

Five-month-old Adam grinned at the splat.

Willa did not grin. This was the first her mother had spoken of any young man. The fact was that neither of her parents had pressed her for an explanation about Adam's father since that first day she'd returned home from the war. Willa had expected them to pepper her with questions about exactly how and when she'd managed to bear a child. She'd expected some word of censure from her parents, but none came. Only once had her mother said she knew that Willa would tell them when the time was right. Evidently right now, her mother thought the time was right.

Adam splashed his hands in play, gurgling and gleeful.

Willa smiled. She couldn't help it. Her son was the light of her life. He was also the spitting image of his father. With his dark hair and big black eyes and a smile that melted her heart, she thought of Levi every time she beheld Adam. Of late, she thought of Levi far too much. She shouldn't, and she knew it. Her smile faded. Levi belonged to another. He'd married another. The notion didn't make her mad, and hadn't since the day she gave birth to Adam, but thoughts of Levi married to someone else—to beautiful, blond Comfort—made her sad. Deeply and irreconcilably sad. For months now, Willa had tried to reconcile in her head and her heart, that Levi was not free.

Free.

Such a powerful word, Willa thought. It held the power of life and death. It held the power of happiness and unhappiness. Bein' free.

Litha Mae scooped her grandson out of the washtub and began toweling him dry.

Willa let her mother take care of Adam, feeling her own energy ebb. It wasn't good to let herself get so melancholy, thinking about Levi and the war, and worrying over Surry.

"Enough, Willa Mae Tyler," Litha Mae declared, handing a diapered and dressed Adam back over to Willa.

Ignoring her mother's pointed comment, Willa walked over to the rocker by the Franklin stove and sank into it, holding Adam. It was time to feed him and put him in his cradle.

"When you're all done with your son, we'll have that talk, Willa. It's time," Litha Mae pronounced, and then reached for her coat. "I'm going out to fetch James in for supper. I think your father should be here when we talk."

"Yes, ma'am," Willa replied, turning her eyes from her mother and onto her son. It was time to talk to her parents about Levi.

It surely was.

CHAPTER FOURTEEN

Although she was ready to unburden her heart and soul to her parents about Levi, Willa knew she'd carry the trauma of the war and her part in it for the rest of her days. Her night terrors told her as much. Waking up in a cold sweat, more and more of late, she saw the faces of so many soldiers that she'd buried, that she'd killed, that she'd tried to save.

No matter that she'd mustered into the army to avenge the deaths of her brothers. No matter that she'd fought for Virginia and the South. No matter that she'd successfully masqueraded as a Confederate soldier for well over a year. None of that mattered. She'd killed. She doubted if she ever could kill again. The thought of pointing a gun and firing at another human being turned her stomach.

That first time so long ago, when she'd followed orders and shot and killed the artillerymen at Ball's Bluff and returned to Waterford in shock with blood on her hands, Levi had been there for her. Willa shut her eyes now as she remembered. Her heart softened, then melted. She could feel Levi's arms close around her, blanketing her with his warmth, his understanding, his forgiveness—and his love. He loved her despite what she'd done. He'd said, "Thee, I love." He, a Quaker, and yet he understood and forgave her. How she wished she could forgive herself.

Willa thought of Surry and their conversation long ago about bein' scared. Surry had been forced into a life of fear because she was a slave. Every soldier who fought in the war, no matter his side, had been forced into a life of fear. Civilians, too, were affected by the war. Every day tired, hungry, and worried for their family and their home, they had been forced into a life of fear. It was just the way of it now, bein' scared.

"Child." Litha Mae put her hand on Willa's. "Come to the table and we'll talk now."

Rescued from painful memories, from a past that haunted her, Willa stared blankly at her mother, needing a moment to come back to the present. She looked over at the table where her father sat. The familiar action of seeing him light up his pipe comforted her and made her feel safe. Pulling herself out of the rocker, she peered over Adam's cradle, checking to make sure he slept easily. Maybe she'd sleep just as easily tonight, after telling her parents about Levi. Taking heart at the thought, Willa took sure steps to join her parents.

Willa had finished. She set Levi's Bible on the table, after months of keeping it safely hidden in her skirt pocket. She hadn't left anything out of her story. It felt good to talk about the past year, about being at the Stone House in Manassas, about Walter and Henry dying there. And about Levi. She folded her hands in front of her, staring at the kerosene lantern flickering on the tabletop, nervous about what her parents would say, unable to look either of them in the eye.

Litha Mae fought tears.

James puffed on his pipe, hiding his emotions.

Skipper and Roscoe scratched to get outside.

James got up and let the dogs out, returning to his seat without a word.

Willa waited. There was nothing else to be said. She kept her focus on the lantern, worrying she might have said too much to her parents. The last thing she wanted was to put her burdens on them. She worried that maybe she had. Unable to stand the silence for another moment, she looked up at her parents. When she saw her mother's tears, and her father's, she finally felt free to shed her own.

In that moment the three grieved together for Walter and Henry, each experiencing their loss anew.

James was the first to speak. "Willa, your mother and I are ble-blessed." His voice caught. "We are blessed to have you home safe. We are blessed to have a grandson. It's a miracle you're home, a mir-miracle," he managed to finish.

"Oh, Daddy." Willa pushed her chair back and hurried to hug her father.

James stood and held his daughter close.

Litha Mae got up and put her arms around them both, her tears unstoppable.

Skipper and Roscoe barked to get back inside.

The trio broke immediately and James headed to the door.

Litha Mae headed over to the cradle to check on a now-fussing Adam.

Willa stayed put, reveling in the moment and in the knowledge that her parents' love was unconditional and forever. As Levi had, they understood and they forgave her. Heartened by the moment, she believed she might know a peaceful night's sleep, at least tonight.

Levi hadn't slept well. Comfort had moved out and left Loudoun County with her family the week before. Maybe that was the reason he hadn't slept well, and not all of the other reasons that kept him awake more often than not. If it wasn't that Benjamin lay buried close by, that Jonah likely already lay buried on some battlefield, that his family continued to suffer, that their Quaker community had diminished in number, he worried that partisans fought all around, all the time. He still suffered insults and threats because he wasn't in the fight, and he worried that food and supplies had run out and that the war raged on, that danger shrouded all of Loudoun County, all the time. He grieved that the life he'd once known as a man of peace slipped farther away with each passing day. He worried over Willa—that he might never see her again.

Free to find her at last, he'd no idea where to look. If he tried to find her in the Confederate army, it would go badly for her and he knew it. He'd no idea the price she'd have to pay if found out as a woman. No, she would have to find him. She'd tried once. Last year she'd tried. He should have held on to her then, no matter that he was married. He shouldn't have let her go. He shouldn't have let her go off to fight, either. He should have kept her safe. Now, he'd no idea on earth where to look for her, or even if she lived.

How could he have been so stupid in the times they were together, not to remember where she was from? She *must* have told him. Levi's insides churned at his stupidity. His inability to remember would cost him any future with Willa, any chance at happiness. He didn't care that she was an outsider. If the elders had finally accepted his divorce, he'd talk to them until he was blue in the face to convince them to allow him to marry an outsider. By all that was right, if he ever found Willa again, he'd never let her go.

Levi climbed out of bed when it was still dark outside and reached for his clothes, mindless of the frigid plank floor. The bed was about the only piece of furniture that remained now that Comfort had gone. He'd let her load up their table and chairs and the parlor furniture to take with her to Ohio. She deserved to have it. Comfort had gone to Ohio to make a new start, and so would he. Furniture could easily be made. His needs were simple. His needs were plain, made more so by the war. Most of all, he needed to find some kind of inner peace and stop being wracked with guilt over letting Willa go and not helping to keep her safe.

He couldn't forgive himself.

He never would.

At least he'd been able to give Willa his Bible the last time he saw her. Maybe the scriptures would help keep her safe. He prayed they did. The cold February wind whistled outside. *More snow today,* Levi thought. Good. Bad weather forced the fighting to cease, for a time at least.

With spring coming, usually a time of hope and renewal, Levi suddenly thought of the familiar passage from Ecclesiastes. *To everything there is a season, and a time for every purpose under heaven*—He couldn't finish the verse; not all of it. He thought only of *a time to die, a time to pluck up that which is planted, a time to kill, a time to mourn, a time to lose* and *a time to rend.* A time for *more* war. There was no room in his head or his heart now to think of hope and renewal. He'd not said a prayer for it, not once.

In the main room Levi put a few of his last pieces of wood in the fireplace and reached for kindling and his matches. Too pre-occupied lately with thoughts of his unprecedented divorce and worry over Willa, he'd neglected to keep his store of wood sufficient. At least it would give him something to do today to keep busy. He'd neglected his appearance too, though he never thought on it much. Although he'd become used to shaving when the war started, he'd let his beard grow. Levi rubbed his face and chin. Willa had never seen him with a beard. What would she think if she saw him now? Levi took down his hand. That's another thing he'd do today to keep busy, work on shaving his beard and doing some laundry. His clothes needed a good wash and so did he. All at once the picture of Willa as she appeared the last time he saw her flooded his vision.

She'd looked like a little girl lost, standing in the rain, in a dress no less, surrounded by enemy soldiers, so fragile, so alone, so frightened. Now he understood her accusing look. She'd known by then that he'd married Comfort. If only he'd said or done something to . . . to what? There wasn't anything he could have done but let her go. The Yankees would have arrested her if he'd said or done anything other than convince them she wasn't a Confederate spy. He'd had to let her go.

Levi threaded his hands through his hair. That needed cutting, too. He swallowed hard, still thinking about Willa. She'd cut off her hair for the war. He remembered running his fingers through her coal-black hair. It was so soft, so lush, despite being short. What he wouldn't give to touch her now. It wouldn't matter to him if she shaved off every hair on her head.

"Lucretia Clement, Caleb Ryan is an *outsider!*"

"Please, Grace, hush. I don't want mother and father to know. Please, Grace," Lucretia begged.

The sisters were clearing the supper table. The plates hardly needed washing. Everyone had eaten all of their meager portions of cured ham and turnip root. The ham didn't go down well for any of them. It was the last of their pet hog, their last connection to happier times before the war.

Thomas and Susan Clement had gone to sit in their chairs by the fire, to read from the scriptures, sometimes aloud, sometimes in silence.

Relieved when she heard her mother begin to read from Psalms, Lucretia couldn't believe she'd chosen this moment to tell Grace about Caleb's letters. She hadn't meant to; the words just came out. Her letter today from Caleb must be the reason. Her heart was full to bursting from reading it. In it he'd said he dreamed of taking her in his arms and kissing her and never letting go. He'd said that dreaming of her was all that got him through his days and nights. But the last part of his letter had captured her whole heart and attention:

Dearest Lucretia, if you'll have me, I want you to be my wife when this war is over. I'm going to ask your father for your hand, I surely am. I love you, sweetheart. You're the star that guides me, the sun that warms me, and the moon that eases me to sleep. I dream of you lying next to me, warming my bed, our hearts beating as one.

Yours always,
Private Caleb Ryan
US Army of the Potomac

"But he wants to *marry* thee!" Grace whispered, pouring the warmed pail of water into the kitchen tub.

"Hush," Lucretia admonished her sister, vigorously scrubbing the plates and cups. "Thee must be quiet." Lucretia chanced a look over her shoulder at her parents and was glad to see their full attention to their Bibles.

Grace had trouble keeping quiet. She hurriedly wiped off the table, then took up another cloth to dry the dishes. "Thee only met him once," she said in an accusing tone.

"I met him more than once," Lucretia snapped back, in a harsh whisper.

Grace almost dropped the plate she was drying. "Lucretia Clement! Has thee . . . has thee done wrong?" Grace didn't mean to say that, but it came out anyway.

"No, Grace." Lucretia exhaled sharply. "I've done nothing wrong."

Grace dried the dishes more slowly. "Please don't be mad, Lucretia," she whispered softly. "I only. . . ."

"I'm sorry, little sister." Lucretia turned to Grace, putting a wet hand on her shoulder. "I know thee feels deeply about doing all that is right. I know thee will be a wonderful leader at meeting. Thee just cares about me. I know that, dear sister."

She smiled warmly, her voice still a whisper.

Grace smiled back, mollified by Lucretia's understanding.

Lucretia turned to the dishwater. "I love him, too, Grace," she said, her throat tight with emotion.

"Girls," Susan called loudly from across the room. "When thee are finished, come read from the scriptures with us."

Lucretia and Grace exchanged secret smiles, then did their mother's bidding.

Spring arrived, at long last. The war began anew. Troop movements started up on both sides, winter camps breaking, with orders being messaged throughout the ranks. Conscription was law in the North and the South, with neither President Lincoln nor President Davis able to rely solely on volunteers anymore. In April of 1862, the Confederate Congress had voted for conscription of "all able-bodied men between eighteen and thirty-five, with subsequent provisions of exemption for owners of twenty or more slaves, by hiring a substitute, or payment of five hundred dollars." In March of 1863, the United States Congress passed the Conscription Act which applied to "all able-bodied men between the ages of twenty and forty-five, with provisions of exemption by hiring a substitute, or payment of three hundred dollars." In both the North and the South there were riots reported because of conscription, with crowds protesting that the draft targeted the poor.

Though conscription was law on both sides, there was one distinct difference between the charges of the two presidents: one made it legal for free Negroes to muster in, while the other did not. United States Colored Troops were forming up at President Lincoln's leadership. No such orders came from President Davis. In spite of the war, and arguably because of it, Negroes started showing up in droves at Union camps, wanting to muster in and fight for their country, patriots all. They would still face prejudice and inequality in pay and duty assignment, but they mustered in nonetheless.

Who was winning this war so far?

The year before, both sides had taken heavy losses, losing as many as 13,000 men on the Union side and 11,000 on the Confederate side at the Battle of Shiloh alone. It would be reported that the Union won the day in April 1862, but at what cost? Five months later, Antietam proved to be the bloodiest day in the war. On that dreadful day over 2,000 soldiers lay dead with 9,549 wounded on the Union side, while 2,700 Confederate soldiers lay dead with more than 9,000 wounded. There had been no clear winner in this battle. General McClellan was considered the victor, but only because General Lee withdrew to Virginia. McClellan's troops were too exhausted to muster any pursuit. The Union was considered the victor, but, again, at what price?

Much of Virginia and the South was already hallowed ground, made so by the spilling of so much blood, by the ultimate sacrifice of so many men and boys on both sides of the fight. Soon the war would spill over into Pennsylvania, to Gettysburg, where the life's blood of a generation would be shed and forever lost, and where every clod of dirt, every shoot of grass would forever be hallowed ground.

Levi sat straight with his shoulders squared at meeting. He refused to cower or look away from the disapproving eyes of some of the Friends. They all knew of his divorce. For all he knew, some of them knew about his work with the Underground Railroad, too. They were few in number now, and half of the benches at the Fairfax Meetinghouse sat empty. His father sat alongside him, while his mother and sisters sat across, with the other women. The elders sat in benches apart from them all. Levi nodded to the elders. The elders stared blankly at him, with the exception of one, who returned his nod.

On this First Day, Levi intended to sit quietly and wait for any leading in the spirit that might lead him to find Willa. Desperate and feeling caught about what to do and where to begin to try to find her, he believed that if he prayed hard enough at meeting, the Word might come. He'd tried everything else; at least he'd tried to think through everything else he might do. So far, he'd come up with nothing, no idea he could act on. He'd no notion which direction to go. Levi shut his eyes to better listen for any sign, any leading of the spirit.

The meeting was quiet; not even a cough among the forty-or-so gathered members.

The door of the meetinghouse creaked open.

Levi opened his eyes and turned to see who'd entered, who was late for meeting.

Lucretia and Grace shrieked and raced for the door.

So did his mother.

Thomas Clement dropped his Bible and grabbed Levi's arm for support.

Levi put a hand over his father's, then slowly guided his father to a stand, not believing whom he saw in the meetinghouse doorway, not believing it was *Jonah!* At that point, others at meeting stood and started for the door, joyous at Jonah's return.

Thomas collapsed back onto the bench.

Levi saw his tears and knew that his father didn't want the others to see. Levi sat back down. "Jonah's come home, Father. He's come home," Levi reassured him quietly, his tone hoarse with emotion.

"Jonah?" Thomas muttered in disbelief.

"Yes, Father. Come with me now, and we'll welcome him home." Levi urged his father to stand. He knew his father no longer shunned Jonah; not since Benjamin had been killed. Jonah was alive. That's all that mattered now.

Thomas clutched Levi's arm hard, then let go and followed Levi into the crowd gathered around his son, returned home at last.

"Where's Benjamin, Levi? How come he wasn't at meeting with thee?" Jonah sat next to his brother in the family buggy. The rest of the family followed in the wagon behind. "Is he ailing?" Jonah questioned, anxious to see his twin brother, worried now for him.

"Giddyup," Levi called out, facing the horse and road ahead and not his brother. He'd offered to take Jonah in the buggy, telling everyone it would be better for Jonah, when really, Levi wanted to ride alone with Jonah and find the right time, the right words, to tell him that Benjamin waited at home: buried there. Levi doubted he'd do this right, but then was there any right way? His heart weighed heavily.

Jonah's crutches inched toward the edge of the seat. He pulled them in closer.

"Benjamin joined up with the Loudoun Rangers last fall and got himself killed, Jonah," Levi said straight out, breaking past the lump in his throat.

Jonah unfurled his fingers from his crutches, pulling his fist into a ball. His other hand, too. Suddenly he was on the battlefield again, gut-shot this time, struck down alongside Benjamin. Their blood spilled onto the ground, and they were dying together. Numbed, his life's blood draining out, Jonah slammed his eyes shut, remembering Benjamin. His fingers relaxed, his hands coming together now as if in prayer. And then he cried.

"Does it hurt?" Lucretia asked Jonah, her eye on his leg, or at least where his leg used to be. She, along with her parents and Grace, knew now that Jonah had been told about Benjamin.

"Not so much," Jonah said, uncomfortable that his family

had to see him this way. He didn't want them to fuss and worry over him. He knew he looked a sight, with his blue uniform pant leg tucked around his stump and his shirt hanging on him from weight loss. The time he'd spent in the army hospital hadn't done much for his poor appetite.

"Oh, my dear child." Susan came around behind Jonah's chair and put her hands on his thin shoulders. She kissed the top of his chestnut hair. "Thee is a brave boy." It broke her heart to see her son looking so poorly. It broke her heart that he'd lost the twin of his heart. She thought Jonah handsome as ever, despite the fact that his gentle brown eyes held no sparkle. He didn't wear his usual playful grin under that mustache and scruffy beard, and he'd lost most of his muscle. Food was scarce, but she'd do what she needed to care for her son.

"Jonah's a man now, Mother," Grace corrected lightly, coming to stand beside Jonah's chair. "Thee is brave," she declared admiringly to her brother.

"Thee is the one who's had to be brave here at home." Jonah forced a smile; Benjamin's death lay heavy on his heart.

Grace beamed at him, her face flush with excitement.

Jonah lovingly ruffled her hair. "Thee has almost grown up in the time I've been away. Thy sister, too," he said, looking now at Lucretia.

All smiles for her brother, Lucretia wanted to tell Jonah all about the Yankee soldier she loved, but of course she could say nothing now. She would tell him eventually, but not yet.

Thomas Clement and Levi came inside the house, having stabled the team and secured the wagon and buggy.

Jonah's eye darted toward his father. His father had said nothing to him since he'd returned. Not a word of welcome or reproach. Worried, he pushed himself to sit taller in his chair, lowering his crutches to the floor, out of sight.

Levi charged over to the table and pulled out a chair, flopping into it. "Like old times, brother," he quipped, trying to keep the conversation light. "We've a lot of catching up to do."

"Sure do," Jonah said, his attention on his father as he approached.

Thomas pulled out an empty chair and sat down, taking out his Bible and putting it on the table.

Jonah swallowed hard, on edge.

"Son," Thomas began, his gaze on Jonah at last. "This Bible is thine. I've kept it close since thee left and now I'm returning it to thee," he said, his eyes wet with unshed tears.

Jonah mechanically reached for his Bible, unsure of his father's meaning.

"Thee cannot go to meeting without thy Bible," Thomas said, nodding his head to emphasize his pronouncement.

Jonah breathed easily for the first time since he'd come home. He knew now that his father had truly welcomed him home and back into the fold. His eyes watered. Except for losing Benjamin, he felt whole again, in mind, heart, and body. In the year he'd been gone, he'd felt alone and abandoned by his family and his faith. Not now. Now he felt whole again, but for losing Benjamin.

A hush fell over the room, with everybody alert to the emotion of the moment.

"Girls, I need thee to help me make a peach pie," Susan Clement suddenly said. "I happen to have a jar left to make the best welcome-home pie in the county," she declared, disappearing into the near-empty pantry.

Everyone was all smiles, their relief at the change of subject palpable.

Lucretia and Grace reached for their aprons.

Thomas filled and lit up his pipe.

Levi tapped Jonah on the shoulder. "Like I said, brother, we have catching up to do."

"We sure do. I'd say that for certain," he answered Levi pointedly.

Levi shot Jonah a questioning look. He got the feeling Jonah had something else on his mind besides knowing about Levi's divorce. Levi didn't doubt that the girls had told Jonah all about him and Comfort while he and his father were in the barn.

"Is thee healing all right?" Thomas asked, and then took another puff on his pipe. "I'd like to know about thy injury and how thee survived."

"Me, too." Levi forgot all about Jonah giving him such a queer look moments before.

Jonah settled back in his seat. He hurt bad inside as he thought of Benjamin—real bad. His leg pounded, pain shooting into his stump. A little pain was nothing. He was alive. Benjamin was not.

"Son?" Thomas coaxed Jonah to begin his story.

Jonah reached into his pocket. He couldn't begin any story about how he survived without showing his family what had saved him.

CHAPTER FIFTEEN

Jonah carefully unwound the green grosgrain ribbon and laid it over his Bible.

"This ribbon is why I'm alive."

Hit with a pang of regret the moment his words were out, he wondered if he should say anything more in front of his family, about who had given him the ribbon. Maybe this conversation should be for Levi and Levi alone. Irritated with himself for taking out the ribbon, he should have thought this through first. He only had one brother left and didn't want to injure him with this news. Maybe he could make a joke about the ribbon, saying he found it on the battlefield and bound his leg, himself. Yeah, maybe he could say that.

Thomas stared hard at the ribbon.

So did Levi.

Neither of them knew what to say, they were so surprised.

At just that moment Lucretia turned toward the table, heavy mugs of tea in hand. Taken aback when she saw the green grosgrain ribbon strewn across Jonah's Bible, she all but dropped the hot mugs, but managed to set them down first. "Wh-where did thee get that?" she asked, bewildered at what she saw, thinking immediately that she'd given a ribbon just like it to Willa Mae Tyler; rather, she'd *returned* one just like it to Willa.

Jonah unbuttoned his shirt collar, squirming now. "It's just a ribbon," he said, trying to make light of her question.

"I know, Jonah, but where did thee get it? Who gave it to thee?"

At a crossroads, Jonah didn't know how to best answer.

"What's so important about this ribbon to thee?" Levi questioned Lucretia. "It's just a ribbon, as Jonah said."

"No, brother. It's not just a ribbon. I think it belongs to Willa Mae Tyler," Lucretia revealed, before she could stop herself.

Levi shot up from the table.

The mugs of tea rattled and spilled.

Uh-oh, Jonah thought.

Lucretia picked up the ribbon and began threading it reverently through her fingers. "Brother, I will tell thee about this later. Now we will listen to Jonah." She put the ribbon back down, hoping Jonah would say something, anything, to rescue her from having said too much.

"Uh-oh," was all Jonah could think to say.

By now, Susan Clement and Grace's full attentions had been drawn to the green grosgrain ribbon lying over Jonah's Bible. Susan's eyes went immediately to Levi. Willa Mae Tyler might be the woman her son truly loved. Susan knew from the moment Levi spoke his vows to Comfort that he loved another. A mother knows these things.

"Lucretia, tell me about the ribbon," Levi demanded.

"Levi, *later.* I will tell thee later," Lucretia quietly put to her brother.

"Me, too, Levi. I will tell thee later," Jonah parroted.

"Thee will tell me *what* later, Jonah?"

Lucretia and Jonah exchanged regretful glances. Both had already said too much. Both should have held their tongues and waited until they could speak to Levi in private.

"Tell me, too," Grace insisted.

"And me," his mother said.

"And me," his father enjoined.

Jonah nodded resignedly to Lucretia to go first.

Finished wiping up tea spills, Lucretia returned the wet cloth to the side of the kitchen tub then turned around, facing her family, Levi in particular. She began by explaining how the ribbon had come into her hands, how it had been given to her by Surry Lion, Willa's secret and best friend. Surry had been given the ribbon by Willa's mother, who'd kept her daughter's ribbon after Willa left home. The ribbon had been a gift to Willa from her brothers one Christmas long ago.

Taking care not to mention Levi's involvement with the Underground Railroad, Lucretia chose her words carefully. It was too late to worry what her parents thought of her about having accepted the gift of the ribbon from Surry Lion. The ribbon wasn't plain, and she shouldn't have accepted it. Caring more about the effect of her words on Levi, she told him the truth, all of it. She told him that she'd returned the ribbon to Willa last year, when Willa had come back to Waterford looking for him.

Levi took up Willa's ribbon, touching it, feeling as though he were touching her. His fingers warmed to her softness. She didn't feel far away anymore but close, within his reach, the ribbon connecting him to her. There was something else. He felt a jolt, a charge tensing through the ribbon. Unwittingly, he wound the ribbon around his hand—each circle tighter than the last, each circle drawing Willa closer, ensuring their connection. He'd hold fast to her. Dear God, if he ever found her again, he'd hold fast to her. "Lucretia, where—?"

"Sit back down, brother. There's more," Jonah interrupted Levi.

"No, Jonah, I have to—"

"Levi, what thee has to do is sit back down and listen," Jonah insisted, his tone sure.

Levi's jaw tensed. Angry at Jonah for interfering, he needed to find out where Willa lived. She could have been wounded and sent home by this time. His insides folded, his nerves raw. He suddenly thought of her without an arm or a leg. Dear God! Maybe she'd decided to leave the army on her own and gone home. There was a chance she had. It was a slim chance, but he had the tie to her in his hands and he refused to let go.

"Levi, *sit down*," Jonah flat-out ordered.

Shooting an accusing glance at Jonah, Levi lowered himself into his chair. It was wrong to be angry at his brother, only just come home and wounded. Levi fought for control. He forced his attention to Jonah and listened. He'd listen to his brother and then he'd listen to Lucretia for word of Willa's whereabouts—where she called home—then he'd leave this very day, and find Willa.

"Mother. Father." Jonah directed to his parents. "I pray thee will keep understanding in thy hearts, hearing what I'm about to tell Levi. These are trying times, to get through this war and keep our faith close. Just as thee has forgiven me for joining in the fight, thee must promise thee will forgive Levi for what I'm about to say. Levi is a good Quaker. Levi has been a good Quaker his whole life. Comfort, a leader at meeting, chose divorce. Levi would have stayed with her. Thee both know that. Thee has never had to caution Levi to Mind the Light. Thee must not shun him for what I'm about to say."

The room fell silent but for audible gasps from Lucretia and Grace.

Susan reached over and put a hand on Jonah's arm, nodding her agreement.

Thomas, however, did not. He set down his pipe and dropped his head as if in prayer, saying nothing.

Only seconds ago Levi had wanted to leave, but no power on earth could force him from his chair now. He edged closer to the table, to Jonah.

"I was dying on the battlefield at Manassas. My leg had been all shot up. The fighting was over, I think. I can't remember exactly. I do remember crawling up behind a house and just sitting there. My mind went in and out. I was losing a lot of blood. I knew I didn't have much time. I remember not wanting to die alone. I was afraid to die alone."

Susan clutched Jonah's arm, tears wetting her face.

"I heard someone say, 'Finish him off,' " Jonah continued. "I didn't close my eyes, but forced them to stay open to face the enemy. I saw the soldier leaning over me. I remember telling the gray coat to go ahead and finish me."

Susan wailed out loud.

Jonah kept on. "The soldier didn't kill me, but . . . but saved me instead. The soldier tied this ribbon around my leg, stopping the bleeding." Jonah caught Levi's eye. "That soldier wasn't a man, but a woman-soldier. That soldier was Willa Mae Tyler."

The ribbon around Levi's hand pulsed and tightened.

Gasps broke the silence, from Lucretia and Grace and their mother.

Not from Thomas. He raised his head, opening his eyes to the moment, to what he'd just heard Jonah say.

"Levi, when she found out my name, she told me how she met thee and how she loved thee. She told me she was carrying thy child. 'Adam,' she'd said. 'I've named him Adam.' "

"Adam," Levi repeated in disbelief.

"Before I fell unconscious, I remember she was with me." Jonah paused. "She and my nephew were with me. I wasn't going to die alone. I wasn't scared."

"Glory be. Glory be." Susan Clement whispered prayerfully.

Lucretia ran to Jonah and kissed his cheeks, then to Levi and kissed his cheeks.

Grace, too, immediately showered both brothers with joyous kisses.

Thomas Clement picked up his pipe, relit the tobacco, and took several puffs, fighting to hide his emotions. He'd made the mistake of shunning Jonah before . . . before he'd lost Benjamin to the war. He didn't want to make the same mistake with Levi. Somewhere out there was his grandson. He couldn't shun Levi or his grandson. His whole life Thomas had lived the Quaker way, but the war . . . well, the war had almost broken him, leading him and his family away from peace and Light. Maybe this child was the way back to God, the way back for them all.

"Glory be." Thomas said loud and clear. "Glory be."

Too shocked about the news that Willa had saved Jonah's life, much less given him a son, Levi didn't hear his father.

Jonah did, and in that moment Jonah knew that his father had indeed forgiven both him and Levi their trespasses.

"Lucretia, where is Willa's home?" Levi scraped his chair back and shot out his question.

"Bedford County, between Liberty and Lynchburg, I think," Lucretia answered right away. "Surry Lion is from the Shelby Plantation nearby," she added, only remembering now.

Levi charged out of the kitchen.

"Where is thee going in such a rush, Levi Clement?" his mother shouted at his back.

Levi stopped and turned around in the doorway, his expression deadly serious. "I'm going to fetch my family, if they'll have me."

Lucas dusted off his uniform, anxious to wear it again. Because so many colored troops were mustering in, what with the passage of the Emancipation Proclamation, and with the call of Frederick Douglass, in the *Douglass Monthly,* for men of color to join the fight, Lucas had been ordered back to his regiment. He hoped it was because he'd be joining the fight. He itched to fight. Every time he heard about another battle, especially in

Virginia, he regretted he wasn't a part of it.

Dang it, Lucas wished he'd been in the fight at Chancellors-ville. He wished he could have fought with General Hooker's men. The losses that day were great and the battle lost. No matter. Lucas still wished he'd been in the fight, helping to kill the thirteen thousand Confederates that fell at Chancellorsville. Lucas had heard that Stonewall Jackson himself was dead now. That was something. But General Lee wasn't dead. He was gathering his troops in Culpeper County, Lucas heard tell.

Lucas thought of home. Culpeper County was close to Loudoun County, with only Fauquier County in between. He thought of enemy troops gathering too close to home. He thought of enemy troops knocking down his neighbors' doors, taking food and supplies and whatever else they needed. He thought of his family, of his mother and his father. Lucas knew his father wouldn't let anyone break down his door. He'd die first. That's what Lucas feared the most: that something might happen to his parents. And Surry. If she'd made it north—all the way north—she should be all right now. *If.* Every night, every morning, Lucas prayed that she was safe.

Shouts outside his tent drew Lucas's attention away from Surry and thoughts of home. Still in civilian clothes, he tossed his uniform back on his cot and rushed outside to see what all the commotion was about.

Troops!

Colored troops.

Marching bold as brass, spit and polished as could be!

Lucas hurried over to the edge of the road.

"It's the Fifty-fourth!" someone shouted.

Lucas stood at attention, despite the fact that he wasn't wearing his uniform, and watched the infantry parade by. He'd heard about the 54th Massachusetts Infantry forming up under a white commander, and had longed to be a part of the fighting unit.

And here they were. He fought the urge to don his uniform and fall in, joining their ranks. Filled with an overwhelming sense of pride, he watched the 54th march past. Every soldier was a colored soldier, every single one. Whoops and hollers erupted all around, the soldiers at Camp Stanton, doubtless feeling the same pride that Lucas did.

He wondered where the 54th was going, which battle, which fight.

"Soldier!" he called to one of the passing men in blue. "Where you headed?"

The soldier was even with him now. "Going to Glory," he answered, smiling. "Going to Glory," he said again, and then passed on by.

"They're goin' to South Carolina, I hear," one of the soldiers standing alongside Lucas said. "I hear they're goin' to attack Fort Wagner."

Lucas picked up the longing in the soldier's voice. He felt the same longing to fall in and join the 54th. . . . Going to Glory.

"No, little sister, we can't go and see the Clements," Surry cautioned Penny. Exhausted and travel-weary, glad at least for the warm summer breeze, Surry pulled Penny to hide behind the ferry station until they were given the all clear to board the ferry and head down the Potomac River. Surry was glad for the cover of night. She and Penny must take care until she got the all-clear signal.

"But why, Surry? I want to see Lucretia and Grace. I want to see them," Penny complained, shrugging off Surry's hold.

Surry gently coaxed her sister to hide behind the station. "Penny, you've been such a brave girl. I know you would like to see the Clements again on your way home to see Mama, but you must understand. It's not safe. We can't."

"But why, Surry? Slaves are free now. Why isn't it safe?"

Penny folded her arms rebelliously in front of her.

Surry had already explained things to Penny, too many times to count. Although she was eleven now, Penny was still a little girl. Surry needed to remember that. Despite everything she'd been through, despite having to grow up too quickly, Penny was still a little girl. "Slaves aren't free yet in northern Virginia. If we went to the Clement farm, we might be seen and picked up, and then we couldn't get home to see Mama. Soon we can travel in the open where slaves are free," Surry tried to say as brightly as she could. She knew Penny was disappointed. She was disappointed, too. She wanted to see Lucas again.

Penny frowned, her little face in a pucker.

Surry understood how hard it was for Penny to understand. It was hard for her, too, to remember where slavery was still allowed and where it was against the law. Why couldn't slavery have been abolished everywhere? In Washington, D.C., it was abolished a year ago. Why not everywhere in the country now? Why hadn't the Emancipation Proclamation freed everyone? Surry had asked herself these questions repeatedly on the long journey back home.

She and Penny had struck out from the Elgin Settlement in Ontario, Canada, as soon as they could after they'd heard the news of the slaves being freed in the South—most of the South, that is. Saxonia Shadd had helped Surry carve out a route home using the same Underground Railroad that had brought them to Canada. Because slavery was still the law in the northern states, she and Penny would need to travel just as cautiously on the trip home as they had in coming.

The journey home would be just as dangerous. They could be caught and sold, Surry knew. She doubted anyone would try to return them to their original master, since it would be against the law to do so. No, she and Penny, if caught, could be sold or beaten or killed. It was a hard reality that followed Surry and

Penny on their way back down through the northern states to freedom at home. Once home, once back in Bedford County, she and Penny would be free and safe from capture. At least, this is how Surry saw things.

Still hunkered behind the ferry station, her arms around Penny, Surry listened to the katydids hum across the summer night. No distant guns broke their steady drone. Unaccustomed to gunfire along the route home, once they'd entered Maryland and Virginia, they'd heard the sounds of war more often than not. Going to Canada, they'd left the war behind, but now they walked right into the jowls of beast. This was the way it had to be for freedom to come to all slaves in the country. It would take a mighty beast to gain freedom for all, a mighty and deadly beast.

Just because slaves were free in the South didn't mean the war around them was over. One battle might be won, but others remained to be fought. Even though it would have been safer to stay in Canada, Surry longed to see her mother and her little sisters who had stayed at the Shelby Plantation. Surry prayed they were safe. She prayed for something else: that the cruel overseer and his murdering son were gone—dead and gone. She took heart, thinking of them caught in the jowls of the beast, crushed to oblivion. Such sweet revenge would be satisfaction, indeed. Surry's heart picked up at the thought.

She wished she could fight, just like Willa had. Willa had disguised herself as a soldier and so could she. Surry had wanted to follow the seventy young men who'd left Elgin to go back to America and join Union forces the moment they'd learned of the Emancipation Proclamation, feeling just as patriotic as they did. But there was Penny to think about, Penny and the fact that Surry had never shot a gun or worn pants or acted the tomboy, like Willa. Surry didn't think she'd make a very good soldier. She knew Willa did.

Surry hugged Penny closer. Scared for Willa, Surry had no way of knowing if she was dead or alive.

"Ouch, Surry," Penny protested, pulling out of her sister's grasp.

Surry leaned against the station wall, trying to keep her nerves steady. She must keep together for Penny's sake. They were almost home. Closing her eyes, Surry took comfort from remembering long summer afternoons with Willa, their feet dangling in the James River, fishing poles in hand. Well, Willa did most of the fishing, always accusing Surry of being too girlie. Surry smiled inside and felt the better for remembering Willa's scolding.

She'd scolded Willa many a time, too, for being such a tomboy, saying she'd never get a boy in all Bedford County to take notice of her.

"There, Surry! The light!" Penny grabbed Surry's arm.

"Hush, Penny. We must stay quiet," Surry cautioned, peering around the back of the station. The ferryman was there, signaling with his lantern for them to come aboard. Without another word, she pulled Penny along behind her toward the ferry landing.

"Surry and Penny Lion?" the stony ferryman asked, the moment they'd reached his boat.

"Yes," Surry quickly answered.

"Come on, then," he instructed. "Time's a wasting." He held out his hand to help Surry aboard, and then Penny. "Ya'll go tuck yourself under that canopy and keep low. There's folks aplenty trying to watch for the likes of you."

"Are you a free man?" Surry suddenly asked.

The ferryman undid the rope tie to the landing and then turned back to Surry. "Sure enough," he said, smiling for the first time.

"Such a wonder," Surry said aloud, not meaning to.

The big man tried to stifle his laugh. "It surely is a wonder, Surry Lion."

She grinned up at him.

"Go on now, miss," he ordered more good-naturedly now. "You best hide with your sister."

Surry nodded, and headed for cover under the canopy. Penny was already curled up asleep. Surry balled up her shawl and put it under Penny's head, then settled against the back of the cargo hold. No easy sleep would come for Surry, not with Lucas so near, and yet so far away.

If only this ferry took her along Catoctin Creek, she'd be in Waterford in no time. Surry closed her eyes, her body suddenly infused with pure pleasure at the thought. She imagined Lucas opening the door when she knocked. She imagined his powerful frame filling the threshold. She imagined his handsome visage full of surprise—happy surprise—over seeing her. She imagined him pulling her into his arms. She imagined him kissing her . . . and kissing her and kissing her. She imagined him scooping her up and taking her to his bed. She imagined him undressing her and her undressing him, not a bit ashamed at such thoughts. Her body would open to him, completely and absolutely. She wasn't afraid of him touching her. She wasn't afraid of him wanting her. She wasn't afraid of wanting him.

Her eyes flew open, her body suddenly on fire.

Beads of sweat trickled down her cheeks. Or were they tears?

Surry wiped her face with the sleeve of her blouse and tried to settle herself. No good came from such imaginings. She could think all she wanted about Lucas, but she knew he didn't think of her. Why, she was just one runaway slave among the many he'd helped. He probably didn't even remember her.

Surry sank full against the cargo hold. Now she had new imaginings. She imagined knocking on Lucas's door and another woman answering: his bride. Surry stretched out her legs and roughly thumped her skirt. She'd never been jealous of any woman before. Silly. Ridiculous. But still . . . she was jealous of the unknown face of Lucas's bride. Straightening her spine, she tried to shrug off the unwanted image of Lucas married to someone else, glad that the ferry headed away from Waterford now.

Gunfire!

Surry heard guns in the distance, jarred by the unmistakable sounds. Her head pounded with each explosion.

Penny slept on.

Surry eased back against the hold, glad her sister wasn't awakened. Penny had already been frightened enough on their journey. Frightened herself, Surry turned her troubled thoughts away from Willa and Lucas and tried to focus on the way ahead, the way home. Her mother would be waiting; surely she would be.

Surry refused to think otherwise.

CHAPTER SIXTEEN

"But, Levi, it seems like the whole Union army is moving through Loudoun now," Jonah said, trying to stop his brother from leaving. "Something's going on. Something's starting up besides the ruckus over West Virginia being a state now and all the skirmishes and cavalry fights in Aldie, Middleburg and Upperville. I found out the Confederates were pushed back, but for how long? No telling where Lee's army is, exactly," Jonah lowered himself to sit on Levi's bed, propping his crutches alongside.

"Little brother, the war's over for thee. Thee doesn't need to worry over troop movements anymore," Levi said, paying little attention to Jonah, too busy packing his saddlebag. He didn't need much for his journey but a few items of clothing and a bit of food.

Jonah grabbed his crutches and got himself to a stand, turning on Levi. "Well, maybe I don't need to worry, but *thee* does. Thee could be walking right into a Confederate trap. Thee could be spotted and picked up and forced into the fight, *or thee could just be shot!*"

Levi buckled his saddlebag closed and left it on the bed. He'd been hard on Jonah when he hadn't meant to be. The war would never be over for his little brother. If his missing limb wasn't enough of a reminder, Benjamin's death was. Because of this, the war would never be over for any of their family. Levi stood face to face with Jonah, and saw the strain of the war and his injury in Jonah's tight expression. "Sit back down, little brother," Levi said.

Jonah didn't move a muscle.

"Please," Levi urged. "I need to hear what thee can tell me about troop movements. Everything."

"All right then." Jonah nodded in approval and then sat back down, setting his crutches aside.

Levi took a seat on the nearby bench, then gave Jonah his full attention.

"Thee *has* to go?" Jonah asked, and not for the first time.

"Thee knows I do," Levi shot back, more harshly than he'd intended.

Jonah heaved a sigh, not a bit ruffled by Levi's tone. He knew there was no way he could talk Levi out of going. Levi was in love with a slip of a woman-soldier, Willa Mae Tyler. Jonah understood that Levi needed to find Willa and his son. There was no more powerful force on earth than love, Jonah knew. There was no way the war was going to stop his brother. Not when he knew where to find Willa and Adam. "What's the route thee plans to take?" Jonah made himself ask.

"I'm going the straight route. I'm not going the Underground Railroad route, but straight," Levi answered, his tone easing up.

"Will thee travel at night?"

"And day," Levi said.

"Night would be safer, Levi."

"Yeah, I know."

Jonah shook his head at his brother, his meaning clear.

Levi almost smiled at his brother's concern. Almost.

"I can see thee is taking thy horse," Jonah looked at the packed saddlebags.

"Yeah. It'll be quicker that way."

"Thee would be safer and less visible on foot, brother," Jonah cautioned.

"Yeah, I know."

"What's your route out of Loudoun?" Jonah asked, dead serious.

"Around Middleburg."

"Then?"

"Then into Fauquier County around Warrenton."

"Culpeper County next?" Jonah questioned, his concentration deep. Culpeper could be a real problem. Jonah had a bad feeling about Culpeper County, and it tugged at him.

"Yeah, around Culpeper," Levi concurred. "And then into Albermarle County around Charlottesville, then I'll pick up the route along the James River. Appomattox County is close, but I won't go to Appomattox, but on to Lynchburg in Bedford County," Levi explained step by step, his concentration as hard as his brother's.

"Only thing I'd change, Levi, is to skirt around Culpeper entirely. It will take thee out of the way some, but thee should take another direction. I have a bad feeling about Culpeper. It's too dangerous there, all right?"

Levi felt Jonah's sharp stare and knew his brother was dead serious. Well, so was he dead serious about getting to Willa and his son as fast as his horse would take him. Usually a cautious man, Levi wasn't thinking about his own safety. Reaching Willa and his son was all that was important. Once he'd found them, then he'd think about safety—their safety and not his. Feeling fiercely protective of Willa and his child, he'd do what he had to do to find them.

"All right, brother? Thee will avoid Culpeper?" Jonah said again.

"Sure will," Levi lied. No need to worry his brother any more than he already had. No lie was a good lie, but Levi thought this one might be. Levi got up, ready to go find Willa and his son. Time was wasting, time they couldn't afford. He needed to bring his family home as soon as he could, to this house, where he'd keep them safe from the war that raged everywhere. Woe unto any that tried to cross his threshold and harm his family. Levi's fists tightened at the thought of anyone trying to harm Willa or his son. Much as he tried to relax his fingers and ignore the fight in him, he could not. Much as he tried to shut out the gnawing realization that if anyone tried to harm Willa or Adam, he might harm the aggressors and break with his long-held peace testimony, he could not. He'd do whatever he had to do in order to reach his new family and protect them from harm. If that meant raising his fist against his fellow man . . . Levi didn't want to finish the thought; not now; not yet. His gut wrenched. Quaker and non-Quaker alike, whether they chose to be or not, were all caught up in the angry fists of the war.

"Levi, take this with thee," Jonah said, scooping up Willa's ribbon.

Levi grabbed the ribbon from Jonah, reverently winding it up before placing it deep in his shirt pocket, over his heart. He smiled at Jonah, mentally thanking him for the reminder.

"This, too." Jonah handed Levi his Bible, the one his father had just returned to him.

"Wh—?"

"Thee should take a Bible in case thee is stopped, to help prove thee is Quaker," Jonah explained, holding his Bible out for Levi to take.

Levi reluctantly accepted Jonah's Bible. Jonah was right; it might help to have the Bible with him. "Thanks, brother," he said.

"Well, I noticed thy Bible is gone," Jonah quipped.

"Yeah, I gave it to someone," Levi admitted.

"Could that someone be a pretty woman-soldier named Willa?" Jonah teased.

"Right again, brother," Levi teased back. "I'll tell thee the whole story when I return with Willa and Adam, all right?"

Jonah's smile faded. *If thee returns,* he couldn't help thinking.

Levi picked up his saddlebags and jacket, and set his broad-brimmed hat square on his head.

"Telegraph when thee gets to Lynchburg, Levi. Let us know when thee arrives," Jonah said, his voice unsteady.

"Sure," Levi agreed. "Sure will."

The brothers exchanged knowing expressions. They both knew they might be seeing each other for the last time.

Levi headed for the door then turned back to Jonah. "Thee will keep close watch over our parents and our sisters while I'm gone?"

"Sure will," Jonah agreed. "Sure will."

"Good then. Farewell, brother." Levi tossed Jonah a last smile and then quickly disappeared outside.

Willa watched her son sleep. He was the most beautiful, the most precious little boy in all Virginia. She gently rocked his cradle, though he was fast asleep. The easy motion helped soothe her nerves. Upset at herself for wanting too much in life, when she already had a healthy son and parents who loved her, she wanted more, which was wrong. She was being selfish. Her brothers had lost their lives to the war. Surry was lost to her forever. It was wrong for Willa to feel lost now, to feel lost in a life without Levi. Shouldn't she be grateful she was alive? Shouldn't she be grateful for her son's life? Shouldn't she be grateful for a roof over her head? Shouldn't she be content, here at home with her parents, sheltered for a time from the storm of war? Shouldn't she be grateful she wasn't in the trenches fighting anymore?

Willa let go of the cradle.

She should be grateful and she was but. . . .

It wasn't enough.

She wanted more.

She wanted Levi.

Skipper and Roscoe began moaning, scratching to get outside. Willa padded across the room and opened the door for the dogs. It wasn't yet light out. Willa had gotten up early to feed Adam, but couldn't go back to sleep herself. Her parents still slept in the next room. She didn't want to wake them, so she stepped outside. A brisk walk might help ease her agitation.

The June day would be hot, Willa realized, the moment she felt the sultry air. Dressed in her thick cotton nightshift, too warm already, Willa fought the urge to make a dash for the edge of the James, toss off her shift, and go swimming. The cool, rushing water had always soothed her. She thought again of Levi. He'd pulled her away from the edge of Catoctin Creek when she'd thought of losing herself in the deep rushing waters, tempted to escape the pain of war, the pain of all the suffering and loss.

"Ouch!" Willa stubbed her toe on a sharp rock. For pity's sake! She'd come outside barefoot.

Skipper and Roscoe ran up, excited, trying to lick her hands.

She giggled at their touch. "Go on, now." She gently shooed them off. A far cry from her life in the trenches over the past year, she giggled inwardly at herself now, at the girlie ways she'd adopted since she'd been home from battle. Here she was shrieking over a little stubbed toe when she'd endured far worse. Willa shrugged her shoulders and took in a deep breath, needing to shake off her melancholy. Humph, girlie.

Surry had always teased her because she wasn't feminine. *Look at me now, dear Surry. I surely am girlie now. And look at you:* "bein' free." Willa's heart gave a lurch, as she thought of Surry and all their teasing back and forth about who was a tomboy and who a feminine girl. Surry would surely approve of her wearing a dress every day. A mother now, Willa thought it best to dress like a mother. There was another reason Willa wore a dress these days. It helped put the war behind her, if only a little. Although Willa kept her gray soldier's jacket and her floppy hat tucked away under her bed, she struggled to leave the war behind and look ahead to her new role as a mother.

Not a wife and mother, but a mother all the same.

Wife.

The very thought of the word sent Willa's already-flagging spirits plummeting. She *had* to stop wanting what she'd never have. She could never be Levi's wife. He was married to Comfort Clarke . . . Comfort Clement. Willa remembered the day Comfort shut the door in her face, the day Willa had gone to Waterford to find Levi and tell him about their baby.

Willa had found Levi that day, all right. Rather, he'd found her caught up by Yankee soldiers. He'd kept her from being arrested as a spy. For that much she'd been grateful, but not for the rest. He'd gone off and married someone else. The pain of it hit Willa hard every day, as if it happened yesterday and not over a year ago.

She couldn't hate him. She wanted to hate him, but she couldn't. Now she hated herself for not being able to stop thinking about him and wanting him. It was wrong, but *it was just the way of it:* loving Levi. Her breasts suddenly tingled. It must be time to feed Adam again. But, no, she'd only just fed him. She put her hands to her breasts, touching them through the thick cotton of her nightdress.

Old memories stirred, memories of Levi touching her there. She remembered him removing her bindings and touching her there. The ache that started in her breasts sent agonizing, pleasurable shudders throughout her body to her very core, penetrating her poor defenses, laying siege to her, returning her to the moment when Levi first took her as his. Willa wrapped her arms around her middle to bring Levi closer still. *Thee I love, Levi Clement. Thee I love,* she dared think. *Thee I will always love.*

Skipper and Roscoe got underfoot, jolting Willa out of her stirrings.

She turned then and walked back toward the house, making sure of her step. Soon it would be light. She'd best put the kettle on and start breakfast. She'd best put her attention to useful purpose and think on everything she did have, and not on what she did not.

"Penny, stop!" Surry yelled at Penny's back, unable to keep her sister from running on ahead, up the overgrown lane to the Shelby Plantation. Surry's heart went to her throat. She wanted to chase after Penny but she couldn't; she was too scared to move. The entire trek down from Canada she'd thought about this moment. She longed to see her mother again and dreaded that she might not.

"Surry, come on!" Penny yelled down the lane. "Come on!"

No one came outside of the big house, chasing after Penny. Not Boyd Blankenship or his father. No one chased after Penny with whip in hand, ready to punish her for running away. Surry swallowed back her fear and started walking slowly, carefully, as if expecting the cruel overseer and his murdering son to break out the lash and stop her. Encouraged that they did not, she hoped them dead now; she surely did.

Things had changed. The big house looked run-down, and the grounds forgotten. Surry picked up her step, worried for her mother. Surry no longer worried for herself or for Penny, so focused was she on her mother. Even in the light of day, with her and Penny out in plain sight, no one came chasing after them. They were free now. Free. No one waited at the plantation gates to slap them in irons and enslave them. No one could do that. Emboldened by the realization, Surry caught up with her sister.

"Surry," Penny whispered, close to tears. "I'm scared, Surry."

"I know, little sister, I know." Surry took up Penny's hand and guided her past the seemingly deserted outbuildings; past the kitchen and the barns and the stable and then on past the sick house and the woodworking shop, finally arriving at the slave cabins. Their old cabin looked deserted, lifeless. Surry's insides seized. She remembered when her family had been kicked out of their cabin and sent to a tired shack at the edge of the woods. Surry didn't try their old cabin door, because she was too scared. "Come, Penny." Surry held fast to Penny's hand and broke into a run, making a beeline for the woods and the last so-called home they'd known.

The shack lay in splintered pieces on the ground!

"Surry! Surry!" Penny screeched, hugging her sister for dear life.

"Hush, now," Surry tried to soothe, her arms around Penny, rocking her close. "Hush, now." Instead of tears, a fierce anger welled up inside Surry. *Damn the Shelbys to hell! Damn them!*

With murder in her heart for the cruel white plantation owners who should have kept her family safe, Surry eased Penny away from her. "Come, Penny." Surry struggled to keep her voice steady. "We're going to the big house."

"Sure enough, Surry?" Penny wiped her eyes with her fingers.

"Sure enough," Surry gritted out, then turned in the direction of the brick, white-columned mansion, her fists balled and her step determined.

"Wait, Surry!" Penny pleaded from behind. "Wait for me!"

Surry didn't hear Penny, so bent was she on finding the Shelbys and meting out her own justice for what they'd done to her family, for all they'd let happen to them. She reached the back of the mansion, with the overseer's fine brick cottage set close.

It infuriated her to see the cottage looking so kept up, with daisies blooming out front and smoke wafting from its chimney. Changing course now, heading for the brick cottage instead of around to the front of the mansion, Surry would take care of whoever was inside that damned cottage first. If the Blankenships still lived and were inside, she'd kill 'em both with her bare hands; she surely would.

"Surry!" Penny had caught up with her.

"Go behind the sick house and hide, Penny. *Now!*" Surry ordered.

"But. . . ."

"Go!" Surry knew she sounded mean and angry, but that's how she felt. "Penny, you have to be able to run if—"

The door of the cottage suddenly pushed open.

Surry froze.

So did Penny.

Pitty Pat was the first to rush outside, then Sam, then Esther Lion and then Surry's two youngest sisters, Letty and Nellie. Surrounded at once by loving arms, the grouping so tight no power on earth could break them apart, Surry dissolved into tears of joy along with everybody else. There were no words for such a reunion, only tears.

"My blessed children." Esther Lion spoke first, her voice shaky.

"Mama," Surry managed to say, hugging her mother close. Home at last, in her mother's arms, Surry let fall all the tears she'd been holding inside for the past year. It was safe to let them fall, she was so relieved to find her mother and her brother and sisters alive and well.

"There, there," Esther said, patting her daughter's back, surrounded by the commotion of Pitty Pat, Penny, Sam, Letty and Nellie, all whooping and hollering with glee.

"Mama," Surry said, pulling out of her mother's arms, their

eyes meeting. "Mama, we're free. *Free.*"

"Thank God Almighty," Esther responded, tearing up again.

Surry fell back into her mother's arms, and they both reveled in the moment, in the miracle of their freedom.

Surry suddenly pulled away again. "Mama, where are the others? Have they come home? Where are my brothers?"

Esther dabbed at her eyes with her apron.

The rest of the children all quieted.

Esther heaved a sigh and straightened the folds of her apron. "No way to say it but to say it, dear daughter. Two of your brothers are gone to heaven, and two are gone off to war."

Surry kept her mother's eye. "Which ones?" she managed to get out in a rough whisper.

Esther took up her daughter's hands. "Lemuel and Jasper were shot sometime after they ran away. I don't know if it was slave catchers that done it or the law or just plain bad white folks, but they were shot and killed, all the same. So was Nate Bonner, Surry girl. I'm sorry to say but Nate's gone, too."

"Nate?" Surry parroted in disbelief, her heart wrenching in her tight chest.

Esther patted Surry's hands. "Gus and Silas are all right, far as I know. Remember that, daughter. Gus and Silas are all right."

Penny cried hard, grabbing onto Surry's skirts and not her mother's, so used was she by this time to seeking solace from her sister during their run to Canada and back.

Surry looked at her mother and not Penny. "Gus and Silas . . . they've gone off to war, you say?" she asked, needing confirmation that they were alive.

"Yes, they surely have. They went up north to join in the colored ranks and fight the moment we were freed by President Lincoln. I don't know where or which unit, but I know they've joined the United States Colored Troops. I'm proud of 'em, Surry girl," Esther said, fighting new tears.

"Me, too, Mama," Surry said and meant it.

"Me, too," Penny chimed in brightly, hugging her mother this time.

Pitty Pat, Samuel, Letty, and Nellie's faces all broke into smiles again.

Surry turned to Pitty Pat and Sam. "You two scallywags. What happened after the Confederates put you in that wagon? I thought you'd be taken off to prison or . . . well . . . or worse."

"No, Surry," Sam answered before Pitty Pat could. "We were captured all right, but they sent us back here, back to Master Shelby, and not to prison."

"Praise be." Surry ruffled the top of Sam's head.

"Wait, Surry," Pitty Pat said, and then hurried away from the group.

Surry's attention was still on Sam. "What happened when you were returned here?"

"We got a good lickin' from the overseer, but that's all," Sam said, his shoulders square.

That's all? Surry thought. How brave was her brother.

"Them Blankenships are both dead and gone, daughter," Esther flatly pronounced. "We don't know who did it, but somebody did. Maybe it was the law. Maybe it was runaways. All we knew was that one day they were here, yellin' out orders, whippin' who they could, and the next day they were just gone. Mr. Shelby never got anybody else," Esther said, surprise still in her voice. "Mr. Shelby came and found us soon after that, tellin' us we was free, and then askin' if I'd stay and help look after his family. He's paying me wages, daughter," Esther said proudly. "And he offered this cottage to me and my family. It's our home now," she finished, nodding her head to underscore such a marvel.

"Oh, Mama, praise be," Surry exclaimed, clapping her hands together.

"You've another reason for celebration, daughter." Esther took up Surry's hands again.

Her heart was so full now, Surry couldn't imagine any more good news.

"Someone else is home now, like you," Esther informed, a twinkle in her worn eyes.

Surry stood motionless, not even breathing.

"Willa Mae Tyler is home from the war. Home from the war with her son."

Surry's hands flew to her mouth. She didn't hear anything after *Willa Mae Tyler is home*. It was a day for miracles, unimagined miracles! Her heart skipped so hard, she unwittingly put a hand over it, warming to the realization that Willa was alive, alive and home, so close after so long parted.

Just then Pitty Pat came running up with a dog filling her arms. "Surry, this is . . . this is my puppy . . . and I . . . and I named him Free," Pitty Pat announced, out of breath.

Another miracle! The puppy had grown, but Surry recognized it as the same puppy Pitty Pat had run out into the road to save right before she'd been picked up by the Confederates. Surry took the dog from Pitty Pat and hugged it close. The sandy-colored mutt licked Surry's face, at the same time squirming to be put down. Surry let him go, watching him scamper off, free to roam where he would.

She was free, too. Free to walk out in the open toward Willa's farmhouse.

A day for miracles, indeed.

CHAPTER SEVENTEEN

"Who's that knocking?" Litha Mae, busy making breakfast, set her skillet back on the cast-iron stove. She exchanged nervous glances with James, watching as he went to the fireplace, took down his rifle and walked to the door. They both thought the same thing. Soldiers. It could be soldiers.

Another knock, this one louder.

James looked over his shoulder, first at his wife and then at Willa, who was sleeping in the rocker next to the cradle. She'd been up half the night with Adam. He'd caught cold, scaring Willa to death. They'd both only just fallen into peaceful sleep.

"Willa! Willa!"

James recognized the female voice. He quickly set his rifle down, not needing it this time. This time there were no slave catchers giving chase. Now Surry Lion was free and home safe. *If this don't beat all.* James was so happy to know that Seth Lion's daughter was all right, he almost forgot to open the door.

Surry stood on the porch, edgy as could be. The last time she'd pounded on the Tylers' door, she and Penny had been running for their lives. She remembered the sound of the slave catcher's dogs that awful night, barking wildly, coming closer, ready to rip into her and her brother and sisters. The only dogs at her feet now were Willa's family pets, licking Surry's hands, their tails wagging in excitement.

James opened the door.

Skipper and Roscoe rushed inside.

Surry didn't move.

"You don't need an invite, Surry Lion. Come on in," James greeted her genuinely.

About to explode with anticipation, Surry gingerly stepped over the threshold, spotting Willa's mother and not Willa.

"You're a sight for sore eyes." Litha Mae rushed over to Surry and took up her hands. "It's a blessing you're all right. Is your brother come back with you, too, and your sisters? Are they all right?"

"Yes, ma'am," Surry answered mindlessly, seeing Willa for the first time, still asleep. "Is . . . is Willa all right?"

"Yes, dear," Litha Mae reassured her. "She's just been up most of the night with her son. He's ailing with a cold."

"Her son," Surry repeated, as if in church. "Adam, isn't it?"

"Yes, dear." Litha Mae guided a stiff Surry over to her daughter. "Go on, now, wake her up. This will be better than any present on Christmas morning," she said, beaming.

Surry looked at James and then at Litha Mae, wanting to make sure it was all right to wake up their sleeping daughter.

They both nodded their encouragement.

Surry turned back to Willa and knelt down beside the rocker. She peered over the cradle's edge and saw little Adam, sleeping soundly. He was beautiful, absolutely and positively beautiful. Choking back tears, Surry reached for Willa's hand. "Willa," she whispered so not to wake the baby. "Willa, it's Surry."

Willa stirred, believing herself to be dreaming. Only in dreams could she hear Surry's voice. Only in dreams could she imagine Surry talked to her, trying to get her attention.

"Willa?" Surry said again.

Willa shut her eyes tighter, wanting to stay in her dream, feeling herself being pulled out of it. She didn't want to wake up. She wanted to stay with Surry, if only for a little while longer.

"Surry, where are you?" Willa mumbled, restlessly turning in the rocker.

"I'm here, Willa. Here." Surry squeezed Willa's hand once, then again, harder.

Willa's eyes flew open. She blinked several times, then sat up straight, unconsciously shooing Surry's hand away. What evil trickery, what madness was this? At once she peered over the cradle at Adam. He certainly was real enough. But, surely, Surry was not. This could not be.

"It *is* me, Willa. I'm as real as your son. I didn't mean to scare you," Surry consoled, fighting tears and new fears that Willa didn't want to see her. She backed away from Willa a little. Maybe Willa didn't want a colored girl for friend anymore, even a free colored girl.

Willa shot out of the rocker.

Almost knocked over, Surry quickly stood.

Adam began to fuss.

Litha Mae came round the side of the cradle and took up her grandson, and walked over to the other side of the room. James went with her.

Willa stared wide-eyed at Surry in disbelief, her mouth agape.

Surry started to laugh, more to ease the tension inside her than anything else. But Willa did look so funny, her mouth open like a silly ole catfish.

Willa clamped her mouth shut; then started to laugh herself. "It *is* you," she blurt out. "It truly is," she said more quietly, her smile gone, tears beginning to well.

Surry started to cry, too.

In the next moment they fell into each other's arms, hugging each other tight, dancing around, giggling and crying like two schoolgirls. No one could guess, witnessing the two of them, that one had been a hardened soldier and the other a fugitive slave.

Surry was the first to speak. "You're in a dress, Willa Mae Tyler," she couldn't help but tease.

"At least it doesn't smell like catfish," Willa teased back.

"You cut your hair, Willa."

"I had to. Wouldn't fit under my bummer cap," she joked.

"Well, it's growing back very prettily."

Willa grinned. "Surry, I've never been about pretty."

"Me neither," Surry declared.

"You've always been pretty, Surry."

Surry instinctively touched her cheek right over the scar left there by the murderous Boyd Blankenship. She hadn't thought about that scar for a long time. Quick as she'd done it, she took her hand from her face.

"And your hair is as pretty as ever," Willa complimented. "I'll admit, it's longer than mine, but I'll catch up," she promised lightly.

Adam started to fuss. Willa hurried over to take him from her mother, glad he was cool to the touch and seemed to have no fever. "There, there, little one. Guess who's come home to see you? Your aunt Surry, that's who," she cooed, walking over to Surry.

"I'm . . . I'm his Aunt Surry?" Surry choked out, touched by such an honor.

"Well, you could be his godmother if you want. I prefer Aunt Surry, though," Willa teased, handing her now-quiet son over to Surry.

"Hello there, little man," Surry smiled down at Adam, who let her hold him without protest. "I'm your Aunt Surry, and I'm going to tell you all about what a mischief-maker your mother was," she crooned, completely captivated by the smiling, handsome, dark-haired child. He had her heart already. Surry eased down into the rocker with Adam, wondering just who had captured Willa's heart, that they'd created such a miracle together.

"Willa, it's a beautiful day. Let your daddy and me take Adam into Lynchburg with us. Adam is ever so much better now and I think the fresh air would do him good," Litha Mae suggested. "You girls can have a proper visit and Adam can have a nice outing."

"But it's dangerous, Mama. It's dangerous to leave the farm. You sound like there's no war going on. What if you run into soldiers and they give you trouble? What if there's shooting and you all get caught in the crossfire? No, Mama, it's too dangerous. Adam stays home," Willa flatly declared, walking over to Surry and collecting her son.

James set down his pipe. "Willa, girl, your mama and I will look out for Adam real careful. We will. You don't have to think like a soldier anymore, daughter."

"But we still have to defend ourselves, Daddy. Out here, there's no one watching our backs. We have to do it," Willa shot back, although her insides turned at the thought of having to kill again, even in self-defense.

"I know that, daughter. Don't you think I don't know that? This might not be Shiloh or Manassas, but there are battles and skirmishes going on all over the place," James said, unaware he'd raised his voice. "Don't you think I know that? Don't you think I know that our cattle have been confiscated for the army, along with our stores of hay? Don't you think I know that what little food we can grow is taken from us if we don't eat it first? Don't you think I know the Yankees could come here any day and burn our house, or worse? Don't you think I know that our neighbors' children are dying every day, just like Walter and Henry?"

Willa's heart tugged as she listened to her father, knowing how he grieved for Walter and Henry. They all grieved. None of this was easy, especially for her parents. Bringing Adam into their lives brought them joy they'd lost to the war.

By now, Surry had gotten up and come to stand next to Willa. Her heart went out to Willa's parents; it surely did. War meant hardship for them all, no matter if they were colored or white, free or slave. Even though the Tylers supported the South, Surry knew they didn't hold prejudice against her race. Their sons, Willa's brothers, had died fighting for the South. Surry knew that Gus and Silas could die, too, fighting for the North. "Mr. Tyler, Mrs. Tyler," Surry said respectfully. "I'll be going now and will come back another time. I don't want to intrude—"

"You'll do no such a thing!" Litha Mae interrupted, charging over to Willa and taking her grandson in her arms. "Now James and I are going to take Adam, who is fit as a fiddle this morning, into town to check the mail and see about supplies. You two are going to have a nice visit and that's that," she huffed out.

Adam reached up and poked his grandmother's chin.

Everyone laughed at once, the tension let out of the room.

Willa caught her father's eye. "I know that life must go on despite the war, Daddy. I know," she said, her tone gentle. "I want you to take Adam and have as fine a day as you can."

James smiled at Willa and at Surry. "And I want you two to have as fine a day as *you* can and have a good visit. Litha." He turned to his wife. "I'll just go hitch up the wagon, and then we'll be off," he said, as if it were an ordinary day in an ordinary time, with no war hanging over their heads.

"Levi Clement?" Surry couldn't believe it. Willa was in love with the Quaker in Loudoun County who'd helped her and Penny along the Underground Railroad? Such a coincidence deserved Surry's full and undivided attention. Then, with the added coincidence that Levi and Lucas were from the same town. . . . Well, Surry just could not believe it.

"You tell me all about Lucas Minor, this minute, Surry Lion," Willa demanded.

Still open-mouthed at Willa's news, Surry had to hear everything about Willa's life first. "No. You tell me all about Levi Clement first." Surry plopped down in one of Willa's kitchen chairs.

"All right," Willa quickly acquiesced, having wished for such a conversation with Surry for a long time. She'd wanted Surry's counsel, and now she had it. This was a treasured moment, indeed. "I already told you I dressed as a man to muster in and fight. I already told you I was first sent to the Waterford area. What I didn't tell you was that I met Levi Clement at the Friends' meetinghouse when my unit was ordered to bivouac there and store our weapons. Levi found me out right away, Surry. I could tell that he could tell I was a woman-soldier and not a man. He never let on to anybody, far as I know, that I was a woman in disguise."

Surry sat at rapt attention, hanging onto Willa's every word.

"Oh, Surry, he's the most handsome, the most gentle, the most masterful, the most wonderful man I could ever think to meet," Willa said dreamily, her face all a-flush.

"Tell me, tell me," Surry suddenly said. "I want to know every detail about your first meeting and every detail after that," she insisted, curious about Levi and Willa, even a little envious that they'd had a child together; wishing that were the case with her and Lucas.

"I love him so, Surry. I truly do. I never thought to love any boy. You of all people know that."

Surry laughed. "Especially with you wearing pants all the time. I can't believe Levi Clement noticed there was a girl under all that tomboy getup," she teased.

"Surry, it was the most amazing time, the most unbelievable time of my life, when we . . . when we made love," Willa managed to say, embarrassed to discuss such a private moment, even with Surry.

"Even though I'm completely jealous, I want to hear everything about you and Levi," Surry said, her tone light-hearted and good-natured. "If I'm ever lucky enough to have 'the most unbelievable time of my life' with Lucas Minor, I'll tell you everything, too."

"I do want to know all about your Lucas." Willa put a hand to the table in front of Surry.

"He's not my Lucas," Surry corrected. "But I will tell you all about him after you finish," Surry persisted, folding her arms across her chest, ready to listen.

"The first time I joined in the fight," Willa began, sitting back against her chair, looking at Surry but seeing only the blood of war on her hands. "The first time I'd had to kill, I remember finding my way back to camp, and to Catoctin Creek, and to Levi. He rescued me from the horror of that awful battle. He did that and so much more. That's when I knew for sure I loved him, Surry. It truly is," Willa said wistfully, hugging her middle now, remembering Levi's touch, his essence, his whiskered cheek, his warm, passionate kisses, his body joined with hers.

"And?" Surry said, anxious for Willa to continue.

"And," Willa parroted, forcing herself back to the moment, continuing her story, intent now on telling Surry everything.

"Mercy sakes, Willa, you had Adam out on the battlefield at Harper's Ferry?" Surry was incredulous.

Willa grinned, inside and out, glad to have finished her love story. The ending was already written, and it wasn't a happy ending, not really. While it was wonderful to have Adam, the light of her life, it wasn't wonderful that she and Levi would never end up happily ever after. He was married to someone else. He wasn't free. He didn't want her, anyway. "All right,

Surry, it's your turn," Willa pointedly said, wanting to change the subject away from Levi and onto Lucas Minor.

Surry's gut wrenched, upset for Willa that Levi was already married. She feared the same about Lucas. Surry wanted to tell Willa about Lucas, yet dreaded it all the same. She'd convinced herself he must be married to someone else by now and not free to marry her. Besides, he hadn't kept her from leaving him last year. He could have stopped her.

Surry's heart hurt. She knew the reason he hadn't stopped her was for her own good. Deep down, she knew that to be true. But still, if only Lucas had said something, *anything,* about his feelings during the week they'd known each other, oh, how sweet such a memory would be. Easing back against her chair, Surry heaved a sigh and at last began.

"Penny and I were waiting at the edge of the woods for our next conductor on the Underground Railroad to find us and take us to the next safe station. Penny was sick with fever and we were both covered in poison ivy. I was so scared for her. But then . . . well, then the most handsome, the most gentle, the most masterful, the most wonderful man I could ever think to meet found us," Surry said dreamily, unaware she'd repeated Willa's exact description of Levi.

Willa smiled at her dear friend. Surry was in love with Lucas, all right; same as she was with Levi. Willa would listen intently to Surry's every word. Maybe for dear Surry there would be a happily ever after. If Willa could do anything to make that happen, she surely would.

Levi pulled up his horse just outside Culpeper. He wished now he'd heeded Jonah's advice and bypassed the area entirely. He eased his horse back into the copse of trees, wanting to stay out of sight. The moment he'd come over the last rise, he'd spotted the troops, Confederate troops, thousands of them, camped in the fields around Culpeper. He pulled back farther into the trees, buying time, trying to figure what to do. Ruled by his emotions, wanting to get to Willa any way he could as fast as he could, he hadn't been cautious enough. For the first time since he'd set out from his farm for Willa's, he was scared he might not get to her if he was caught. His heart thudded in his chest, and every muscle in his body was alerted to danger. He'd known the risks, but they hadn't seemed to matter much until now. Faced with the barrier of so many Confederate troops, he needed to find an escape, and quick.

The image of Willa holding their son clouded his vision and his thoughts. All he could see was them. All he wanted was to get to them. Dear God, was that so much to ask? Levi slipped off his black, broad-brimmed hat, needing to pray. He closed his eyes and imagined himself at meeting, waiting for his Inner Spirit to speak to him, to lead him, to guide him. He shut out everything else, craving the silence he needed to better hear the Word.

"Get down from that horse, *now*," a gravelly voice commanded.

Levi opened his eyes and looked straight into the rifle barrel pointed at him, damning himself for letting this happen and getting caught.

"I said *now*," the stone-faced Confederate soldier spat out.

Levi replaced his hat and slid off his horse. More soldiers rode up, easily surrounding him.

"Put those hands up and keep 'em up!" the same soldier yelled.

Levi kept his eye on the wary soldier and the gun pointed at him. He knew the scruffy, worn-out-looking soldier could just as easily kill him as not. The rules of war governed everything these days, conscience be gone. All of the soldiers surrounding him breathed in the winds of war, only them and not any gentle breeze of peace. If the one gun pointed at him didn't kill him, another would. Levi's gut turned in determination. He *couldn't* let himself be killed, not now, not when he was so close to finding Willa and his son.

Of their own volition, his eyes shut and he began to pray for strength and the Way to break free from this stranglehold the war had on him. He prayed for the strength to hold fast to his peace testimony, his last pure tie to his faith, fighting the desire to fight the soldiers trapping him. Levi prayed harder. He'd do anything for love, but would he kill? Unwittingly he reached inside his heavy broadcloth jacket for the Bible Jonah had given him, needing the Word now more than ever.

"I said hands up!"

Levi opened his eyes. The muzzle of the rifle poked into his chest. Slowly, carefully, he raised his hand back up.

The soldier spat some of his tobacco chew to the ground, but kept his gun on his prisoner. "You some kind of preacher man?" he accused more than asked.

"I'm Quaker," Levi answered.

"They're cowards," one soldier called out.

"Yeah, they don't believe in fightin'!" another gritted out.

Levi's jaw tensed. He'd heard this before. Schoolyard bullies, all of them.

"Is that so, Quaker man?" The soldier with the gun on him poked it harder into his chest. "I think you just might be a spy and not no Quaker," he snarled disrespectfully.

"I'm no spy," Levi said.

"Well, I say you are," the soldier said, poking the rifle barrel harder. "Spies get shot," he said, his tone cold as the grave.

"I'm no spy," Levi repeated, his tone steady.

"C'mon, Gabe, we gotta get goin'," someone said.

"What say we shoot this son of a bitch first?" The soldier, Gabe, stepped back from Levi but didn't take his eyes off him.

"Keep your hands up and walk over yonder so we can all get a good shot at you," he ordered flatly, as if killing the enemy had become routine as filling his boiler cup with coffee.

Levi didn't move, refusing to go willingly. The other soldiers slid out of their saddles and took up their rifles. Just then a bugle call sounded from camp, drawing their attention. Levi bolted then, breaking through their line, and took off in a run.

"Stop, you son of a bitch!" someone shouted at his back.

Levi kept running.

"You bastard coward!" he heard from a rider on horseback, coming up behind him.

"Get him boys!" another yelled.

Levi kept running and running until he couldn't anymore, stopped by a blow from behind and knocked unconscious.

CHAPTER EIGHTEEN

Levi was coming to. Dazed and disoriented, he instinctively tried to bring his hands to his head to stop the pain. His head felt split open. He couldn't move. His hands were tied. He was tied; trussed up like a wild Christmas turkey, shoved in the back of a wagon. Each movement, each new rut hit, scraped against the side of his face, jarring him back to consciousness. The light was poor. He managed to lift his head a little and bring his fuzzy vision into some kind of focus. *Gray.* At first all he could see was a gray blur of arms and legs. He blinked hard through swollen lids. He realized then, he wasn't dead and he wasn't alone.

Someone laughed menacingly. A gray leg shot out and kicked him in the stomach.

Levi's body jackknifed.

"Better get used to that," the same voice taunted. "Where you're goin' you'll need to be tougher than what I see."

Levi tried to sit up, and finally managed to do so. Two Confederate soldiers sat across from him, leaning against the side wagon boards. Their hands were bound behind them, but not their feet. Levi stared at their untied, booted feet, waiting to see if either of them would try to kick him again, still trying to regain full consciousness.

"That's just for starters, what I just done to you."

Levi stared hard at the wild-eyed soldier across from him, no matter that it made his head hurt worse. The soldier looked like he'd been roughed up, too. His grubby, bearded face crooked into a smile. The soldier next to him kept his head hung down, unmoving and saying nothing. Levi could see blood on the soldier's jacket. The wagon jerked over another rut, momentarily breaking Levi's focus. He shoved himself into a corner of the wagon for support.

"No funny moves."

Levi stared at the rifle barrel in front of him, and then at the stone-faced soldier who held it. The guard had appeared out of nowhere.

The soldier who'd kicked Levi snickered.

The big man holding the rifle pointed it at that soldier now. "You shut up," he ordered and jabbed the rifle barrel in the soldier's chest. "You shut up, you yellow-belly, or I'll do it for you."

The soldier stilled and hung his head meekly, same as the man tied next to him.

Levi watched and waited, unable to do much else. He was a prisoner, just like the other two men.

"What are you lookin' at, yellow-belly deserter?" the guard spat out, bringing his rifle back to Levi.

Levi didn't move, but kept his eyes locked on the guard. He refused to hang his head.

"You cowards make my stomach turn," the guard snarled at Levi. "You pretending to be a preacher man or something to get out of fightin' makes me sick." The guard spat in Levi's face.

Levi refused to look away, especially now.

"I'd just as soon shoot the lot of you 'stead of botherin' to take you to Castle Thunder. Hell, you'll die there soon enough anyways." The big guard smirked, seemingly amused by what he'd just said.

Castle Thunder? How far away is Castle Thunder from Bedford County and from Willa? Levi fought to keep his thoughts clear.

He feared that each turn of the wagon wheels took him further away from Willa. "Where is Castle Thunder?" Levi asked.

"You don't know about it, do you? You don't know that it's hell on earth, do you?" The burly guard crouched down to be level with Levi, his gun still ready. "Well, boy, now just why do you need to know? You ain't ever gonna leave there," he said, his tone malevolent.

"Where is it?" Levi repeated.

The guard started to laugh and stood back up. He set his rifle up against the driver's wagon seat, and then turned back to Levi.

Levi watched and waited to hear where Castle Thunder was.

"I'll tell you where it is you're goin'." The guard rubbed his beefy hands together, making fists and cracking his knuckles. "You're going straight to hell in Richmond, boy." And then he buried his fist in Levi's jaw.

Levi braced against the first hit, and the second, fighting with everything in him to remember *Richmond . . . Richmond . . . Richmond . . .* before he lost all consciousness.

"Oh, look, Willa! Adam's taking a step!" Surry called out excitedly.

Willa spat out the clothespins in her mouth and charged through the lines of laundry she'd just hung. Quilts and sheets flapped in the stiff morning breezes. Willa beat past them to reach Surry and her son. The moment she did she fell to her knees alongside Surry, clapping her hands together gleefully at her son's first steps.

Adam toddled over to his mother, his little face all smiles.

"My precious boy." Willa hugged her son tightly, and then gently set him away from her so he could attempt more steps.

"*My* precious nephew," Surry chimed in, her tone lighthearted and full of pride.

Willa hugged Surry, almost knocking the both of them over. They were like two little girls again, as if happy to have finally caught that ever-elusive catfish together.

"Willa Mae Tyler, let go of me," Surry suddenly said. "You'll make me get my skirt and blouse all mussed, and I need to be neat and tidy today."

Willa smiled and plopped down to sit on the cool September grass to watch her son.

"Oh, all right." Surry sat down next to Willa as gingerly as she could, not wanting to wrinkle the new Lindsay-Woolsey skirt she'd just made.

Willa's heart warmed to her forever friend, remembering that time so long ago on the banks of the James when Surry didn't want Willa to get her new dress all fishy-smelling. Surry was going to see her beau, Nate Bonner, later that night.

Nate Bonner was dead now. The truth of the sad events in Surry's life weighed heavily on Willa's heart. At least now Surry was free, and many in her family had survived slavery and the war . . . so far. Maybe, just maybe, Lucas Minor has survived the war so far, too.

It was Willa's dearest hope that Surry would one day end up with the man of her dreams and live a long and happy life in the arms of Lucas Minor. As for herself, Willa knew there could never be any such happy ending for her and Levi Clement. He was married; end of story. It broke her heart that Adam would never know his father. Maybe the right thing to do would be to visit Levi—after the war, of course—and give him an opportunity to know his son. Her heart wrenched, watching little Adam, knowing Levi was missing this wondrous moment in his son's life.

"What has you so sad, Willa? Where's your smile for Adam and his big day?" Surry worried about the turn of Willa's thoughts, guessing correctly where they'd wandered. "Look at your little man." Surry lightly jabbed Willa in the arm. "Next thing you know he'll be running so fast you won't be able to catch him."

Willa smiled again, rescued from her dreary thoughts.

"Don't you even have one word of encouragement for me today, Willa Mae Tyler?" Surry stood up and straightened her skirt.

Willa got up, too, making sure Adam stayed close. "Of course I do, Surry, except you don't need my help anymore as far as schooling. You're the teacher now," Willa pronounced.

"If not for you, I wouldn't be any teacher now and you know it," Surry corrected. "I am anxious to see how many children show up for school. I've put the word out to all of the ex-slave children I could, and we'll see how many actually come today. I'm that appreciative that the Shelbys are letting me use the old sick house for a schoolroom. It cleaned up nicely, and we've built tables and benches, enough for twenty children if need be."

"Surry, I'm so proud of you. How wonderful it is, what you're doing, giving the children an opportunity to learn," Willa said.

"Shucks," Surry tossed out, deliberately using the slang expression, her smile bright.

"I'm being serious, Surry," Willa chided. "You have been through so much, and now look at you. You're going to do so much for others. You've a generous heart, Surry Lion. That you do." Willa nodded to underscore her words.

Surry's smile faded. "I've a good reason for my so-called generous heart now, Willa. I'm free, and bein' free means . . . everything."

Willa understood. Her throat tightened with emotion. She didn't want to cry, not now, not in front of Surry on Surry's big day. Surry was free, but she didn't have everything in life, not yet. She didn't have the man of her dreams. Jolted by the thought, Willa suddenly wondered if she should write to Lucretia Clement in Waterford and perhaps inquire about Lucas Minor. She didn't dare think of mentioning Lucretia's brother Jonah. By now, the army would have told the family that Jonah had fallen at Manassas.

Her heart sank at the thought of Jonah dying and how the Clements must have grieved. Doing her best to think of the living, and of helping Surry, Willa tried to focus on her letter to ask after Lucas. There was only Lucretia to ask. Willa couldn't write to Levi; not with him married. There was no one else in Waterford Willa knew or who might even answer her query. Lucretia knew Surry, and Lucretia might be able to help her and give Willa information about Lucas. What with the war and communication being sparse at best, still . . . Willa thought she should try to write to Lucretia. Yes, she surely would. This very day, in fact.

Adam toddled back to Surry and Willa, unsteady on his feet, but still able to keep standing. The moment he ran into their skirts he turned himself around and started off again.

Willa and Surry laughed out loud, both marveling at how well little Adam took to walking.

"I'm off now, too, Willa. I don't want to be late for my first day of school."

Willa hugged Surry for luck. "Have a wonderful First Day," she said, only afterwards realizing she'd used a Quaker reference. First Day was Sunday, and this wasn't Sunday, but it was Surry's first day of her job as an official teacher. Willa thought of Levi and wished with all her heart she hadn't. Still, there was nothing to be done for it. She had to write to his sister and find out about Lucas Minor for Surry's sake. No matter that writing to Waterford would be a reminder that she'd never be with the man of her dreams, ever again. She had to do this for Surry.

"I'll come by tomorrow and give you a full report," Surry

told Willa, and then walked over to little Adam and gave him a kiss on the top of his dark head of hair.

Adam protested, apparently not wanting anyone to stop him from his new-found-fun of walking.

Willa scooped him up in her arms then. "Wave bye-bye to your Aunt Surry, Adam," she instructed and raised his hand in a waving motion.

"Bh-bh," Adam dribbled out, and waved his chubby little hand on his own. "Bh-bh," he muttered again, smiling brightly at his Aunt Surry.

Surry's heart melted. She waved back. "Bye-bye, little man. Bye-bye," she said again, then turned and quickly made her way down the lane and onto the road leading to her plantation school.

Willa kissed her son on his apple cheek and then whisked him inside the house. She had a letter to write.

Willa didn't mind heading into Lynchburg on foot. It was a pleasant-enough day, and her parents would take good care of her son. The exercise would do her good, too. For some unexplainable reason, she didn't think about any dangers along the road or of meeting up with soldiers. She had the letter on her mind, the letter she'd just written to Lucretia Clement. It was addressed to General Delivery in Waterford, and Willa hoped that would suffice and her letter would be delivered successfully. The mail anywhere was sketchy at best.

The last time she'd traveled to Lynchburg, it had been on horseback, a lifetime ago it seemed. That's when Willa found out that Walter and Henry had been killed at Manassas. That was before she'd mustered into the army. That was before she'd killed . . . and killed . . . trying to avenge her brothers' deaths. That was before she'd been consumed with hate for the Yankee enemy. Now, walking briskly along the road into the city, dressed in a dress as was fitting, she couldn't muster hate for anyone on either side of the war.

She loved the South, but she understood the northern cause and couldn't hate them for it. Surry was free now. The North had freed Surry, not her beloved South or her beloved Virginia. The war confused her nowadays. She saw no clear lines between friend and foe. All she could see clearly was the blood being spilled on both sides. It broke her heart over and over every day, and would until the war ended. God only knew when that would be.

After a two-hour walk, Willa made it to the post office in Lynchburg. Anxious to mail her letter, she hoped she had enough money with her. She had a twenty-five-cent bill in her pocket, printed in Richmond, Virginia, dated April 14, 1862. Her father had some of the printed Confederate money, and Willa hoped it would be acceptable currency in Lynchburg.

Carefully removing her letter from another pocket, Willa handed it and the twenty-five-cent bill to the postmaster.

"Here, miss," the postmaster said, giving her two ten-cent bills in change through the cage window.

Relieved to have her letter to Lucretia Clement posted, Willa turned to leave.

"Oh, miss," the postmaster called out.

Willa immediately pivoted and slowly re-approached the window cage.

"You're Willa Mae Tyler?" The wiry postmaster stared out over his spectacles.

"Ye-yes," she answered haltingly.

"I have something for you. It's been here a spell," he added, and passed the sealed letter under the window cage.

Willa couldn't imagine who would be writing any letter to her. The last time she'd received a letter here, it was to tell her about Walter and Henry. There was no one else in the family off to war, yet she was scared to death to take the letter. It couldn't be good news. It just couldn't be.

"Miss," the postmaster said. "I don't have all day. Ya'll take your letter. There's someone in line behind you."

Willa slowly crooked her head and saw that there was, indeed, someone behind her. She turned back to her letter and reluctantly picked it up. Without seeing who it was from, she pocketed the letter and quickly exited the post office. The letter settled in her dress pocket like a dead weight. She wanted to take it out and throw it away. She hated that she was such a coward. Maybe the news wasn't bad. Soldiers walked past her on the street, dressed in Confederate gray. That didn't matter to Willa; she had to look for a place to sit and read her letter. She must, whether she wanted to or not. Spotting a park of sorts to one side of the cotton mill she'd just passed, she found a bench and sat down. Her palms were damp with nervous sweat. She wiped them on the skirt of her dress and then removed the letter from her pocket, at once trying to bring her vision into focus.

The letter was from Jonah Clement! Jonah didn't die!

Willa's hands went to her mouth in surprise, the letter dropping into her lap. Jonah Clement managed to survive Manassas. Such a miracle. Stunned by the revelation, Willa didn't think about why Jonah might be writing her. Moments later, she did. Slowly, cautiously, she took the letter back up in her hands and opened the envelope. Her heart beat wildly in her chest, fearing the unknown. She forced herself to read Jonah's words:

Dear Willa Mae Tyler,

I survived because of thee and thy ribbon. I'm home now in Loudoun County because of thee. There are no words to thank thee for thy kindness.

I will ever be thy servant in this life. I lost part of my leg, but the rest of me is just fine. Waste no time in pitying me. I'm a whole man in my heart and mind and have thee to thank, only thee.

I must ask thee now to prepare for my words.

Willa swallowed hard, filled with dread. Yet she'd no choice and had to read on.

This is about Levi. Thee must know as I know that my brother loved thee.

Dear God in Heaven. Jonah said *loved.* Hard to see through the tears already stinging her eyes, it was all Willa could do to read on.

When I returned from the war, I told Levi about how thee had saved me. I gave Levi thy green ribbon to prove it. Thee needs to know that Levi and Comfort divorced. The details are not important now.

Shocked, Willa tried to comprehend what she read. Levi wasn't married anymore, and him a Quaker . . . divorced. The news didn't sink in. Jonah had said *loved.*

I told my brother that thee carried his child. I told Levi about Adam. When I did, Willa, Levi couldn't get to thee and his son fast enough.

He set out for Bedford County as Lucretia said it's thy home. Levi set out for Bedford County to fetch thee and Adam and bring thee both home, here to Loudoun County. This is the sad news I must share, Willa. Levi was to telegraph me from Lynchburg when he arrived safely. That was almost three months ago. I fear, as does our family, that Levi has met with an untimely death. War being war, my brother must have been killed, either by accident or on purpose.

Willa's hands shook, making it hard to hold the letter. What she read couldn't be so. No, it couldn't be. Yet, her hands shook. The very core of her being shook. Somehow, she read on.

I am writing thee to make sure thee knows that my brother loved thee and his son. If he could have, he would have found thee. It is this that I wish thee to know. Our family grieves for Levi, but we rejoice in the birth of his son. Thee is not Quaker but thee and thy son will always be in our hearts and prayers.

I am sorry to have brought thee this sad news.

With thee in grief,
Jonah Clement
Waterford, Loudoun County, Virginia

With thee in grief, Willa read again. *With thee in grief.* The mind-numbing truth of Jonah's news about Levi, about Levi dying somewhere between his home and hers, refused to sink in. She couldn't let it. She wouldn't.

Mechanically folding the letter and replacing it in its envelope, she put the letter back in her pocket and sat on the unforgiving iron bench, staring straight ahead at nothing. The noontime sun did little to warm the deadly chill slicing through her shaken body. She hugged her arms around herself and stood.

It would take two hours to walk home. She must start out now. Willa looked in all directions, trying to remember which way to go. Which way was the way home? For the life of her, she couldn't remember why she couldn't remember. Of their own volition, her feet started to take steps along the James. She stared into the dark waters, watching the powerful current ebb and flow, fighting the urge to slip into the inviting water. But it would feel, oh, so wonderful to disappear into nothingness; surely it would. The dark waters called to her, drawing her in.

Willa stumbled over the rocks along the riverbank, mindless of impediments. She thought she heard gunfire and instinctively crouched down, waiting for the all clear. Men lay dead around her, so many wounded, so many hurting. She must get them all into the water where they'd be safe from harm.

One reached for her arm. "There, there," she consoled, crawling to the water, tugging the wounded soldier. Blood ran everywhere. The thick red ooze coated her hands, her face, her whole body, weighing her down, slowing her progress to the water. Willa fought her panic. The soldier still had a hold on her, then another grabbed on, then another, and then everything went dark and deathly quiet. And, then, blessed oblivion.

CHAPTER NINETEEN

Levi eased his right arm up enough to see if his shoulder was re-broken or not. He worked through the pain, intent on getting his arm moving again. His filthy, bloodied shirt chafed against his torn skin. Accustomed to his wounds, he knew he was one of the lucky ones kept prisoner in Palmer's Factory at Castle Thunder in Richmond. He was still alive.

There were hundreds and hundreds of other prisoners, yet many others had died since he'd been there. The men jailed with him were hardened to the core. Levi would hear someone callously yell out that "A fellow here wants to get his discharge," when a man died. Life in the prison meant daily brutality for the Union prisoners of war and deserters held along with him. It went especially badly for prisoners believed to be spies or criminals. Levi was neither, but it made little difference to the war-hardened guards.

From being let out in the exercise yard by the latrines, in the common area of the prison, Levi knew all about the other two buildings inside the fenced compound that made up Castle Thunder. Gleanor's Tobacco Factory was the largest hold where Confederate army deserters and political prisoners were kept. The other smaller building was Whitlock's Warehouse. That's where they kept women and Negro prisoners. His insides turned when he thought of what might have happened to Willa if she'd been captured as a spy or a prisoner of war and put into Whitlock's Warehouse.

He held on to the fact that she was not in prison in Richmond, but in Bedford County with their son. He refused to think that she was anywhere else but safe on her family farm. He refused to think that something might have happened to her and his son along the way and that they might not have made it to safety. The only thing that kept Levi going, the only thing that kept him alive in this hellhole and stirred his broken body to move another day, was his belief that Willa and Adam were all right and were waiting for him to come and fetch them and take them home to Loudoun County.

How much time had gone by? Eight weeks? Twelve? Levi couldn't remember anymore. Most every day he was dragged out of his communal cell and beaten by the guards. They would spit on him for being a Yankee spy or call him a coward or just hit him to occupy their time. Levi took their punishment and didn't fight back or utter a word of complaint. This angered the guards, he knew. They wanted him to cry out in pain, but he wouldn't give them the satisfaction. Most times he'd just pass out from the beatings and wake up in his cell on the cold, unforgiving, stone floor.

The other prisoners never had much to say. For some inexplicable reason they didn't start fights with him, almost as if they had a grudging respect for his ability to withstand the frequent beatings. Sometimes he'd overhear other prisoners plotting their escape, but there was no escaping Castle Thunder. Too many guard boxes dotted the surrounding walls. No one got out alive. Prisoners either died from malnutrition and disease, from brutality, or were shot trying to escape.

Determined to stay alive until he could figure a way to get free, Levi ate the maggot-infested bread and graying bits of dried meat and did what he could to get fresh water to drink. It was up to the guards to dole out fresh water, and Levi usually didn't get his fair share. He'd taken to asking other prisoners for a bit of their water and sometimes they actually gave him a drink from their tin cup. Not too proud to take their help, Levi needed to stay alive to get to Willa and Adam. One thing Levi had in his favor: at six foot five and well-muscled, he could withstand the lack of decent food and brutal beatings better than most jailed at Castle Thunder. He'd wasted away to a point but still had some muscle left for the fight he needed to get free. The way of it in prison for many was kill or be killed. No one had killed Levi yet, and he hadn't killed anybody . . . yet. He wondered if he could if pressed. He knew he'd have to fight his way out of Castle Thunder. He didn't know if he'd have to kill to do it. Despite becoming hardened himself in the brutal prison, having to break with his long-held peace testimony was the only thing that struck fear in Levi's heart.

Today he was more afraid than ever. Today he'd make his break.

A new guard had taken over his cell block, a dark-haired, bearded guard who appeared to be about Levi's size and his height. The other prisoners had been taken out to the exercise yard and Levi was alone in his cell. He'd just been thrown back in the cell after his interrogation and beating. He hadn't lost consciousness this time. If he had, his plan wouldn't work. He waited for the guard to approach, praying with everything in him that the guard would come soon, before the other prisoners returned. Levi's window of opportunity to escape wasn't much, but it was all he had.

The door to the cell block creaked open and then shut hard, the loud, iron clang reverberating throughout the damp, drafty enclosure. Levi lay down on the stone floor as if passed out. He waited. His only chance was to wait, to be patient and not make any mistakes.

The guard unlocked Levi's cell door and came inside.

Levi lay still as the grave.

The guard walked over to Levi and nudged his side with his booted foot. "Are you dead yet, fella? I cain't figure why you're not dead yet. You're either a coward or a spy, and I'd kill you myself if I get the chance. Ain't no way you're no man of the cloth, pretending to be a preacher man to get out of fightin'. You make me sick." The guard jabbed Levi again with his boot.

Levi felt spittle on his face and made sure he didn't flinch.

He waited . . . just waited.

The moment he knew the guard turned his back, Levi leapt up and put his muscle-tensed arm around the guard's throat, pressing tight to cut off all air and force the man to pass out. The move had been done to him enough times during his torture for him to know it should work. The big guard struggled, but Levi's strength proved too much, and the man soon slipped to the floor. Levi worked quickly, removing the guard's clothes, making sure to take his ring of keys, too. Before Levi stripped out of his filthy, torn remnants, he took Willa's ribbon from his shirt pocket. Jonah's Bible had been taken from him, but not Willa's ribbon. He'd managed to keep it hidden.

Levi changed into the guard's Confederate uniform: boots, hat and all. Everything fit all right and shouldn't draw any notice. He dressed the still-unconscious guard in his own clothing and left the man on the floor, on his side with his back to the door so no one would think anything different when they returned.

In the next second Levi had the door to the cell locked shut and the main door to the cell block, too. He charged along the dark passage, knowing the way to the exercise yard. Once outside, he walked swiftly along one side of the yard, to the gate near the latrines. The back gate was the only way out. Levi had been watching it for weeks. Whenever a guard approached it, another armed guard would unlock the gate and let the guard through, no questions asked. Levi had seen this done over and over. He didn't chance looking out over the yard now, not want-ing any of his cell mates to recognize him. When he reached the gate he stood there and waited, his determined heart steady and his breathing sure.

"Hey there, soldier. I never seen you before. Where ya'll go-ing in such an all-fired hurry?"

Levi didn't falter. He instinctively put his hand over one side of his face, as if in pain.

"Bad tooth, huh? Going to the medic?"

Levi nodded yes.

"Hope he fixes you up. Take a good swig of John Barleycorn before they tie that string to your tooth and yank it out," the guard joked, and then laughed out loud.

Levi moaned, indicating he'd do just that.

"Take the quick way to the medic and don't go out the main gate but the one here, yonder," the guard said, pointing to another gate in the very back of the fenced compound. "You're new so you likely don't know the guard there. Just tell him I sent you. Tell him Jasper sent you, and look this way and I'll give you a thumbs-up. We're not supposed to be using that gate, but the guard there knows me and he'll let you."

Levi couldn't believe his good luck. He did just as Jasper instructed, and before he knew it, he was outside the fenced compound, outside the dreaded, deadly Castle Thunder, free to walk the streets of Richmond. He was free to escape Richmond and get to Bedford County and find Willa and his son!

On provost duty in Baltimore city, Lucas chomped at the bit to fight. God, how he wished he'd been at Gettysburg in Pennsyl-vania to help turn back General Lee or at Fort Wagner in South Carolina in July with the 54th Massachusetts. Half of the six hundred colored troops in the 54th had made it out alive. Even if he'd gone to Glory with those killed, he surely would be happier than he was here, on provost duty in Maryland. Lucas felt far away from the war and he hated it. Let some other unit besides his 19th regiment keep the watch in Baltimore City, and let his unit be sent to the fight.

As it stood he, along with colored recruits from southern cities in Maryland and the eastern shore, were stationed in Baltimore City. His captain had taken sick a few months back and died from it, was all Lucas knew. Lucas had liked the captain, respecting him above all others, and wished the captain could have fallen in battle and not from illness. If his captain still lived, Lucas believed he could get the transfer he so desperately wanted.

Lucas had even thought of deserting and joining up somewhere else, but he'd be tracked down soon enough. He'd thought of leaving and going home. Hell, he'd likely be caught and shot as a coward. He wasn't any coward. He was a proud soldier in the United States Colored Troops, and wanted only to serve his country and his people. Some of his people were free now. Those in the southern states were free. By God and by damn, Lucas wanted to fight the enemy until *all* the slaves in *all* the states were free. He wanted something else even worse: to see Surry Lion at least one more time before dying for his country and his people.

It made him crazy worrying and wondering where Surry was and how she was. His insides churned every time he thought of the beautiful runaway slave. What if she'd met someone? What if she'd gone and married another man? A girl as beautiful as she wouldn't be waiting for him come the end of the war. No sir. No way. Despite the truth of it, that Surry wouldn't be free to marry him if he survived the war, Lucas daydreamed about her anyway. He imagined her lustrous, dark eyes shining for him, her soft, ripe lips opening for his kiss, her sweet and smooth-as-honey skin begging to be tasted. He dreamed of her long hair curling over her shoulders and shimmering down her slender back, waiting for his touch. He imagined her as his and it made him crazy. Crazy for her.

Aw hell. There was nothing to do but keep at his post in Baltimore City and wait for any opportunity to join in the fight to end slavery. At least he could fight and help make the country a better place for Surry to live in; a place where she'd know freedom and be safe at last; thank God Almighty, safe at last.

Willa regained consciousness on the hard ground. Men bent over her, all soldiers in gray jackets with gray faces. She'd tried to save her comrades and take them with her into the river. Had she saved them from her nightmare that Levi was dead? Searing pain shot through Willa's heart. It was the pain of death. Levi's death. She struggled to remember what had just happened to her at the river's edge. When she did remember, she wished she hadn't.

By accident or on purpose, Jonah had said in his letter. Either way, Levi was dead.

"Let's get you up, miss." One of the soldiers put a hand under her back and helped her to stand. Another soldier flanked her other side, his arm out to help steady her.

"You all right?" someone else asked.

Her knees buckled.

The soldiers quickly re-steadied her.

Her legs didn't want to support her. Her head spun. She wanted to slip away, yearning for the sleep of death, yearning to be with Levi in heaven. She could see him so clearly, waiting for her. How handsome. How tall. How welcoming. But no. He wasn't beckoning for her to come to him, but motioning for her to stay with their son. Adam. Remembering Adam kept Willa on her feet and stopped her from breaking free of the soldiers and disappearing into the dark waters of the James. She had to get home to her son. A part of Levi lived in her son. She must get home to Adam. Willa easily shrugged off the holds on her and started walking down the street, sure of the way home.

"Miss, let us take you home," one of the soldiers called out, and soon caught up with her.

Willa slowed her step but kept on walking. "I'm all right. Thank you for your help. I'm all right, and I know the way home," she said, and picked up her step again.

The soldier didn't pursue her.

She picked up her step even more, trying to stay ahead of the tears rising up inside her. As fast as hot tears rained down, she'd wipe them away, doing battle with the place in her heart that gave her a reason for being, the place where she'd kept Levi safely hidden. That place inside her was empty now but for a sea of tears, hot, horrible, heart-wrenching tears.

Willa ran now, as fast as she could. She ran until she'd cleared the city of Lynchburg, until she'd made it down a good stretch of the dirt road home. She ran until she collapsed in an exhausted, grief-stricken heap in the road, the reality of Levi's death catching up with her. She let herself cry openly then.

"Thank you for coming, Surry," Litha Mae soberly greeted, then ushered Surry inside the Tyler farmhouse.

"Where is Willa, Mrs. Tyler?"

Little Adam toddled up to Surry, beaming at his aunt.

Surry bent down and picked him up. "Such a good boy," she cooed and kissed his warm cheeks. She hugged him tight until he protested, then set him back down on the floor to play.

"Willa's in her bedroom, Surry. She's been there since she got home yesterday evening," Litha Mae told her, taking Surry's arm to direct her toward the closed door. "Willa hasn't had anything to eat or drink, and I'm not sure she's slept a wink."

Surry mutely nodded and reached for the door handle.

"You might want to read this first, Surry."

Surry pivoted around, seeing a letter in Litha Mae's outstretched hand. Reluctantly, Surry accepted the letter. She didn't have to read it. She knew that Levi Clement was dead. She knew that Willa wished herself dead, too. Surry had grieved along with Willa the moment Mr. Tyler had come to the plantation to let Surry know what had happened.

Willa had been through so much, first losing her brothers, then fighting in the war, then meeting and falling in love with Levi, then managing to carry their babe to term and give birth to him in the middle of a battlefield, bearing up despite the fact that Levi was married to another woman, only to be forced to endure the news of Levi's death. Surry's heart clinched. She felt so sad and so ill-prepared to give her forever friend encouragement in this dark moment.

"I'm taking Adam to the barn. James is there. You go on in with Willa now, Surry. She needs you," Litha Mae said, choking back tears.

Surry nodded her acknowledgment and then turned toward the bedroom door, taking great care to place the folded letter in her skirt pocket. Swallowing hard for courage, she turned the cold metal handle and opened the door, then slipped inside the bedroom. It was quiet as a tomb and almost as dark. Surry walked right past the bed to the room's only window and opened the shutters. Sunlight poured inside.

"No. Don't," Willa whispered feebly.

Surry took deliberate steps to Willa, who was lying faceup, fully dressed, with her hands folded over her chest as if the undertaker had placed them so. Her tear-soaked face was red and her eyes puffy and swollen. Surry eased herself down on the bed and caught Willa's cold hands in hers. She immediately started rubbing them to help Willa get warm.

Willa turned her head to look at Surry.

"I know," was all Surry could think to say. "I know."

Willa grasped Surry's fingers hard. "Surry, stay with me. Please," she whispered pitifully.

Surry lay down next to Willa and then took her in her arms, much as a mother would a child. "There, there," Surry tried to soothe as she rocked Willa. "There, there."

Levi found what fresh water he could in streams, but not much food. Berries were scarce and the forests gave up little else. He could try to hunt for rabbit or squirrel, or even a fowl, but he didn't want to waste his energy. He'd been on the move since he escaped Castle Thunder days ago and wouldn't stop for anything but hiding from troops he encountered, no matter their colors. Forced to stop at those times, he couldn't risk being captured and sent back to prison. He'd be executed for certain, no questions asked this time. Still clad in the uniform he'd used for his escape, Levi looked like any other Confederate soldier, with two exceptions: he was more unkempt than most, and he wasn't with any unit and, therefore, could easily be pegged as a deserter.

Getting to Willa and Adam—he had the way fixed in his memory—kept Levi going despite his hunger and exhausted state. Weak from malnutrition, poor sanitation, sleep deprivation, months of brutality, and consumed with worry for Willa and his son, Levi knew he needed to keep going, no matter what. In the recesses of his mind he knew his family back home must believe him dead by now. As soon as he could, he'd contact them. He remembered, he was supposed to have telegraphed Jonah from Lynchburg.

I have to find Willa first. . . . His troubled thoughts trailed off. He hadn't prayed in a long time, having almost given up on God. Almost. Somewhere between escaping Richmond and being on the run, Levi realized God was within; the Word was within. Levi struggled to find the Light within and gather the strength he needed for the fight of his life: finding Willa and his son.

Hidden in the underbrush on the outskirts of Lynchburg, relieved he'd at last made it to the port city along the James, Levi couldn't risk going into the city and finding a telegraph office. He hated that he couldn't telegraph Jonah yet. He might be spotted and arrested.

No, he couldn't risk going into Lynchburg. *Willa first . . . Willa first. . . .* The mantra played out in his head. Dizzy from exhaustion and run-down from his still-healing wounds, Levi had trouble standing and keeping his footing. He shook his head hard, needing to think straight. It was just after dawn, and he had enough light to see his way. He'd search out every farmhouse between Lynchburg and Liberty until he found the right one. Until he found Willa.

James Tyler set down his hoe and picked up his rifle, fixing the approaching stranger in his sights. He could see now that the man was a Confederate soldier. James always kept his rifle handy when he was away from the farmhouse. Too many horror stories had made their way to his kitchen table, stories of houses ransacked, livestock taken, women molested, and families killed. No, sir, he wasn't going to let any soldier, Yankee or Confederate, harm his family. Willa had finally gotten past the news that Levi Clement was dead and was trying to get back to some kind of normal life. Hah. His gut turned. Nobody could lead any kind of normal life until the war ended. No telling when that would be.

The soldier came closer.

Skipper and Roscoe barked wildly and circled the soldier as he walked.

James readied his rifle, the tall Confederate still in his sights.

The morning sun disappeared behind a cloud. James waited to be sure of his shot. The scruffy-looking, bearded soldier didn't appear to have a gun. In fact, the soldier looked sick, real sick. James relaxed his trigger finger and let the soldier come closer. "Hold up there!" he called out over Skipper and Roscoe's barking.

Mindless of the dogs at his heels, Levi saw the gun pointed at him. He heard the man tell him to hold up and so he did. He couldn't risk getting shot and killed, not when he was so close to Willa.

"You, there, what do you want?" James yelled. The ragtag Confederate had stopped a good twenty yards away. Able to get a better glimpse now, James thought the soldier looked close to death and lowered his rifle.

Levi's mouth felt like cotton. He tried to moisten his chapped, cut lips but couldn't. Swallowing past a dry, raw throat, he needed to answer the farmer before he got shot. "I-I want to find . . . to find Willa Mae Tyler," he shouted with everything left in him. Close to passing out, feeling his body weave and his mind cloud, he forced himself to stay upright.

"Who are you?" James instinctively demanded.

"Le-Levi Clement," Levi managed to answer.

James let his rifle fall to the ground and hurried to Levi. Willa's Levi.

Dazed but on his feet still, Levi breathed easier when the farmer dropped his rifle.

"Son, you're *Levi Clement?*" James repeated in disbelief.

Levi nodded, blinking hard to keep his vision in some kind of focus.

"Then you've found Willa Mae Tyler. She's my daughter," James reassured Levi hoarsely, his throat tight with emotion.

"She is thy daughter?" Levi felt the hand of God reach out to him and to Willa in that moment, guiding them both out of the wilderness and showing them the way home, the way home to each other. Overcome with relief that Willa hadn't died in the war but was home, here, Levi almost collapsed to the ground.

James caught Levi and helped him stand. "Son, I'm going to get my wagon and take you to the house. You sit down here and wait, all right?"

"No," Levi squared his shoulders and shook off the help offered. "I'm going with . . . with thee." It took effort to talk, but not to start walking. Suddenly infused with the energy he needed to reach Willa, he felt blood pump through his heart again and out to every vein in his body, keeping him on his feet.

"All right, son," James reluctantly agreed, and walked alongside Levi, finding it hard to keep up, despite the boy's obvious ill health. Shocked as he was that the boy wasn't dead, James couldn't imagine his daughter's reaction, and worried for her sake. From the looks of Levi Clement, he might not be alive come morning. What kept the boy on his feet now was nothing short of a miracle.

Skipper and Roscoe ran on ahead home.

Mind the Light and keep walking, Levi. It was Willa's voice that sang in his heart and head now, at long last guiding him home to her.

CHAPTER TWENTY

Willa hurried with the wash. Surry would be over shortly, and Willa wanted to hear every detail about how the school at the plantation fared. From reports so far, despite the war, twenty children attended school when they could. *Twenty!*

How wonderful that Surry could pass on her skills to the ex-slave children. A few adults came to school, too. Willa couldn't wait to find out how they were all doing with their classes. She hung out the last of Adam's diapers. He napped inside the house and would be awake soon; another reason to hurry. No matter that her mother was inside the house making biscuits and worrying over the poor store of preserved goods they'd need for the coming winter, Willa didn't want her mother to have to watch after little Adam. Humph. He wasn't so little anymore. He was more than a year old now, and Willa knew he was going to grow tall and handsome just like . . . just like his father.

Willa bit her lip hard, refusing to cry. She had too much to do today, and there was no time for tears. She'd made a pact with herself not to cry over Levi except at night when she was alone in her bed, letting herself remember him then: his warmth, his smile, his powerful arms drawing her toward him, his deep, delicious kisses, the rich timbre of his voice that rippled down her spine and awakened her passion. She'd remember him stirring her body until she wanted every part of him touching every part of her. Then she'd let herself cry for him, only then. Biting her lip again almost to the point of bleeding, Willa turned to empty the washtub. She'd learned to get through her days without Levi, one chore at a time. Finish one chore and then go on to the next was just the way of it now.

Skipper and Roscoe came running up so fast, Willa just missed dumping out the wash water all over them. "Oh, so you two want a bath, do you?" She smiled. It felt good to smile. The dogs took off. Willa reset the empty tub and looked in their direction, wondering what the scallywags were up to.

That's when she saw her father coming toward the house. He brought someone with him. A man in uniform, a tall man.

Willa let out a sharp gasp. Her body went numb. She shut her eyes and spun around, turning her back on the apparition coming toward her. She hadn't counted on this, on losing her mind to grief and conjuring up Levi's ghost! *All right, Willa Mae Tyler,* she lectured silently. *Go inside and see to Adam. Just see to Adam, and you'll be in your right mind again.* "Just see to Adam," she mumbled aloud, opening her eyes and taking careful steps toward the house.

"Willa!"

She froze. She knew that voice. Ghost or not, she knew that voice. She bit her lip harder still, fighting for calm. Trembling inside and out, she stepped onto the front porch. "Just see to Adam," she quietly whispered, "and you'll be in your right mind again."

"Willa, love."

Every nerve in her body jangled. She shut her eyes tight, afraid of whom or what she'd see if she opened them. In that impossible moment, a calm stillness washed over her, coaxing her to settle, suspending her in another time and place where all went quiet but for the voice calling to her. If this was death coming for her, taking her to join Levi, so be it. Slowly, deliberately, with all fear gone she turned around and opened her eyes.

Levi held out his arms for her.

She ran into them.

James wiped tears from his eyes and stepped away to give his daughter and Levi a few moments of privacy, shooing Skipper and Roscoe into the house.

Levi pressed Willa's body to his, the feel of her slender shape telling him she was flesh and blood, alive and not dead in some trenched-out grave on the battlefield. He felt whole again; complete, with Willa a part of him. He didn't care that he cried. He didn't care that she'd see his tears. They were for her . . . his Willa, love.

She cried, too. He felt her cry against his chest, against his heart, infusing life into his withered soul. But then suddenly, without warning, Levi felt her slip away from him. He strained but he couldn't hear her cries. He couldn't feel her warm body close. He blinked hard but he couldn't focus. Then, all went black.

Willa slumped to the ground under the weight of Levi's body. Fighting panic, instinctively remembering her army experience, she scrambled out from under him and rolled him onto his back, immediately checking his breathing and feeling for a heartbeat. She found one! *Thank God. Thank God.* Levi had passed out, but he was alive.

Working quickly, she ran her hands over his body, pressing hard through the rough fabric of his disheveled Confederate uniform, checking for bullet wounds and injuries from canister fire. Streaks and splotches of dried blood were obvious, but she didn't see any signs of fresh bleeding. When she examined his outstretched limbs and ran her fingers behind his head, feeling for injuries, she realized what had happened to Levi all these months. He'd been in prison. That's why he looked so bad now.

That's why he didn't get to her earlier. He hadn't been killed, but captured and tortured. He'd broken out and found her, but . . . Willa lay her head down on Levi's chest and held fast to him. *Please, Dear God, don't let him die. Not now. Please, Dear God.*

"Two days Levi's been unconscious. What if he never wakes up?"

Willa stirred the oatmeal for Adam's breakfast, giving voice to her worries. Her parents were inside her bedroom, caring for Levi. Adam's cradle had been moved back out to its original spot by the fireplace. With no doctor nearby, Willa's parents had ministered to Levi, refusing to let her bathe him and see to his wounds, saying it wouldn't be proper. Ridiculous! Proper? Humph. She'd lain with Levi and had a baby with him and now her parents won't let her see to his needs, not wanting her to see him naked? Ridiculous. Willa stirred the oatmeal harder, a splat of the hot porridge finding her hand. "Ouch!"

Adam toddled up, doubtless responding to his mother's cry.

Willa set the spoon down and scooped her son up in her arms. Land sakes! She could have accidentally burned Adam. "Time for breakfast, my baby boy," she said, putting him safely in the wooden high chair her father had made.

Just then her bedroom door opened and her parents came out, closing the door behind them.

"How is he?" Willa shot out her question, at the same time overseeing Adam trying to spoon oatmeal into his mouth.

"Hard to tell, Willa. He's not awake yet," James answered honestly, entering the kitchen area and pouring himself a mug of coffee from the pot set on the iron stove.

"I think he's better," Litha Mae said encouragingly. "I think he'll wake up anytime now." She nodded her head to Willa to affirm her opinion.

"Whoops. No. No." Willa guided the spoon to Adam's mouth instead of letting him flip another spoonful of oatmeal onto the floor.

"Willa, I have something for you that I found in Levi's shirt pocket." Litha Mae held out the green grosgrain ribbon to her daughter, careful to keep her emotions hidden.

"Oh, Mama." Willa reverently took the ribbon in her free hand.

"You let me finish here with Adam." Litha Mae nudged her daughter away and sat down next to Adam's high chair.

Willa pressed the ribbon to her lips. The tie that binds. Such a journey her Christmas ribbon had made. And now, to have Levi return it to her, the same ribbon Walter and Henry had gifted her. . . . Overcome with emotion, she slipped down into the nearby rocker and quickly dissolved into tears, clutching the ribbon tightly over her heart. If Levi lived, it would be like Christmas every day. Such a present she wished for now, such a miraculous present.

"Willa, dear, we're taking Adam and going over to the Shelbys," her mother announced matter-of-factly, as if nothing was amiss.

"Oh." Startled out of her worry and melancholy, Willa scrambled out of the rocker and hastily pocketed her ribbon.

James walked over to the door and pulled down his jacket and hat. "Mr. Shelby has work for me, and I'm taking it. We need the money, and it's good, honest work," he asserted, more to himself than to his daughter.

Litha Mae took Adam from his high chair and pulled down his little coat and wool hat, dressing him warmly for the outside. "Now, Willa, dear, you keep an eye on Levi, but I don't want you staying in there with him for very long. It's not proper," she said, catching her daughter's eye.

Willa nodded she'd obey.

"I'm going with your father to visit with Esther Lion and see Surry's schoolhouse," Litha Mae added. "I think it's a fine thing what Surry is doing. Yes, indeed."

Willa nodded to her mother yet again, but said nothing. She watched them all leave, throwing a kiss to her son before the door closed behind him. Feeling a twinge of guilt, Willa knew she would most definitely not obey her mother's wishes. Her family would be gone much of the day, and she couldn't resist spending every minute of that time seeing to Levi. Proper or not, she padded toward her bedroom door the moment she believed it all clear to do so.

Deftly, she creaked open the door and peeked inside the room at her bed. It was empty! She charged inside, fearful for Levi. Was he dead and gone and her parents didn't have the heart to tell her? Rushing over to the shutters, she threw them open to better glimpse the grave situation, seeing but not seeing. Dizzy with fright, her head reeled.

"Looking for me?" Levi teased from behind her.

Willa spun back around and saw Levi all right—stark naked but for a bit of sheeting draped low around his waist. Far from dead, every inch of his powerful, scarred body looked very much alive. Lean from his rugged ordeal, he still had muscle enough to stir her passion. His handsome, mischievous grin and penetrating, slate gaze lured her ever closer. Mindless of whether it was proper or not, she took slow steps toward him, amazed at how changed he was from only two days ago. Her parents must have bathed him and shaved him and tended his wounds, their healing hands working wonders.

Only inches from him, Willa stared up at Levi, feeling the joy of every Christmas morning in the whole of her life all gathered up in this one moment. She dared not touch him. What if he wasn't real? What if all of this was a dream, a Christmas wish that would disappear the moment she touched him? She couldn't bear it if he left her again. Her hands trembled at her sides. She held them firm, too scared to find out what would happen if she touched him.

Levi watched her, drinking in every detail of her beautiful face, her beautiful hair, her beautiful body, clothes and all. He'd seen her in a dress once, last year in the rain. He'd thought her comely out of her soldier's disguise, but he never imagined the effect she'd have on him as she did now—all woman and all his. Her dark eyes sparkled for him. Her caught-up, ebony hair asked for his touch. Her rosy lips begged for his kiss. Her lithe, slender curves demanded him to take her in his arms and take her to bed. His loins stirred. Lost in love and lust for Willa, every part of him ached for her.

Struggling to keep his control, Levi reached for the top button of Willa's dress and began undoing it.

Mesmerized, Willa let him.

He slipped the dress off her shoulders and then to the floor. "Kick off your shoes," he gently commanded.

She did.

Undoing her hair, Levi let the dark locks fall around her shoulders and partway down her back. He resisted the urge to lose himself in the feel of her hair, in the taste of her kiss, and quickly removed her underclothes and carried her to the bed.

Willa had no time to react to being naked in Levi's arms. She'd no time to react to anything but the feel of Levi's flesh against hers, wanting to feel all of him inside her, filling her with his love. Her skin burned where he touched her. Her female center ached for him, waiting for him to set her on fire.

Levi tenderly lay Willa down on her bed and then eased himself over her, taking care not to crush her under his weight. He kissed her gently at first, but neither of them craved gentleness. His bruising kisses deepened.

Her mouth opened for him. *She* opened for him. He tasted

wonderful, just as she'd remembered. He felt wonderful, hardening over her. Arching up to him, kissing him and kissing him and kissing him, she ran her hands down his back to his buttocks, brazenly guiding him to her.

Levi muffled his laughter against her soft, wanton lips, knowing she was ready for him; knowing she wanted him. He let out a guttural moan, ready to penetrate her tight, silken sheath, filling her and claiming her as his.

Willa cried out the moment he entered her, at last breaking their kiss. Breathless, lost on wave after passionate wave of impossible pleasure, reveling in the moist, hot beads of perspiration coating their fused bodies, she died over and over in Levi's arms, a happy women, indeed.

Their passions spent after making love a second time, the reunited couple fell into exhausted, satisfied sleep in the safety of each other's loving arms.

Willa was the first to awaken. Merciful heavens! What time was it? Adam! Her parents! Instead of languishing next to a still-sleeping Levi, much as she wanted to, she bolted out of bed and gathered up her clothes. In a panic, she couldn't imagine the scene if her parents came home and walked in on her and Levi!

"Come back to bed."

Levi's deep, sleepy command sent shivers down her spine. But it didn't matter; she must ignore him. She hurried with her shoes, frustrated that their ties were in a tangle. "Levi, my parents will kill me if they find me in here with thee!"

Levi's heart wrenched. She'd said *thee.* Still, he couldn't help but chuckle at what else she said: that her parents would kill her if they found them together.

Upset with Levi for taking her words lightly, Willa had to laugh herself, when she thought about what she'd just said. Her parents surely would not kill her. She and Levi were adults and had a child together. They'd both been through hell in the war and survived.

No, she wouldn't die on this day because she'd slept with the father of her child, even though they were not married. It was wrong in the eyes of Victorian morality, but it was the most right thing she'd done in the whole of her life. Calming down, fully dressed, she plopped down on the side of the bed.

Levi sat up and pulled her close for another kiss.

"Oh, noooo," she teased and scrambled out of his reach. "I'm going to the kitchen to begin supper, with my parents none the wiser when they return. Adam surely will be—"

"Adam!" Levi blurted out, not letting Willa finish. It was his turn to hop out of bed and find some clothes to put on. He wanted to be dressed properly to meet his baby son for the first time.

"More new recruits, huh?" Lucas remarked to the soldier standing guard with him outside the appointed building in Baltimore City. "Hope they don't bolt when they find out their pay isn't the same as whites and that they might not get a uniform and proper shoes, leastways not all of them."

Lucas tried not to be bitter about the inequality between white and colored soldiers, but it was a hard pill to swallow. Sure, he was glad to see so many Negroes, free or still slave, muster into the Union army. It made him even more proud of his people, but he wasn't glad to be standing here and watching them. A few short weeks and then he'd be in the fight. That was the rumor going around camp. A few short weeks and his regimental battalion would head for the conflicts in West Virginia and Virginia. Chomping at the bit to fight, Lucas would soon get his chance. He might also get a chance to check on his family at home. If the battle took him anywhere near Waterford, he'd do his damnedest to see if his parents were all right.

He thought of Surry then.

He wished he hadn't.

He wished he could shake his worry for her and the undeniable fact that he'd fallen in love with her based on a memory, a memory after knowing her for only one week. For Lucas, it had been time enough, but he doubted Surry Lion even remembered his name.

He had to forget Surry. He believed he could, once he was in battle. When he fought and probably died for his people and his country, then he could put memories of the beautiful runaway slave to rest once and for all.

Esther Lion worried for her daughter. Surry's days were filled with teaching the ex-slave children at the plantation. But her nights. . . . At night when everyone was asleep, then Esther would hear her daughter sob into her pillow. It broke Esther's heart. There were so many reasons for all of them to cry every night into their pillows, too many reasons, but being a mother, Esther had a feeling something else upset her daughter. Tonight, after supper and after everyone else had gone to bed, Esther would talk to Surry. Esther had her suspicions this was over a young man who'd stolen Surry's heart.

Dressed in the close-to-fitting dark pants and a white, heavy-cotton shirt he'd found hanging on a peg in Willa's bedroom, Levi hurried out to join Willa and wait to meet Adam for the first time. It was late afternoon now. Levi had never been so nervous. So far, he hadn't been any kind of a father to his son.

What if Adam didn't take to him? What if Adam shunned him? Levi was nervous, all right. Just then he thought of his family back home and realized he needed to telegraph Jonah and let everyone know he was alive. Tomorrow, first thing, he'd get to Lynchburg and send his message. But first . . . first there was Adam.

Returning to the bedroom, unmindful of Willa's curious stare, Levi checked his appearance in the square of mirror over her dresser. As much as he appreciated being cleaned up by Willa's parents, and as much as he thought he looked better without his unkempt hair and scruffy beard, was it enough not to scare his son? When he heard the front door to the house open, Levi's heart leapt to his throat. In the back of his mind he realized he hadn't met Willa's mother yet, either, but his thoughts were on Adam now, only Adam. His nerves on edge, he walked cautiously back into the front room.

A kerosene lamp burned brightly on the kitchen table. Levi looked at it first and then his eye was drawn to the dark-haired, handsome child peering at him from around the bottom of one of the chairs. Levi stepped closer and then dropped to his knees near his son, only vaguely aware there were others in the room with them. Sitting back on his heels, Levi had never felt this kind of a pull on his heart, not even with Willa. His eyes watered with love, a father's love.

Adam toddled out from behind the chair rungs and walked toward Levi, his little face all smiles and curiosity.

"This is your daddy, Adam," Levi heard Willa say. "Go to your daddy."

Adam apparently didn't need much coaxing and walked straight up to Levi, then unceremoniously plopped down in front of him and looked up at his father. More curious now, Adam's smile turned into a frown.

Levi froze, absolutely captivated by his son.

"This is your daddy," Willa said again.

Adam kept his eyes on Levi. "Da-da-da," he blubbered out, smiling through little bubbles he'd drooled.

Levi put shaking hands around his son's middle, his fingers

steady the moment he did. "Yes, da-da," he parroted, and drew Adam into his arms.

Adam squealed in delight. "Da-da-da-da," Adam babbled, poking at his father's face and laughing all the while.

Levi kissed his son's forehead and hugged him tight, no longer nervous that Adam wouldn't take to him, and at once fiercely protective of his son. It was just the way of it between father and son.

Over the next weeks, Levi continued to grow stronger. But, to keep away from Willa and her bed, it took a fortitude he didn't think he had. Her parents had laid down the law that they could not live together as man and wife until they *were* man and wife. Despite his faith, Levi thought of having a civil ceremony in Lynchburg or whatever would make her parents happy, but Willa would have no part of it. She had it set firm in her mind to become Quaker and have a Quaker marriage ceremony. In her mind it was the right thing to do.

Her parents trusted their daughter's mind and heart. And so it happened that the Tylers at long last agreed to let their daughter and their grandson travel with Levi to Loudoun County, to his farm and his family. The war slowed during the winter, but didn't stop. The trip would be dangerous in winter, but more dangerous come spring, Levi believed.

When Willa told Surry her plans, Surry's reaction was instinctive and immediate. Like Willa, Surry knew her mind and her heart, and asked Willa if she could go, too. Surry was determined to go to Waterford and wait for as long as it took for Lucas to come home. She needed to be there waiting for him, willing to take the chance that he'd come home and might not want her, the way she wanted him. Life was short. Levi Clement had almost died. Willa had almost missed out on a life with the man of her dreams. Well, Lucas Minor was the man of Surry's dreams and she'd risk losing everything for the chance to have every-thing.

It was a difficult good-bye, the day that Levi pulled the wagon and team—loaned by Mr. Shelby—with Willa, Adam, and Surry on board for the treacherous journey across war-torn Virginia into Loudoun County. Unhappy they'd travel unarmed—Willa refused to take a gun for protection—James didn't like it, not one bit. He knew Levi would lay down his life for his daughter, but he still wouldn't rest easy until he knew they'd arrived safely in Loudoun County.

Esther Lion had come to bid her daughter good-bye with all four of her daughters and Sam in tow. Esther hated to see Surry leave, but she hated her tears at night more. Finding Lucas Minor would surely dry Surry's tears. Penny had agreed to help teach Surry's pupils until a proper teacher could be found. Litha Mae offered to help Penny if need be.

James and Litha Mae unwittingly took each other's hand as they watched Willa and Adam pull away from them, knowing they'd worry every moment until they got word all four pas-sengers on that wagon were all right. Willa promised to let them know. She promised them something else: that she would marry Levi Clement in a Quaker ceremony as soon as possible, mak-ing everything right in their eyes and the eyes of God.

When the war ended, for surely it had to end someday, James and Litha Mae would make regular visits to Loudoun County to visit with Willa and her new family. Although it was hard for them to watch her leave home for the last time, they didn't doubt her purpose, knowing their daughter was following her heart.

As for doubts, the one to convince after a safe journey home and a joyous reunion, the one parent who needed convincing was Thomas Clement. Since losing Benjamin to the war, he'd softened toward Jonah and accepted him back into the fold, despite Jonah having taken up arms against his fellow man. Thomas had even accepted Comfort and Levi's divorce. Comfort had put forth her case and convinced the elders to allow the divorce and make their appeal to Yearly Meeting.

But now, even though Thomas was overjoyed that Levi was alive and had come home with the woman he loved and with his son, Thomas had his doubts that Willa Mae Tyler truly wished to become Quaker, willing to sacrifice so much to live a plain life, a life of peace. She'd been a soldier and had masqueraded as a man, killing many people. Jonah had killed and Thomas had forgiven Jonah. But could he forgive Willa? Could he believe that she had peace in her heart now; peace and only peace? Would their Quaker community accept her? Would Yearly Meeting grant permission? Thomas would have to accept the decision from Yearly Meeting, and so would Willa Mae Tyler.

Times grew tougher, especially in the South, not only for the exhausted, beaten-back troops, but for civilians, too. Food ran short and tempers ran high. Too many husbands and sons and brothers—and in some cases, wives and daughters—had been cut down in battle, never to return home. The blood of too many young Americans washed across the countryside, their souls cast upon the unending tide of war.

Breaking from winter quarters, troops were again on the move in the spring of 1864. At long last, Lucas was in the fight. His 19th regimental battalion had advanced out of Baltimore City to Harper's Ferry to join the battle, inflicting serious damage on enemy cavalry. The next month, the 19th marched to Manassas, and then saw their first major conflict in the Battle of the Wilderness in May. The battle lasted three days, with neither side claiming victory. Lucas watched many in his unit die over those three days, hardening him even more for the fight, seeing firsthand the price they all paid for freedom.

After the Battle of the Wilderness, those left in Lucas's unit were assigned to guard duty with the 9th Army Corps. Lucas saw action aplenty with the 9th, repelling Confederate cavalry and engaging in frequent skirmishes with the enemy. Rumor had it that the 9th was going to join up with the 25th Army Corps and head toward Richmond. That would be the battle of all battles, Lucas knew.

Taking the capital city of the confederacy would be the end of it for the South, Lucas believed. He couldn't wait to help end it and return home to Waterford. He hoped to God his parents would be waiting for him, both surviving the war and hard times. He knew Surry wouldn't be waiting in Waterford or anywhere else—not for him anyway. His gut turned. He had pure hate in his heart for the man he imagined her waiting for. Every day he woke up, every day he went to fight, he tried to forget Surry, but every day he survived the fight, he'd collapse on his bedroll and dream of her.

Willa chased down the street after Adam, catching up with him in front of Lucas Minor's house, used now as a school for the Negro children in the area. Surry had gone to meet Lucas's parents soon after her return to Waterford and said straight out to them that she'd come to Waterford to wait for Lucas to return home from the war.

Arletta and Nathan Minor welcomed Surry into their home immediately, and later offered Lucas's house to her to live in and to use as a school. Surry cherished such an opportunity and quickly came to cherish Arletta and Nathan Minor. They were wonderful people and loved their son. Surry had come to love them and hoped they loved her, if only a little.

Willa hoped with all of her heart, as she finally caught up with Adam out front of Lucas's house, that when Lucas came home, he'd be happy to find Surry there waiting for him. There was always the chance he would not. What would happen to her dearest friend then?

With Adam in hand, forcing her spirits to brighten, Willa pushed open Lucas's front door and stepped inside the schoolroom. Her white bonnet askew, she quickly straightened it, feeling the brunt of all the children's surprised stares. Even Surry gave Willa a disapproving look. Best friend or not, Willa had interrupted her classes.

"Surry." Willa tried to keep her voice to a whisper but it was impossible. "Surry, I'm getting married tomorrow at the meetinghouse at noon, sharp," she blurted across the classroom. "Will thee stand up with me?"

The lesson plan fell from Surry's hands. She rushed over to Willa and gave her a crushing hug.

The children giggled.

Adam broke free of his mother's hold, wanting to explore and play.

Willa and Surry hugged each other close, neither able to let go of such good news, each spilling out tears of joy onto the other.

Surry finally pulled away, keeping Willa's hands in hers. "Of course I'll stand up with you. What kind of a forever friend would I be if I did not?"

Willa grasped Surry's fingers tightly. She swallowed hard, choking back tears. "Thee is my truest and dearest friend. I couldn't . . . I couldn't get married tomorrow without thee," Willa managed. "Thee is a part—a part of my heart unto eternity, Surry Lion." Willa smiled through new tears.

"As you are a part of mine, Willa Mae Tyler," Surry whispered back. "As you are a part of mine unto eternity," she repeated, and hugged her forever friend to her.

In that moment both Willa and Surry realized their friendship was a gift, a special gift to them from Above that no one and no color barrier and no war could ever take from them. Theirs was a gift of friendship unto eternity.

"Tomorrow then," Willa said quietly and pulled out of Surry's embrace, her heart brimful to bursting with gratitude for her rich bounties. She had Surry for friend and Levi for husband; at least tomorrow she would be married. More anxious than excited, Willa searched the room for Adam and quickly collected him. "Tomorrow, then," she tossed out to Surry and then hurried out of the schoolroom.

Surry closed the door behind Willa, heaving a deep, contented sigh, happy beyond happy that tomorrow Willa would marry the man of her dreams. Surry looked around at the children. They all grinned at her. She bent down and scooped up her lesson plan from the floor where she'd dropped it. "All right now, you still have to do your ciphering, so pick your slates back up, all of you," she informed her pupils, trying to sound stern when she felt anything but.

The front door flew open yet again.

"Willa Mae Tyler, I—" Surry couldn't finish. She couldn't breathe. She couldn't feel. She couldn't think. The lesson plan slipped from her hands just as before. Only this time it wasn't Willa come back. It was Lucas!

Dressed in Union blue, Lucas dropped his haversack in the open doorway and set his rifle against the outside frame. He couldn't breathe. He couldn't feel. He couldn't think. It couldn't be but it was. It was Surry waiting for him!

Surry froze.

Lucas froze.

Time stood still for them both, precious time, time neither of them dreamed they'd have together. They drank each other in, reluctant to take a step closer, fearful this was only a dream.

The children started to clap their hands, excited to see their very first soldier in the United States Colored Troops.

The whooping and hollering of the children brought Surry and Lucas back to the reality of the moment, the reality that this was real and not a dream. The two quickly fell into each other's arms and at long last had their first kiss, a kiss filled with the promise of many more to come.

It was the best of times.

EPILOGUE

"Until death I am thine."
The Quakeress Bride
Elizabeth Clementine Kinney, 1840

"Oh, the water's like ice!" Surry scooted back from the edge of Catoctin Creek, enough to clear her feet.

"Thee is such a girlie, Surry Minor," Willa teased. She had her feet full in the water, watching while Adam and her two-year-old twin daughters, Adelaide and Lydia, did the same. "Stay right by me, children," she lectured them.

Surry tried to get her three-year-old son Seth to come away from the creek's edge, but the little guy refused. Strong like his father, Seth ever gave Surry fits. "Willa Mae Clement, I suppose you'll try to stick a fishing pole in the children's hands next!"

"Like this one?" Willa said; laughing and taking up one of the poles she'd contrived.

"Humph." Surry sat back down next to Willa, giving up on her friend and on her rambunctious son. She'd stay right at the water's edge with him, much as she thought the creek too cold, despite the sweltering hot day.

"Here, Surry, have a worm," Willa teased and tossed the squishy worm into Surry's lap.

Surry yelped in protest and managed to swat the worm away. She turned to Willa intending to get mad at her but couldn't.

Willa always had a smile for her.

Surry smiled back and held out her hand, however reluctantly, for another worm.

Willa reached in the tin can and handed Surry a new worm, and then handed over her pole for Surry to bait the line, keeping a close eye on all of the children. Surry was expecting, and Willa kept a close eye on her too, especially on these outings to Catoctin Creek and into the hills beyond. Blessedly, with the war over, it was safe to explore the woods surrounding Waterford.

It had been two years since the war that divided the country and tore families and friends apart had ended. The South surrendered to the North with General Lee surrendering to General Grant at Appomattox Courthouse in April 1865, not far from Willa's home in nearby Bedford County.

Much had been won in the war, but much had been lost.

Slavery had ended but not all prejudice and bigotry. The Emancipation Proclamation was a beginning, only a beginning. A generation of young men and women fighting on both sides had given their lives for this beginning. Walter and Henry had given their lives. Benjamin had given his life. Surry's brothers, Gus and Silas, had given theirs. Private Caleb Ryan had given his. Thousands upon thousands of soldiers, white and colored, had given their lives. Many civilians had lost their lives, too, caught in the crossfire of war. Fertile farmland had been burned and all but destroyed along with livestock and homes.

Waterford had not been spared, suffering terrible losses in the Burning Raid of 1864, with over two hundred barns and eight mills destroyed along with their remaining store of hay and grain. Those cattle, sheep, hogs, and horses that were not slaughtered were driven off by Union forces under General Merritt, all in retaliation against Mosby's Rangers. Colonel John Mosby and his men had been using Loudoun County as their base of operations for their raids against northern troops.

General Grant wanted him caught, killed, gone. Mosby had been wounded but not killed or captured.

Willa remembered meeting the infamous partisan leader, plumed hat and all, the day he spared her life, but not the lives of the Yankees escorting her to Goose Creek. Mosby and his men fought on until the war ended; even afterward, Mosby refused to surrender, disbanding his Rangers instead. Willa respected him for fighting for his cause. She respected soldiers on both sides of the battlefield, no matter the color of their coat or their skin, for fighting for their respective causes, right or wrong.

But now . . . now was not a time for war, but a time for peace, a time for love.

Willa doubted she'd ever find the right words to thank God for Levi and her children and the contented, peaceful life they now shared. Every First Day she'd sit quietly at meeting, surrounded by her family and all the Friends, and wait for the right words to come, to properly thank God for her blessings, vowing to ever Mind the Light. When Levi would take up her hand to leave meeting, she knew the hand of God had brought them together and would never let them part, even unto death.

Willa watched Surry put her line in the creek flow, recalling the time when they were girls of seven, sitting along the James much like now, and Surry asked her what bein' free meant. Willa hated having to find out and tell Surry. She remembered how Surry had cried. It still hurt, remembering.

The children splashed their feet in the water.

"Now, all ya'll stop that. I'll never get my fish if you scare them all away," Surry lectured, good-naturedly.

Willa smiled at the scene, at the happy children, at Surry's attempts to catch that smelly fish and let old hurts go. She was finally able to, knowing that Surry's children would never have to ask their mother the same question Surry had asked her on the banks of the James.

It was just the way of it now: bein' free.

ABOUT THE AUTHOR

With her three children grown, **Joanne Sundell** and her husband live part-time in Colorado and part-time in California where their first grandchild, Max Preston Fessler, just came into the world!

E-mail Joanne: author@joannesundell.com